The Bacheloress

The Bacheloress

Woman in Progress 1

by
Victor Margueritte

translated, annotated and introduced by
Brian Stableford

A Black Coat Press Book

Edited by Peter Gabbani

English adaptation and introduction Copyright © 2015 by Brian Stableford.
Cover illustration Copyright © 2015 Mike Hoffman.

Visit our website at www.blackcoatpress.com

Introduction

La Garçonne by Victor Margueritte, here translated as *The Bacheloress*, was originally published by Ernest Flammarion in 1922. The novel became a huge best-seller, eventually selling 750,000 copies, but owed its immense success less to its innate literary merits—although they are considerable—than the immense scandal that it caused, when it raised a storm of negative criticism and loud calls for it to be banned on the grounds that it was pornographic and deeply offensive to morality. The era when books were prosecuted on those grounds was past in France, but the opprobrium was deflected in an unprecedented fashion, when the members of the Conseil de l'Ordre de la légion d'honneur took it upon themselves to decide that the decoration previously given to the author should be revoked.

That decision further amplified the fuss surrounding the book, seeming to many people to be far more scandalous than the novel itself, and the storm of protest became a fierce contest in which very different ideologies clashed. The author, who was deeply hurt by the insult, added a note to the copies issued after the print run reached 150,000, three months after the book's initial publication, in which he attempted to defend the text against the charge that it was pornographic, and against the allegation—more pertinent to the issue, and perhaps more serious—that he had dishonored France by besmirching French womanhood, thus losing his moral entitlement to an award that was, by definition, conferred for honoring the fatherland.

Those later printings also carried a copy of an open letter by Anatole France addressed to the Conseil, protesting vehemently about the withdrawal of the award and insisting that Victor Margueritte was still an honor to his nation, because of what he had written, as well as the author's own reply to the letter informing him of the Conseil's decision, which concluded with opinion that the members had covered themselves with "ineradicable ridicule." Presumably, they agreed, as they never took similar action again. That did not, of course, prevent the original perpetrators of the protest from continuing to oppose, strenuously and steadfastly, the explicit description of sexual acts in fiction, especially in contexts that challenged the "official" moral attitude to such acts, and thus threatened to assist in the modification and evolution of such attitudes.

The descriptions of various sexual acts contained in *La Garçonne* are, in fact, a trifle more explicit than were commonplace at the time, although the work done by the text, in collaboration with hundreds of others, did indeed assist in the progressive evolution that has accustomed modern readers to finding such descriptions routine—even in England, where the publication of a book like *La Garçonne* would have been unthinkable in 1922, and remained unthinkable until the famous breakthrough in 1963 when D. H. Lawrence's *Lady Chatterley's Lover*—originally published in Italy in 1928—was finally allowed legal publication in its homeland. *La Garçonne* was translated into English by Hugh Burnaby in 1923 as *The Bachelor Girl*, for a U.S. edition published by Alfred Knopf, but that edition was inevitably bowdlerized, as the passages describing various sexual acts that had caused so much offence in Paris could not possibly be reproduced in a mass-market book published in America, so the present edition is the first unexpurgated edition in English. The story was filmed several times, but standards of film censorship were even tighter, so the film versions were similarly filleted. The fact that *La Garçonne* proved so much more shocking in France than similarly-explicit contemporary texts, however, has far more to do with the context of the acts described than the terms of their descriptions, and with its situation within a long literary tradition of accounts of female sexual behavior produced by male writers.

The tradition of masculine literary accounts of female sexuality is by no means entirely confined to France, but France has an exceptionally rich tradition of extended character studies of women who kick over the traces of conventional sexual morality. Even English is not entirely devoid of such works, but Daniel Defoe's tongue-in-cheek *Moll Flanders* (1722) was unsupplemented for a long time, and such eventual tentative ventures as Grant Allen's *The Woman Who Did* (1895), H. G. Wells' *Ann Veronica* (1909) and Michael Arlen's *The Green Hat* (1924) are exceedingly pale by comparison with their French equivalents. The intense French fascination with high-class whores, stimulated by spectacular exemplars prominent in the court of the Sun King and his successors, produced numerous literary reflections in the 18th century, most archetypally *Manon Lescaut* (1731) by the Abbé Prévost, but the tradition acquired an important new twist with the advent of Naturalism, when Émile Zola pioneered what his manifesto claimed to be the a quasi-scientific analysis of the motivations involved in human behavior. Zola's most famous application of that method of the sexual component of female psychology is *Thérèse Raquin* (1867), although it is arguable that the method had been used before Zola and that a precedent of enormous importance had already been put in place by Gustave Flaubert in *Madame Bovary* (1856). Several other writers in the nascent Naturalist tradition had a particular interest in analyses of female psychology, most obviously the Goncourt brothers, whose *Renée Mauperin* (1864) was followed by several other detailed character studies, culminating in *La Faustin* (1882), written by Edmond alone, after Jules' death. Joris-Karl Huymans also contributed significantly to the tradition in *Marthe* (1876) and *Les Soeurs Vatard* (1879)

The earlier Romantic tradition, seen by some critics as a rival superseded by Naturalism, had, of course, produced its own archetypes of heroic feminine delinquency, most notably Théophile Gautier's buoyant *Mademoiselle de Maupin* (1835) and Alexandre Dumas *fils'* tragic *La Dame aux Camélias* (1848), but they had an inevitable methodical inclination toward the sentimental that the Zolaesque approach wanted to set aside in favor of a supposedly clearer and more objective analysis of the problematics of female sexuality and attending male attitudes. Zola's "scientific" approach was partly based in idiosyncratic theories of heredity, but as the science of psychology evolved, especially the idea of the unconscious, a school of "neo-Naturalism" emerged that employed more intimate analytical instruments, and brought the tradition back to a significant overlap with the Symbolist fiction that descended from Romanticism. It was the neo-Naturalist school to which Victor Margueritte and his brother Paul were affiliated, and to whose evolution *La Garçonne* can be seen as exemplary and central.

Victor (1866-1942) was the younger brother, Paul having been born in 1860—he died in 1914—and Paul had already established a solid reputation as a notable writer of the Naturalist school before Victor made his debut. Initially, in fact, Victor had seemed more likely to follow in the footsteps of their father, General Jean-Auguste Margueritte, who had made a name for himself fighting in Algeria before being killed at the battle of Sedan in 1870; Victor joined the Spahis in 1886 and after a spell at the École Militaire in Saumur he became a lieutenant in the dragoons, but he resigned his commission in 1896 in order to devote himself to writing. Almost all of his early work was done in collaboration with his brother, with whom he wrote numerous novels and several plays between 1896 and 1907, but he published a dozen solo novels thereafter before achieving a new notoriety with *La Garçonne*. The latter was not his first excursion into the relevant literary terrain, his first solo novel having been *Prostituée* [Prostituted] (1907) and *La Garçonne* having been closely preceded by *Un Coeur farouche* [A Wild Heart] (1921). His interest in the politics of marriage was long-standing; the essays he had written in collaboration with Paul had included several on the topic in question, including "Le Mariage libre," reprinted in *Quelques idées* [A Few Ideas] (1905).

Any consideration of *La Garçonne* as a literary work, therefore, ought to take into account the fact that it was a result of an extremely long process of extrapolative gestation, and that its heroine, Monique Lerbier, has a rich literary ancestry—in which, significantly, almost all of her predecessors had ended up dying ignominiously. Having said that, however, it also needs to be recognized that there were some strikingly original aspects to Monique's portrayal, and to her narrative treatment, which react very sharply to the precise period in which the novel was seeded and engendered: the five years following the end of the Great War.

It seemed in that period to everyone, but with a unique agony in France, where so many of the war's archetypal trenches had been dug, defended and filled with blood, that the society that had existed before the war had been ripped to shreds, and that a new one was in the process of an exceedingly difficult birth. The war was remembered in France not merely with horror but with intense bitterness, and there was a fervent desire to attach blame, not only to German militarism but to the forces native to France that had permitted the war to happen and had profited from it. Victor Margueritte was by no means alone, among French writers, in stigmatizing "profiteers" and politicians who had, allegedly, not only wanted and orchestrated the war, but were still reaping its benefits and spending them lavishly, while those who had fought and suffered through five terrible years from 1914 to 1918 were continuing to struggle and suffer.

What was truly shocking about *La Garçonne* in 1922—and remains veritably shocking today—is not so much the reckless behavior of its heroine, who is far more sinned against than sinning, and is explicitly represented as the victim of a mental aberration occasioned by ill-treatment and excessive sensibility, but the portrait the novel paints of the irredeemably corrupt social milieu in which she is, in essence, a mere lamb marked for slaughter. The novel really does besmirch the honor of French womanhood, in no uncertain terms, not in the character-study of Monique, but in the exceedingly hostile and contemptuous portrayal of her peers, especially Michelle Jacquet/d'Entraygues and Ginette Morin/Hutier, who are offered to the readers not as luckless strays but as supposedly accurate types of a "new woman," created and shaped by post-war society.

The notion of the emergence of a "new woman" pre-dated the war by several decades, having been loudly trumpeted by Henry James, and similarly detailed by the Margueritte brothers in *Femmes nouvelles* (1899), but precisely because of her prior existence there was a keen consciousness of the fact that her evolution seemed to have entered a crucial new phase in 1919. In the U.S.A., largely untouched and tremendously advantaged economically by the Great War, the phenomenon seemed largely benign, extensively celebrated as it was in the idea of the "flapper," who had existed before the war but only came into her own in the "Roaring Twenties." In England, also untrenched although by no means unbloodied, the tabloid press celebrated the activities of the socialites they called "Bright Young Things," whose Bohemian recklessness was seen as an inevitable and arguably necessary release after years of nightmare. In France, the view seemed much darker, even—and perhaps especially—to the writers who had cheerfully glorified the Bohemianism of pre-war Paris, and who saw the license of the new era as a much more malign phenomenon by comparison. Félicien's Champsaur's *Tuer les vieux, jouir!* (1925)[1] is one of the more outspoken complaints about the new corruption of youth, and has no doubt at all that the blame for that purulent corruption lay exactly where Victor Margueritte had put it.

The problematics of the new sensibility are neatly encapsulated in the title of *La Garçonne*, in a way that makes it difficult to translate. If *garçon* were construed as "boy" then a *garçonne* would be what was and still is known in English as a "tomboy," but in the context of the novel the word means "bachelor," and the whole point of the story is to analyze and complain bitterly about the double standard conventionally employed in the judgment of the behavior of bachelors and

---

[1] Translated as "Kill the Old, Enjoy!" in *Homo-Deus*, Black Coat Press, ISBN 9781612273518.

unmarried women. In that sense, the term *garçonne* was a ne-
ologism, as is made very clear when the comedian Briscot,
nonplussed by Monique in her new guise, has it on the tip of
his tongue to call her a *garce* [slut] but discreetly extends the
word to *garçonne*—and then immediately corrects himself by
observing that she is not merely *a* garçonne but *the* garçonne:
a new model, something unprecedented and unique.

It is perfectly understandable that the Knopf translation
should have been entitled *The Bachelor Girl*, but the diminutive effect of the appellation "girl," like the diminutive suffix
of the modern American "bachelorette" and the English
"ladette," carries a note of implicit dismissal and minimization
that is not appropriate to the case in question; that is why I
have substituted the less orthodox "bacheloress"—which becomes all the more appropriate if it is deemed to be not (yet) a
real word. Perhaps something more appropriate would exist if
the double standard of which the text complains were not still
toxically active, and if the argument of the book did not seem
so direly pertinent even today. The author's optimistic hope
that progress might be made in that respect has proved, of
course, far wilder than he was prepared to assume, although
that does have the arguably-advantageous effect, from the
viewpoint of the modern reader, of maintaining the discomfit-
ing effect of the novel.

The author went on further to promote that optimistic
hope by publishing two further books that were marketed as
sequels to *La Garçonne*, *Le Compagnon* (1923; tr. in an edition uniform with this book as *The Companion*) and *Le Couple*
(1924; tr. in the same uniform edition as *The Couple*) which
inevitably benefited from the publicity of the scandal, but
failed to achieve anything like the same success, partly because they were content to be less explicit in matters of sexual
description. The three novels were given the collective title of
La Femme en chemin [Woman in Progress], allegedly repre-
senting three potential stages in the feminist quest for equality
between women and men; the second provides a counterpart to
La Garçonne in offering a contrasting character study of a

woman more powerfully armed with virtue, who does not have to recover her sainthood after a catastrophic fall, while the third extrapolates the quest of both characters into the future, in order that the children they have raised in the assumed path of righteousness might assist in providing a tentative resolution of sorts.

The preface to *Le Compagnon* states that that novel was always intended as part of a couplet whose other component was *La Garçonne*, and was, in fact, started first. An early draft of part of the text appears as "La Femme en chemin" in the periodical *Oeuvres Libres* before the author set it aside in order to write *La Garçonne* from beginning to end before resuming work on its expansion. The same preface contends that the couplet was envisaged from its inception as a continuation of the theme of the much earlier couplet constituted by *Prostituée* and *Jeunes filles* (1908), and that those early solo novels also picked up themes from two separate novels written by the brothers in collaboration in 1897 and 1899, the latter being their study of *Femmes nouvelles*. There was no plan when the new couplet was first conceived, however, to add the third volume converting the couplet into a trilogy; that was an afterthought.

In spite of these observations, and its pre-planned relationship with *Le Compagnon*, as well as its position within a long sequence of works spanning its author's career, and many predecessors in the same genre by other hands, *La Garçonne* can perfectly well be considered in isolation, as a unique and highly exceptional item in the history of French literature—which, although standing on the shoulders of giants, was enabled thereby to discover and map new horizons. It remains very readable today, partly because the problems it identifies as having been intensified by the consequences of the Great War were not solved, as he hoped they might be, by a pattern of future events akin to that described in *Le Couple*. Because the fundamental issues remain problematic, even in the 21st century, to a much greater extent than Victor Margueritte must have hoped, the novel still has the capacity to shock, although one is bound to assume, given that progress does happen, that the balance of outrage and sympathy in modern readers' reactions to the novel is likely to be tipped in the latter direction.

This translation was made from a London Library copy of the Flammarion edition of *La Garçonne*, identified on the cover as one of the 365th thousand. The library's original printed catalogue lists the book as being held in the Librarian's Room—the *enfer* in which the administrators routinely file books considered too indecent for public display—but the copy I borrowed is a later one, donated in 1976 and placed on the open shelves. Contrary to the library's usual policy, however, that copy was left unbound and placed in a cardboard slipcase, apparently still being judged as an item apart from its companions on the shelf.

Brian Stableford

THE BACHELORESS

PART ONE

I

Monique Lerbier rang.

"Mariette," she said to the chambermaid, "my coat..."

"Which one, Mademoiselle?"

"The blue one. And my new hat."

"Shall I bring them to Mademoiselle?"

"No, lay them out in my room..."

Alone, Monique sighed. What a chore this sale would be, even if she did find Lucien there! It was so nice in the small drawing room. She laid her head on the cushions of the sofa again, and resumed her reverie...

She is five years old. She is eating dinner in her room, at the little table where "Mademoiselle," the regent of her life, serves her and supervises her every day. This evening, however, Mademoiselle is on leave. Aunt Sylvestre is replacing her.

Monique adores Aunt Sylvestre. For one thing, the two of them are not like the others. The others are women. Even Mademoiselle! Maman has given her that name. "Even though you're a widow, because a governess must always be called Mademoiselle."

Aunt Sylvestre and Monique, by contrast, are girls. She is a little girl, although she thinks that she is already grown up, and the Aunt an old girl...very old! The proof is that she has wrinkled skin and three hairs in her chin, on a wart like a chick-pea.

15

Then again, Aunt Sylvestre always brings black nougat, almonds and burnt honey every time she comes from Hyères. Monique doesn't know exactly where Hyères is, or what it is. Hyères is like Yesterday[2]—a long way away. Only today counts, and today is a celebration. Papa and Maman have gone to the Opéra, and before then they have been invited to the restaurant.

The Opéra is a palace where fairies dance to music, and the restaurant a place where one eats oysters. It's reserved for grown-ups, Aunt Sylvestre says.

But here comes a fairy...no, it's Maman, appearing in a low-cut dress. She has white feathers on her head, and she looks as if she is dressed entirely in pearls. Monique touches the fabric, ecstatically. Yes, tiny, very tiny pearls, truly! She would like to have a necklace of them.

She caresses Maman's neck as she leans over to say *au revoir*. "No, no kiss, because of my lipstick! And as the small hand moves up toward the velvet of her cheeks, the impatient voice orders: "Don't touch! You'll smudge my make-up."

Behind her is Papa, all in black, with a big white V emerging from his waistcoat. It's a funny shirt, in shiny cardboard. Maman tells Aunt Sylvestre, who smiles as she listens, a long story, but Papa taps his foot and says: "With your mania for spending three hours putting black on your eyelashes and pink on your fingernails, we'll miss the overture!"

What opening? The oysters?[3] No. As soon as Maman and Papa have gone, without kissing her—Monique is disappointed—Aunt Sylvestre explains that it's the overture of the music. Music opens, then?

Thoughtfully, Monique asks: "What is it, then?" and Aunt Sylvestre who has taken her onto her knee, explains: "Music is the song that comes from everything...from oneself,

---

[2] In French, Hyères is far more like *Hier* [Yesterday] than it seems to be in English. It is a commune in the Var, in the far south of France, the oldest resort on the Riviera.

[3] *Ouverture* [overture] also means "opening," hence the error.

when one is happy…from the wind when it blows over the forest or the sea. It's also the concert of instruments, which recalls all that. And the overture is like opening a big window to the sky, so that the music comes in and you can hear it. Do you understand?"

Monique looks at Aunt Sylvestre tenderly, and nods her head.

Monique is eight. She has been coughing for a long time. She often coughs. So, when she goes for a walk by the sea, Mademoiselle—who is no longer the widow but a Luxembourgeoise whom she doesn't like, with cheeks like red balloons—has orders not to let her play bare-legged in the rock-pools where the shrimp wriggle, and not even to let her run away from the tide over the sand that hardens as it gets wet. She can't pick up the fresh seaweed that smells of the ocean, or the seashells whose nacreous ears contain the sound of the waves. "What do you want to do with those dirty things? Throw it away!" Maman declared, once and for all.

Monique can no longer read whenever she wants to—because of her headaches. On the other hand, she has to do an hour of scales regularly; it does no good to say that it drives her mad; it appears that it's a discipline for the fingers. Well, if this is a holiday, Trouville is more tedious than Paris!

Besides which, she sees much less of her parents. Maman is always in the automobile, with friends. And in the evening, when she has dinner—which is rare—she leaves immediately afterwards to change her clothes and go dancing at the Casino until very late…so, in the morning she sleeps. Papa? He only comes on Saturday, by the husbands' train. And on Sunday he stays with Messieurs for his business.

The biggest bore is when Maman "goes to the beach." They watch the lines going back and forth on the boardwalk. One would think it were a linen shop. The mannequins show themselves off, all the same, in packed rows. The people who form circles, sitting around near wicker huts or tents, exchange greetings with the people walking. When they arrive at the end of the boardwalk they turn round and come back. What are they following? Monique doesn't know. Another mystery. The world is full of them, if she can believe the replies given to her incessant questions...

For the moment, she is amusing herself, not far from the maternal hut with little Morin and a comrade whose name she doesn't know. They have baptized her Toupie because she is always twirling on one foot, singing. Crouched under the distracted gaze of the Luxembourgeoise, all three of them are building a sandcastle with towers and a moat. In the middle stands a curly-haired little body named Mouton with his spade over his shoulder. They have put him there in order to stand still, telling him: "You're the garrison."

The rule of the game is that when the castle is finished, the garrison will be free, and in his place they will lock up, as a prisoner, whichever of the three of them allows herself to be caught. But the castle isn't finished. Mouton stamps his feet and, without waiting for its completion, carries out a vigorous sortie. Toupie and little Morin flee. Monique, who relies on her faith in treaties, hasn't budged—with the result that when Mouton wants to imprison her, she resists. He shoves her...blows and cries...

The Luxembourgeoise, who comes running, receives her share of blows. Then the Mamans come running. They separate the combatants and, without listening to the confused explanations, which are contradictory in any case, they shake them. Mouton, who proves stubborn, receives a slap. At the same time, Monique feels a hand that strikes her on the wing: *click! clack!* "That'll teach you!" Her face smarts.

Flabbergasted, she looks at the enemy who has just abused her strength. The enemy, satisfied to have equilibrated the misdeeds and the punishments...is her mother! Is it possible? Rage and amazement divide Monique's soul. She has made the acquaintance of injustice. And she suffers from it, like a woman.

Monique is ten. She is grown up. Or rather, her mother declares, shrugging her shoulders, she is an intolerable child, with her fantasies, her vapors and her nerves.

For a start, she does nothing like everyone else! Hasn't she torn her lace dress and caught cold last Sunday playing hide and seek in the grounds of Madame Jacquet's house, with Michelle and young scapegraces? Old Mechlin—a real bargain at 175 francs a meter. And yesterday, at the pastry shop, didn't she take it into her head to take a large brioche, nearly a kilo, from the display to give it—outside, on the sidewalk—to a little girl in rags who was devouring it with her eyes? Instead of good bread!

She had tried in vain to pay for it out of her savings: it wasn't charity, it was extravagance; and even, fundamentally, false generosity. It was necessary not to give the unfortunate a taste, and in consequence a regret, for what they couldn't have...

Monique is pained by that reasoning. She would like the whole world to be fortunate. She is also chagrined; the members of her own family don't understand her. It isn't her fault if she has a character that doesn't resemble those she sees around her! And it isn't her fault either, if, because of her hollow cheeks and stooped back, she doesn't do honor to her parents. "You're growing up like a weed!" she hears repeated, incessantly...

If this goes on, she'll end up falling ill; they've promised her that! She accepts the idea with resignation, almost with pleasure. To die? That wouldn't be any great misfortune. Who loves her? No one.

Except Aunt Sylvestre.

In the Easter vacation, when, after a bad bout of bronchitis and three weeks in bed, Monique awoke so weak that she could no longer stand up, the aunt was there! And when the doctor declared: "This child needs to live in the country for a long time, in the Midi if possible, by the sea—the climate and life in Paris are no good for her..." the aunt cried: "I'll take her with me! I'll take her, Hyères is excellent, isn't it, Doctor?"

"Perfect—the ideal place..."

It was immediately agreed. And Monique has so much joy in thinking that she will be transplanted into the sun, to be with her true mother, that she doesn't think of being saddened by the fact that her father and mother don't manifest any regret.

Monique is twelve. She has the plaits and check dresses of a schoolgirl. She is the top pupil in her class, in Aunt Sylvestre's school. Instead of gray, foggy streets, the garden extends, rising up the slope of the hill. The sun dresses everything with a splendid lightness. It shines over the Chamaerops palms, like giant ferns, and over the spiny rackets of the cacti, over the blue-tinted or yellow-edged aloes, which look like enormous bouquets of zinc. The sea is the same deep blue as the sky; they fuse together in the distance.

Easter has come around again, flowery Easter! Jesus advances on his little donkey, through the swaying green branches. The ground is like a single carpet, bright and multi-colored, of roses, narcissi, carnations and anemones.

Tomorrow Monique will be all in white, like a little bride. Tomorrow! The celebration of her spiritual wedding! The good Curé Macahire—she cannot pronounce his name seriously[4]—will admit her, with her companions of the catechism, to Holy Communion.

She has tried to penetrate the beautiful legends of the Testaments; she has succeeded all the better because she has had as a tutor her great friend Elisabeth Meere...Zabeth, who is a Protestant, made her first communion four years ago, and her fervent rigor adds a singular exaltation to the mystical fever with which Monique is burning. Both of them, in the adoration of the Savior, are discovering love, obscurely.

Monique's is all confidence, abandonment and purity. She goes forth with an ingenuous intoxication on the open

---

[4] Because it is similar to that of the stock villain of melodrama, Robert Macaire.

wings of her dreams. She only has one puerile anxiety: that of not profaning, by biting into the snowy host in passing, the invisible but present body of the Divine Spouse.

It is also necessary, Abbé Macahire has firmly recommended, that she confess her bad thoughts in advance. She has had two of them that she has tried to drive away. The vile flies settle unceasingly on the lily of her expectation. Her pretty dress! Vanity. And the eggs—the Easter eggs! Gluttony. First of all the big one, in chocolate, that she received from Paris, and then the medium-sized and small ones, in sugar of all colors, and even one real egg, hard-boiled in hot water, for which it is so amusing to search through the bushes and flower-beds of the garden.

It is a big occasion for Aunt Sylvestre, who has been preparing treats and surprises for a week, for the whole school. It's also her fashion of communion. At least, that's what Abbé Macahire complains, adding: "What a pity that such a worthy woman is a miscreant!"

It is necessary to believe that that is not a very grave sin, since Monsieur le Curé seems to pardon her for it. It would annoy Monique a great deal to go to Paradise while Aunt Sylvestre went to Hell! But all those ideas make her head ache...

She is happy, and the weather is fine.

Monique is fourteen. She does not remember having been a sickly child. She is as robust as a young plant that has found its soil and is growing thickly.

She is at the marvelous age of reading, in which the imaginary world reveals itself, and when youth envelopes the real world with its magic veil. She has no notion of evil, so vigilantly has her educator weeded that naturally healthy soul. She has, instead, a sentiment of and appetite for good.

Not a dreamer, but a believer—no longer in God, however, for in that matter she has disengaged herself from the contradictory concepts of Abbé Macahire and Elisabeth Meere. She has gradually converted herself to the reasoned materialism of Aunt Sylvestre, while retaining, like her, a spiritual imprint. But she also manifests—the ferment of her double and initial mysticism—a tendency to the absolute. Thus, she has a horror of lying, and a religious adoration of justice.

She still has Elisabeth Meere as a great friend. The latter has changed her religion, from Lutheranism to Zionism. For three years she has been infatuated with Monique, all the more so because she has desired her hopelessly. She is due to leave school soon, and her hypocrisy recoils before the adolescent's evident purity. Her kisses would like to be emphatic, but dare not.

Monique, whose has a sentimental crush on the art teacher—a former Prix de Rome resembling Alfred de Musset—is as far from suspecting Zabeth's inclinations as the similarly-hidden salacity of Monsieur Rabbe, the fake Alfred.

It is a June day. Night is falling. It is still so warm in the garden that they have moist skin under their dresses. After dinner, Monique and Zabeth follow the lavender path that rises up to the big red rock, which overlooks the salterns and the sea beyond. In the distance, the Monts des Maures are visible, blue against the green sky. Out at sea there is a little orange sail, and in the sky, heavy coppery clouds.

"It's stifling," says Zabeth. Nervously, she plucks a perfumed leaf from a fruiting orange tree and bites into it.

They breathe in the odor of the tall eucalyptus; it mingles, in waves, with those of argeles and cystopteris ferns: all the intoxication of the Provencal soil.

Monique loosens her bodice and then raises her bare arms, searching in vain for a cool breeze. "*Zut!* Now my shoulder-strap's broken. The chemise slips down, revealing her breasts. They lift up their small but perfect roundness. On her blonde skin, veined with blue, the pink nipples are erect.

Zabeth sighs. "Another night when we'll sleep badly, even going to bed in the nude. Do you know that your breasts are getting as big as mine?

"No?" says Monique, delighted.

"Yes, look! Only yours are apples and mine are pears..."

Zabeth rapidly bares her gilded bosom, in which the heavier fruits are displayed in tacit offering. She compares the elongated forms and brown, hard nipples with the satiny elegance of Monique's breasts. Her hand cups them and caresses them softly.

Monique smiles at the agreeable sensation without analyzing it and without understanding...but as Zabeth's fingers clench she says: "Stop it! What's got into you?"

Zabeth blushes and stammers: "I don't know...it's the storm!"

For the first time, Monique experiences a strange disturbance. Swiftly, she closes her bodice. At the same time, a distant voice rings out. It's Aunt Sylvestre, calling: "Monique! Zabeth!"

Zabeth buttons herself up, embarrassed.

"Hello!" Monique replies.

The voice forms an echo, coming closer.

The storm has passed.

Monique is seventeen. She counts: one...two...three years the war has lasted, already. Is it possible? The third long vacation since Hyères has come, like a big hospital in which the wounded are reborn.

She is pursued by the haggard eyes that the sun causes to blink, on emergence from their eternal night of fear. She does not understand how those who fight can accustom themselves to the frightful death that is their lives. She does not understand either how those who put on a semblance of fighting a little—so little!—and those who do not fight at all accept the suffering and carnage of others.

The idea that one part of humanity is bleeding while the other amuses and enriches itself upsets her. The big words agitated over all of it like flags—Order, Right, Justice—complete the fortification within her of her nascent revolt against the social lie.

She has passed the final examinations of her studies brilliantly, having pursued them between her incessant and ingenious means of devotion—not only on behalf of the convalescents of the Hyères but also the obscure crowd which is prey to all the evils in the fetid bed of the trenches.

Now, a new existence is beginning: Paris; courses at the Sorbonne. Monique has returned to the family home. She has said goodbye to Aunt Sylvestre, the boarding school, the garden, to everything that has made her an alert young woman with a bold and pure gaze and fresh cheeks. Adieu to the gentle past, where, in acquiring health, she has also acquired a soul.

Her old bedroom in the Avenue Henri-Martin, nicely prepared, has caused her a real pleasure. She has been touched by the welcome of her father and mother. She feels that she counts, now, in the eyes of her parents; she does them honor... Aunt Sylvestre has sown; they will harvest. Happy herself, she no longer holds their detachment or their egotism against them. She loves them on principle...

For the first time since 1914 they have gone to stay in Trouville. Monique devotes her month of August to serving as a voluntary nurse at the auxiliary hospital, number 37. She is so absorbed during the day by her occupations, and in the evening by her books, that she pays no heed to others. Those she observes the least are the ones closest to her: her mother, always running around, her father, always absent. The Lerbier factory is doing war work and, it seems, making millions manufacturing explosives. And to think that in the meantime, under cover, refugees and spectators are tranquilly and frenetically painting the town red, coupling and dancing the tango, dancing the tango and coupling, in Deauville!

Monique is nineteen. The nightmare has come to an end. Such an expansive force, such a need for blossoming, is within her, that, since the armistice, she has almost forgotten the war.

Self-contained more than ever, and increasingly less involved in the existence of her parents, she is following courses in literature and philosophy, actively practicing sports—tennis and golf—and amusing herself the rest of the time making artificial flowers, using her own method.

The social group of which she is reluctantly a part declares her to be an eccentric, not to say a poseur, because she does not like either flirting or dancing. Monique, conversely, judges her friends to be more or less unconscious fools, and profoundly depraved. Dig like Michelle Jacquet into the trouser pockets of her boyfriends? Or, like Ginette Morin, lock herself away in every corner with her girl friends? No thank you.

If she were to love, Monique would only love on a grand scale, giving herself to it entirely. She has not yet encountered that. Among all the men that her mother mentions to her—having decided to marry her off as soon as possible—there is really only one name: Lucien Vigneret, the industrialist; but although she has taken pleasure in distinguishing him on several occasions, he has not even noticed her...

Lying on her divan, therefore, Monique dreams. In superimposed visions, her life files past on the mysterious screen: hallucinatory precisions detached by memory from the backcloth of forgetfulness, and reincarnated...

She thinks about those vanished doubles of herself. Today, she is twenty, and she is in love.

She is in love, and she is going to be married. In a fortnight, she will be Madame Vigneret. The dream is being realized. She closes her eyes and smiles. She thinks, emotionally, still confused, about the Mairie and her official celebration, and the mind-numbing tra-la-la of the lunch at which, with lewd innuendos, a crowd of people will congratulate her, doing nothing to her happiness.

Ingenuously, she has allowed herself to be taken, has given everything, two days ago, to the one who is everything to her...a hasty, painful embrace, but of which she retains a proud joy. Her Lucien, her faith, her life! She is going to see him again in a little while, at the sale. Her entire being reaches out toward the sweet moment.

She has acted, since she loves him, as he desired. She is happy and proud to be, from now on, his "wife," to have demonstrated confidence by that supreme proof of abandonment. Wait? Refuse herself until the calculated evening of consecration? Why? What creates the value of unions is not the legal sanction but the determination of choice. As for *propriety*...a week sooner, a week later...!

Propriety! She smiles, with a malicious blush, on imagining the peremptory word sounding in her mother's mouth. If she knew!

Monique shivered; the door opened. Madame Lerbier appeared, her hat on her head.

"Not ready? You're mad! The auto is here. Have you forgotten that I'm dropping you at half past two at Foreign Affairs?"

"There, Maman—I only have to put my coat on."

Madame Lerbier raised her eyes to the heavens and moaned: "I'm going to be late for my meeting!"

II

"Ginette!" Monique exclaimed.

"What?"

"Your flirt!"

"Léo? Where? One can't see anything in this crowd."

"At Hélène Suze's stall, choosing a cigar..."

"I can hear their dirty talk from here! Look at them smiling!"

"It doesn't seem to bother you."

"Me? It amuses me."

"Don't understand!"

"Ginette Morin laughed. "Monique, I adore you! You never understand anything! Deep down, you're just silly, in spite of your independent airs."

Ginette had already turned her back, showing her merchandise and smiling at a short, plump, long-haired man: Jean Plombino, the king of profiteers.

"A cravat, my dear Monsieur? Oh, not to hang you...to await that of the Légion d'honneur. Or these pretty handkerchiefs? No? This box of gloves, then...?"

Under the bouquets of enormous chandeliers, sparkling in the icy foliage of their droplets, a continuous rumor rose up in the white and gold sequence of the reception rooms. The mythological characters on the large tapestries, alternating with the red damask of the walls, seemed to be contemplating the crowd with astonishment as it circulated or bunched up from one counter to the next, filing the immense gallery on the ground floor of the Ministry—transformed into a saleroom for the day—with a hubbub of voices and eddies of elegance. Parisian High Society, assembled there, was buzzing like a vast swarm of hornets.

Jean Plombino, a Papal Baron, was listening distractedly to Mademoiselle Morin. He sensed Monique's gaze posed upon him; he bowed low, his hair plunging. He was the widower of a Sicilian orange-seller and was looking for an educator worthy of his new wealth for his only daughter.

A poisonous mushroom of the war, but a Jewish mushroom and hence very attached to the familial soil, the "Baron" retained, in his monetary fetishism, that of conjugal virtue. Beneath her bold appearance, he had discerned Monique's rectitude and honesty: qualities all the more precious in his eyes because he had always lacked them, and knew how rare they were in the display of young women awaiting husbands, or, by default, lovers. One only had to reach out! Prices marked; just choose.

There was only one inconvenience in regard to the little Lerbier, whose blonde radiance fascinated him: her imminent marriage to Lucien Vigneret, the automobile manufacturer. A good pedigree, evidently, but what a woman-chaser! It was only a matter of time. Who could tell? Perhaps, one day or another, a divorce? And then, for want of a wife, what a mistress! The Plombino millions would make her forget his ugliness, that of a pachyderm with moist skin. A man with an annual income of twelve hundred thousand francs is always sure of a warm welcome...

Vexed by the cold greeting with which his demonstration had just collided, he redoubled his lewd attentions to Ginette Morin. She was a piquant brunette, whose company, in bed...

He had only imagined her there by way of a pastime. In fact, to the same extent that Monique appeared to him an enviable companion, Ginette inspired no confidence at all in him. For trifling, that was another matter! His lip drooping at that idea, he licked it.

Stimulated, he acquiesced: "A box of gloves? Why not? Especially if you let me try them on."

"Six pairs would take rather a long time."

"I don't think so..." He laughed coarsely.

Her eyes widened in astonishment. "What's funny about that? They're glacé kid, seven and a quarter..."

"That's not my size."

28

"Evidently!" She laughed in her turn, insolently, at the spectacle of the stout hands he displayed.

Jean Plombino, who had hoisted more than one sack onto his shoulder when he had been a stevedore in the Genoa docks earning three francs a day, had at least retained the wit not to blush at his plebeian origins. The humility of old spiced the self-congratulation of his fortune with pride.

"Not everyone can have your fairy-like fingers," he mocked, "even by paying the price."

Ginette was silent; what was he insinuating? And what did that reference to commerce mean, coming from him? What if there were a good reason for it? Baronne Plombino? Repulsive as the animal was, in that case, one might consider it...

But the Baron continued; "Ah! Here comes Léo, the arbiter of elegance! Bonjour, Monsieur Léonidas Mercoeur...Mademoiselle Morin is waiting for you."

"It's Hélène Suze's fault," said the newcomer, excusing himself with a complicit wink. "I was carrying out your commission, Mademoiselle."

"And?"

"Understood."

What a threesome! she thought. Behind her imperturbable gaze, the evening was mapped out: the pleasure of a smoke at Anika Gobrony's place, the novelty of cocaine, and whatever might follow...!

She imagined it with a confused precision, in her unhealthy curiosity as a quarter-virgin in search of all the vices.

The Baron sensed that he was excess to requirements. Taking a blue banknote out of his wallet, he said: "For your good works, Mademoiselle, with my respects to your mother."

"At least take something. Here, this sachet. Carnation—my perfume."

"As a souvenir, then. As for the gloves..." He pointed at Mercoeur. "They're for him. Your size will fit him, I'll wager."

Beaming, he waddled to the next counter, where Madame Bardinot and Michelle Jacquet were making amicable gestures to him.

"There's no longer an aristocracy!" pronounced the distributor of worldly verdicts, with an elegiac bitterness. "Money has leveled everything. It's the reign of universal boorishness."

Léonidas Mercoeur—Léo for short—floated, by definition, above such miseries. Fattened since the age to please by the generosity of his mistresses, before fruitful speculations in military supplies had definitively sheltered him from need, as well as from enemy fire, in 1915, the former hairdresser promoted to chronicler of society lived on his income: thirty thousand bullets, in State bonds. His war chest. Since having experienced the pleasure of auxiliary services, he continued it in civilian life. As Madame Bardinot's bidet-emptier, he met his minor expenses—double his income—a part of which she obtained from her lover, the banker Ransom. That did not prevent the handsome Léo, the confidant of old women and tutor of the young, from fishing in the troubled waters of every encounter, to some small benefit.

Purchasers interrupted their private conversation. Proud of being more well-patronized that her best friend, young Jacquet, whose urchin profile she could see at the next counter, Ginette spared no effort, her eyes sparkling as she leaned forward. Her neck bare and her breasts visible under light crepe, it seemed that with every object sold, to all comers, she dispensed a little of herself. An arrogant satisfaction was mingled with her sensual excitement; she would have the largest receipts of the evening!

"Wait there, Léo! You haven't told me anything."

Perceiving Max de Laume and Sacha Volant heading toward them, he whispered very rapidly: "Tomorrow, six o'clock, at Anika's. We'll have all the time in the world, since your parents are dining at the Élysée."

"Rendezvous?"

"With Hélène Suze at the tea-rooms in the Place Vendôme."

"You're a love!"

He was bowing ceremoniously, taking his leave, when an increase in the agitation and the murmur caused them to turn their heads. People moved aside, making way. Like a tall ship, the stiff, smooth statue of John White, the American billionaire, appeared, escorted by a small rolling sloop—that was the wife of General Merlin, in person, the President of the Oeuvre des Mutilés Français, who was doing the honors—and followed by a noisy fleet of aged gentlemen and beautiful ladies.

"Here come the serious clients," joked Léo. "I'm off!"

Having turned her back to Ginette and disinterested herself in her exploits, Monique was surprised to see the wave of officials unfurling in her direction. Where were they headed? Doubtless for the counter of the director of the sale, Madame Hutier, the Vice-President of the Oeuvre? No! It was in front of her own display of artificial flowers that the cortege came to a halt.

Pale with jealousy, Ginette hastened to the rescue, and Madame Hutier came running, simpering.

"May I introduce our dear Vice-President, Madame Hutier, the wife of the former minister," said the General's wife, turning to John White.

The billionaire's bony face did not move, save for a mechanical jerk of the neck in honor of the unknown governor.

"Mademoiselle Morin," the daughter of the illustrious sculptor.

In spite of her engaging reverence, Ginette saw her name assessed by the same indifferent dip.

"Mademoiselle Lerbier."

An expression of interested suddenly relaxed the angular features.

"Ah...chemical products? I know...and these little things?"

He inclined his long body over the tiny marvels— narcissi, roses and anemones—like a flowering of gems in a doll's garden.

"Mademoiselle Lerbier amuses herself making them. A veritable artist…and so Parisian!"

The General's wife, surprised to see the automaton that she had been ferrying around for twenty minutes, without any other result than the occasional "oh" and his minuscule nods, come to life, seized the opportunity that she had been seeking thus far in vain to interest her visitor in the destiny of the Oeuvre.

"She's one of our most devoted collaborators. The injured men adore her."

Really? thought Monique, who had only been to the great Hospice de Boisfleury once, and had come back so distressed that she had not had the courage go to back since. *That's a bit strong!*

But with a military glance, the General's wife invited her to understand and play along. At the same time, John White enveloped her with a sympathetic gaze. He had picked up a tiny hawthorn twig. He examined it curiously.

"Aren't those white petals lovely?" gushed the President. "Notice the delicacy of tone. One can't tell whether it's ivory or jade."

"It's only dried breadcrumbs and paint," Monique rectified.

"Oh!" said John White. "Really? I'll keep it."

And while he handed the delicate jewel to the stout Madame Merlin, he took out a checkbook and a pen from the inside pocket of his jacket, and impassively signed and detached two checks, one for five thousand francs made out to the stupefied Monique—"For the hawthorn"—and the other, for ten thousand francs, to the President, whose rounded face was glowing like the full moon: "For the wounded."

Then, having smiled at Monique without saying another word, he distributed a triple nod of the head, collectively, to the counter, and resumed his route, without manifesting the slightest desire to pause at the next stall, in spite of the prostrations of Madame Bardinot.

It was, however, appropriate to offer a glass of champagne as soon as possible to the donor. The President, satisfied, now disdained superfluous demonstrations. Pressing behind the American sailing ship and the pilot sloop, the wave of the cortege flowed toward the buffet.

"You've never said, my dear, that you were in correspondence with America," said Madame Hutier, reproachfully.

"Me? I've never heard of John White."

"That's true," attested a newcomer.

Monique turned round upon hearing the voice that, for her, immediately drowned out all the rest.

"But John White must have heard of Monsieur Lerbier's invention," Lucien Vigneret concluded.

Monique was suddenly enlightened. A pink flush suddenly animated the delicate pallor of her complexion.

"What! You already know?"

"It's the big Event!"

"I can't get over it..."

As usual, Ginette said to herself, returning to her business, convinced that the whole thing had been prearranged.

Meanwhile, Madame Hutier, indulgent to the success and to consecrated love, hastened to leave the lovers to their confidences. *What a lovely couple—and so well matched!*

Monique and Lucien mimed the exchanged of a kiss with their lips. Beneath the banality of words, she heard nothing but the song of her happiness.

"Don't look for midday at two o'clock," Vigneret continued. "It's not to merit your smile, although it's well worth the check that John White forked out. The blow was aimed at your father. The fellow must think that the integration of nitrogen into agricultural fertilizer has a profitable application on American soil. And as John White, Francophile, would rather deal with Aubervilliers than Ludwigshaven...you get it?"

"Well, the dollars will be welcome."

With a bitterness that surprised her, he remarked: "Certainly. Gold is always welcome, especially when, under the dollar sign, it's louis that are returning."

"They're returning to our industry what we've spent on armaments. A fine misfortune. All the same, it's not the fault of New York that Paris and Berlin were at war."

He agreed: "You're right, Minerva."

He was joking, with that nickname given as much to her logic, whose categorical affirmations he feared, even while holding them in esteem, as to her beauty...

Minerva! She detested the comparison, under which she divined a reticence: an ill-defined point at which their characters could not succeed in reaching accord. The only shadow on her love! She looked at him. He smiled.

"It's very unkind," she murmured, "to tease me every time I talk seriously. Fundamentally. I don't care about anything except us."

He contemplated her, flattered.

She murmured: "You're the present, the future, my body, my soul...it's so good to have absolute confidence in one another. You'll never deceive me, will you, Lucien? For one thing, eyes like yours couldn't, wouldn't be able to lie! Tell me everything you're thinking! Lucien...Lucien! Where are you?"

He took her hand, kissed her on the wrist for a long time, and murmured: "Present!" And in the same breath he modulated: "I love you!" But he was thinking: *She's tiresome, with her mania for sincerity. That promises pleasure for the future...perhaps I've been wrong not to be more frank with her. I ought to have told her everything, about Cléo. Or, at least, asked her father to tell her part of the truth. It's too late now...*

I love you: at the incantation of the magic words, Monique relived the unforgettable hour: the two of them alone, by chance, in the apartment where they would soon be living, and into which she was taking so much pleasure in moving. She had only one desire, but dared not formulate it: that the opportunity would come up again.

Little by little, without divining the road that he was following in an inverse direction, she recapitulated, going over everything, day by day, that would conclude by uniting them: their movements, their rendezvous. That evening, the daily visit. Tomorrow at five o'clock, the furrier; then a glance at the Empire furnisher recommended by Pierre des Souzaies; then tea at the Ritz...

She pulled a face. "What a pity you have an engagement in the evening! It would have been so nice to dine with us, and after the theater, to celebrate Christmas Eve. I'll keep your place anyway...you know, box 27. Alex Marly in *Ménélas*."

"It will be impossible for me to get out of it. But I assure you that's important business."

Yes, the licensing of his new car, the sale to be made, with the Belgians having come expressly from Antwerp. They would settle it more easily in the agreeable atmosphere of a supper. He had told her all that, and she admitted it as one of the tedious necessities of his profession.

"Next year, of course," she specified, wagging a menacing finger, "we'll no longer be apart."

She saw herself, after the intoxication of the honeymoon, collaborating even in daily labor. They would share everything, cares as well as pleasures.

"Swear?"

"Of course!"

At thirty-five, Lucien Vigneret was approaching marriage as one approaches a harbor after a stormy voyage. With the certainty of being loved, he savored the calm of mind in advance, and the satisfaction of the senses. He viewed the perspective of that stability as something akin to the warmth of a pair of slippers. He was only thinking of his own happiness.

Monique's? He was convinced that he would ensure it, while enjoying himself, with tenderness, attention and, soon, the absorbing presence of children...absorbing for the mother. For, even about children he scarcely cared, already having one abandoned daughter in the world: a responsibility that weighed upon him no more heavily now than his last dog, which had been run over. His greatest torment at present was the inevitable rupture, at least in appearance, with his mistress Cléo, a milliner…a young woman that he had debauched, and then set up in an apartment, who was counting on marrying him some day.

A jealous, impetuous nature—just like Monique!—but franker and more spontaneous: liable to stick, he thought, especially since he had conquered her without reserve. He feared some explosion, on one side or the other, at the Mairie. How could that be avoided? By keeping her suspicions dormant until the end…between now and then he would be the master, with the patent in his pocket, of the Lerbier business. Afterwards, he would see! Ready to harness the two of them discreetly to begin with…

Lucien Vigneret, shrewd calculator, was counting on a considerable coup in the association with his future father-in-law: a pact concluded in principle, of which Monique unwittingly was the stake.

Afflicted by the general financial crisis, the Lerbier factory, beneath its brilliant surface, was tottering. What remained of its war profits had melted away in the pursuit of a new invention. Lucien nevertheless judged that he would be making a magnificent deal in giving in exchange for the contract the unpaid five hundred thousand francs of Monique's dowry, and only bringing to the Lerbier-Vigneret Company five hundred thousand of fresh money. The transformation of nitrogen, diligently exploited, would be solid gold—hence his undissimulated ill-humor at the disquieting generosity of John White, a possible shareholder. After the marriage, as much as he wanted! Until then, the girl had, in Vigneret's eyes, the full value of the patent—but no more than that.

In treating her in that fashion, he was neither better nor worse than the majority of men.

He was about to say *au revoir* to Monique when she held him back, with a spontaneous supplication.

"Maman's coming. Stay. You can come with us."

In her ingenuous fervor, she was enjoying the precarious moment, like a nun regarding eternity. Did not Lucien, with his decided bearing, his muscular slimness and his jet eyes, hold sway over everything? The most handsome man, beside her. Even Sacha Volant, the former aviator turned racing-car driver, and even Antinous, alias Max de Laume, the literary critic of the *Nouvelle Anthologie Française*, paled by comparison.

Indeed, she perceived them pressing around Ginette.

Mademoiselle Morin inspected Monique's stock scornfully. Although the end of the sale was approaching, it was still more than half full. Pointing to an empty space in front of her, she said: "You're too late. I don't have anything left to sell."

"Yes!" protested Sacha Volant.

"No. What?"

"That!"

He pointed to the rose that was wilting in her waistband.

Max de Laume underlined, with an ambiguous smile: "Your flower."

"Too dear for you, my young friends," Ginette riposted.

"Indeed!" they exclaimed. "How much? Name a price."

"I don't know. Twenty five louis? Is that too much?"

"It's nothing," Sacha Volent assured her, gallantly. "I say thirty, and cheap at the price!"

"Forty!" said Max de Laume.

"Fifty!"

Mademoiselle Morin judged the equivocation, if not the auction, sufficient, and, detaching the rose, which Sacha Volant was already getting ready to seize, she handed it to Mercoeur, who had just reappeared.

"Judged, Messieurs!" she said, with a mocking grimace. "I'm not selling it. I'm giving it away."

In the large reception rooms, where the crowd was less dense and the rumor was attenuated, the charity sale was finishing with private receptions. The orchestra of the Garde Republicaine had succeeded the famous jazz band of Tom

Frick. Foxtrots and shimmies were quivering between the tables in the main hall where the buffet was. Around the counters, where groups had formed in accordance with sympathies, bursts of laughter and voices resonated more loudly. One might have thought it, after the bustle of the afternoon, the enthusiasm of a select party, in which high society was closing ranks. The five or six hundred representatives of all the sacristies and all the headquarters were there. They were at home.

"Your mother isn't coming," said Vigneret. "Six o'clock! I need to run. Indispensable business." The rendezvous with Cléo, at her place, was at quarter past six. He only just had time.

"Until this evening, then," she sighed. "Don't be too late."

"Half past nine, as usual..."

He drew away under her tender gaze. When he had disappeared, Monique experienced the sensation of an abrupt isolation. What was she doing in this fair of all the vanities and all the corruptions?

The luxury and stupidity that was on parade there, beneath those governmental chandeliers—together with the loud adding up of the receipts, proclaimed by everyone with the closing of cashboxes—sickened her. The gilded banner: *For the Benefit of the French Wounded* did not succeed in eclipsing, in her memory or her sensibility, the atrocious vision of the great Hospice de Boisfleury.

Familiar as she had been, once, with suffering and hospitals, that spectacle—the human woodlice dragging themselves along or hopping on crutches, trunks maneuvering on wheels, huge facial wounds; all that debris of men who had once had intelligence, hope, love, and no longer had anything but formless stumps, pulp features, blank eyes and tortured mouths—was an intolerable memory. It pursued her with an unspeakable horror. A war crime, stained with filth that all the gold in the world and all the pity of earth could never efface from the bloody forehead of humankind!

38

The shrill laughter of Ginette Morin rose up. At the same time, Monique perceived her mother. She hurried to meet her.

Madame Lerbier, blooming in her furs, advanced non-chalantly.

"Let's go, quickly!"

"What's the matter?"

"I feel sick."

"It's not surprising with this heat," Madame Lerbier commiserated. "Come on! You can wait while I make a little tour?" And as she was stifling, she took off her sable stole. The pearl necklace appeared around the fleshy neck.

III

"It's tiresome," said Madame Lerbier, as they went down the broad steps of the Ministry. "Your father has kept the auto. Since he's not coming back with us, Lucien might have thought of leaving you his."

"Bah! We'll find a taxi."

"I have a horror of those machines! They're dirty, and one's risking death every two minutes..."

"We'll go on foot then." She laughed.

Her mother looked at her sideways.

"In any case, Maman, if taxis disgust you, there's always the tram on the other side of the bridge."

"Very witty!"

Monique was well aware of her mother's horror of democratic means of transport: promiscuity, slowness... It had a bad odor, and it was never-ending!

She shrugged her shoulders. "You'll admit that a nice limousine..."

"Obviously! An income of a hundred is better than fifty, fifty than twenty-five, and so on... But the auto, you know! Even if Lucien didn't have one, I'd have as much pleasure in marrying him."

"A thatched cottage and a heart! You're an idealist, and you're young. I'm looking forward to the time when you have a daughter to marry off." She moaned. "Hail that one! Hail it, then! Hey! Driver...!"

Disdainfully, the man clad in leather passed by without making any response.

"Brute! Bolshevik!" She took her daughter as a witness. "That's where it's taking us, your socialism."

Despairingly, she was contemplating the quay, swept by the bitter wind, when a sumptuous coupé drew up at the sidewalk level with them, in response to the appeal of a crier. At the same time, Michelle Jacquet, who came out behind them,

40

shouted: "Madame! Madame! Would you like me to give you a lift home?"

"What!" Madame Lerbier exclaimed. "You're alone?"

"Madame Bardinot, to whom my saintly mother has confided me, has been abducted by Léo."

Madame Lerbier could not help saying: "Naturally!"

"Oh," observed Michelle, while she installed herself beside the driver, "I don't think that'll go any further. Léo's making eyes at Ginette; to punish him, he can soon be given a successor. Isn't that so, Monique?"

"I haven't noticed anything."

"She only has eyes for her Lucien. My fiancé doesn't inconvenience me, you see. Only the Marquisat d'Entraygues springs to Mère Jacquet's eyes. For the price of my dowry she could as easily have got a Duc!"

Madame Lerbier tutted, scandalized. "Oh, Michelle, if your excellent mother heard you talk like that about her future son-in-law…"

"Her ears would fall off."

"The young women of today have no respect for anything! In fact, why haven't we had the pleasure of meeting her today?"

"Her Thursday, you know."

Michelle avoided that solemnity, as much as she could. A meeting place for old and young Messieurs on the make or itching to show themselves off. Various shades of bluestocking also appeared there. Madame Jacquet, the author of a little book of Maxims, was a member of the Societé George Sand, which awarded a literary prize of fifteen thousand francs.

"Her Thursday, that's true," repeated Madame Lerbier, with compunction. As much as she scorned Madame Bardinot, while cajoling her, she revered the wealth of Madame Jacquet. She was a former dancer who had eventually extracted herself from prostitution, with her famous pearl necklaces and her town house in the Avenue du Bois, married to an ambassador. He had died senile during the war, and she wore demi-mourning with majesty, as the official father of Michelle, inherited along with everything else. By virtue of her freethinking salon, frequented simultaneously by the Nuncio and the President of the Sénat, Madame Jacquet had become influential. She made academicians and brought ministries down.

While Monique, enclosed in her daydream, responded with monosyllables to the gibes with which Michelle clawed her young friends, Madame Lerbier allowed herself to be cradled, indolently. An excellent vehicle, after the fatiguing afternoon engagements... An exhibition of English portraits! The crowd, in which one could hardly see anything! Then the new Tea-Dance Hall in the Rue Daunou—not a single table free! And from five to six, to finish off, Roger's divan...

A frisson ran from the nape of her neck to the hollow of her back. She smiled mysteriously at the narrow mirror that sent her reflection back to her, above the crystal and gold compact. The wrinkles under the skillful make-up and severe massages were no more evident there than the kisses of a little while ago...

Uniquely preoccupied with her person, Madame Lerbier, at fifty, had but one aim: to look as if she were thirty. It was thus that, a distracted housekeeper, she presided with detachment over the running of her household, satisfied as long as the money came in every month. What might her husband do or think? That had no more existence for her than the secret being of her daughter. In spite of, or because of, her smiling egotism, she was nonetheless, in general opinion, the beautiful and good Madame Lerbier. Thanks to her art of appearing to live more fully than others, and her dress sense, she was even spared malevolent gossip.

"*Au revoir*, my darling, until tomorrow," Michelle said, kissing Monique. "We'll see you at the theater? *Au revoir*, Madame."

"My regards to your mother."

"Don't worry! She'll have a smile when she knows we've come back together. She likes you."

Madame Lerbier swelled up even further with pride as she went past her braided concierge, who bowed deeply.

42

Those testimonies of social consideration, from the top to the bottom rung, seemed to her as necessary as breathable air. She could not imagine that there might be any other atmosphere than that of prejudice, within which and for which she lived...

The elevator stopped. The door of the apartment opened at the same time. It was Aunt Sylvestre, who had just come in, prudently, via the stairs, and who had heard them.

"You see," joked Madame Lerbier, perceiving her sister. "We're not dead!"

The old lady retained two fears from her provincial reclusion: that of cages suspended with their panels of buttons and their comings-and-goings on cables, and that of road junctions to be crossed in the midst of autobuses.

"Your Paris," she declared, "is a madhouse!" She tapped Monique's hand.

After kissing her, the latter said: "At least you enjoyed yourself at the Français?"

Every time she made the trip, Aunt Sylvestre treated herself to a classical play.

"That's the only thing lacking in Hyères...otherwise, it would be the terrestrial paradise. Admit it!"

"I admit it."

Monique kissed the old parchmented face again. Much more than her mother, she thought she was the daughter of that worthy woman. Hyères! Yes...the harmonious past rose up in her grateful memory. Her schoolgirl room...the classroom, open to the blue...and the garden, and the great rock: a belvedere from which she had thought one might be able to discover the world!

"Well," said Aunt Sylvestre, "look at you, my little cabbage. You have letters..."

Monique picked up a pile of envelopes from the lacquered tray and darted a glance over them.

"Nothing. Always advertisements!"

She was amused by the addresses, in which "Madame Vigneret" was already juxtaposed with her maiden name, variously scrawled. There were offers of all sorts, from the visiting cards of information agencies (Discretion and Celerity!) to good wishes from the women of the market, and advertisements for brassieres.

"You don't think that publicity indecent? Tell me, Aunt! I think newlyweds should be left in peace. The ceremony is nobody else's business, after all. Come on—we'll chat while I get dressed. It does me good to be able to speak with an open heart. It seems to me that I'm wiping away mud!"

She finished putting on a silk dress—one of those ample tunics that hang by themselves in supple pleats along the lines of the body.

"I like that!" she said. "How comfortable it is! One could believe that one were naked, and it's as chaste as a Greek robe. Do you remember the archaic Diana in the Musée de Marseille?"

"With the stole falling to her feet? Yes."

Gripped by a need for exuberance, Monique had seized her bewildered aunt around the waist, and, sketching out a dance, she began to sing.

> We won't go back to the woods!
> The laurels have been cut!
> The beauty that is here,
> Let's go to collect...
> Come and join the dance!
> See how we dance!
> Leap! Dance! Embrace
> The one that you desire![5]

Then she burst out laughing, and the worthy old woman was willfully kissed on the nose and on the chin, with a benevolent gaze...

---

[5] The words are those of a traditional children's song, lines of which had been quoted in numerous previous literary works, including a poem by Théodore Banville and the title of a novel by Édouard Dujardin.

"Oof!" said Aunt Sylvestre, sitting down again.

Now, her arms raised, along which the long sleeves had slipped back uncovering the gilded armpits, Monique put up her hair. She resembled, with her young firm-breasted bosom, a statuette of Victory at the prow of her destiny.

"Did you see that there's a letter under the advertisements?" asked Aunt Sylvestre. She turned it over. "It has a strange appearance..."

"No—show it to me."

The envelope was greasy, of coarse paper, the handwriting unwieldy. It reeked of anonymity.

With a disgusted expression, Monique opened it.

"Well?" exclaimed Aunt Sylvestre, before the expression of astonishment, which reddened with indignation.

"Oh—read it."

"I don't have my spectacles. Go on—I'll listen."

With a scornful voice, which took on an involuntary hint of anxiety as she went along, Monique read:

"*Mademoiselle, it's sad to think that someone is deceiving a young woman like you. The man you're about to marry doesn't love you. He's making a business deal. You aren't the first. He already has others on his conscience. If you don't believe me, ask Madame Lureau, 192 Rue de Vaugirard. She's the mother of the girl he seduced and abandoned after she gave birth to a little girl. Today he has another mistress. Her name is Cléo. He goes to see her every day. She knows nothing, and they love one another very much. I thought I ought to inform you. A woman who feels sorry for you...*"

With a swift gesture, she tore the denunciation into little pieces.

"Into the fire—that's all that's worth!"

"Why must there be such villainous souls?" murmured Aunt Sylvestre. "What can malevolence not invent?" The precision of the first item of information, however—the name and address—preoccupied her. Perhaps, all the same, it was worth checking? She promised herself to do so, without worrying Monique in advance.

45

Divining her plan, however, the latter became annoyed.

"No, no!" We won't do Lucien the insult of such a suspicion! He told me that there was nothing serious in his bachelor life. To suppose him capable of such an action for a single instant would be to diminish myself! And as for the so-called Cléo..."

She smiled. Had her father not affirmed, after Lucien, that that was ancient history? A caprice concluded before their love commenced...

Dinner was very cheerful. Monique joined in chorus with her Aunt's pleasantry with so much enthusiasm that Madame Lerbier sometimes looked at her covertly. Her daughter's nervousness appeared to her to be more exaggerated than usual tonight.

"Monique!" she said, showing her the back of the chambermaid, who was shaking with laughter. On the service trolley, the plate of *foie gras* in port was quivering.

But Monique was in full flow. "Say, Papa, do you know what Ponette has baptized Léo: the *mec plus ultra*."[6]

Monsieur Lerbier raised his bird-like head. "No?"

"Michelle heard her!"

"Who's Ponette?" enquired Aunt Sylvestre.

"Madame Bardinot."

"Why Ponette?"

"A derivative of Paulette...because she's easy to mount."

This time, Madame Lerbier thought it necessary to take exception, for form's sake. "It's frightful how badly brought up you are!"

"Trapped, Aunt! If you hadn't taught me to tell the truth!"

"Pardon me! Your mother's right. Even for the truth, there are manners."

"Especially for the truth," Madame Lerbier overbid. "First of all, what is it, the truth?"

---

[6] *Mec* is a slang term for an elegantly-dressed man, less contemptuous than the English "fop"

"What I believe to be true," said Monique, incisively.

"And there you are! She has the monopoly! What do you say, Schoolmistress?"

Aunt Sylvestre agreed with her sister.

"It's also," Monique conceded, less by way of excuse than explanation, "that that milieu disgusts me! Fortunately, Lucien bears no more resemblance to those puppets than I do to those dolls."

She searched with her gaze for her aunt's approval.

"You need to know, however," said Madame Lerbier, determined to have the last word, "that with your manner of speaking and acting solely at the whim of our inspirations, you pass for a lunatic. Fundamentally, you're a *bacheloress*. Look at your friends, Ginette and Michelle. They're true young ladies—Michelle especially."

Monique put down her glass. She had nearly choked. Taking advantage of the chambermaid leaving, she said: "Their husbands won't be getting any gifts."

Madame Lerbier tutted, scandalized. She would have liked Monique, while not being an absolute white goose, to have maintained until marriage the decent ignorance that a mother would discreetly enlighten on the eve of the great day. Under the pretext of scientific education, however, that frankness did not recoil before anything—even, if necessary, calling the most secret organs by their names. No! Whatever Aunt Sylvestre might think, certain chapters of natural history ought to be limited to the vegetable realm, so far as young women were concerned. To anatomical precisions, Madame Lerbier preferred, in spite of its pseudo-danger, the dormant shadow: modesty. That was it—the modesty of mystery! Modesty: when she had uttered that great word, she had said it all.

"You cause me a great deal of pain," she murmured.

"It's necessary to face facts, Maman. Since the war, we've all become 'bacheloresses' to a greater or lesser extent."

Monsieur Lerbier abstained from intervening in such matters. He had resolved the sexual and sentimental problem

47

within the family by making a separate existence. Afterwards, and above all, the inventor had but one idea: to double the cap of the impending bankruptcy—and in order to do that, to conclude the marriage without delay.

In the meantime, it was necessary finally to inform his daughter of the agreement for which she was paying the expenses. How could he do that? She was counting on the promised dowry to contribute to the expenses of the household, at least to subsidize her personal expenditure...

At that idea, Monsieur Lerbier lowered his head. However, as they went into the drawing room, he straightened up. His wife was telling him about John White's liberalness. He asked for all the details.

"Aha!" he said. "I'll write to that Maecenas immediately, to thank him and invite him to visit the factory. We might even have him to lunch that day?"

He envisaged a golden prospect. Might he not obtain more from Vigneret by playing him off against White, and *vice versa*? Not to mention that he might then involve Ransom and Plombino...

He rubbed his hands. That needed examination! He forgot that Monique's love, a card already played in the game, was at stake. Had he thought about it, it would not have worried him overmuch. In business, his mildness became ferocious.

"Tuesday, do you think, my dear? We might also invite Plombino and Ransom, with the Minister of Agriculture..."

"And Lucien!" exclaimed Monique. "What are you doing? If it's a matter of your discovery..."

"Lucien as well, naturally."

She took advantage of him lighting a cigar, while the women sat down at the card table to play bezique, finally to let go of the preoccupation that was tormenting her.

"By the way, Papa, speaking of Lucien, I received an odd letter this evening...an anonymous letter."

Monsieur Lerbier turned round. "That's classic! What did it say?"

48

Without taking her eyes off her father, Monique summarized the letter. While she was speaking, her throat contracted, Monsieur Lerbier raised his arms to the heavens, but made no reply.

"In sum, Papa, what if the accusation is true? What if there really is a Mademoiselle Lureau in the Rue de Vaugirard?"

With a conviction that was semi-sincere, he declared: "Don't you think that I know him? One doesn't give one's daughter to someone without obtaining all the information..."

She breathed deeply.

"I was sure of it! It's the same for this Cléo, isn't it?"

Sensing dangerous ground, Monsieur Lerbier only advanced prudently. He affirmed: "You can't think that a man, at thirty-five, has always lived like a hermit. I don't say that your fiancé can't have had little adventures, like everyone else...oh, of no importance! All that's finished, buried, with his bachelor life..."

"There's still one thing that bothers me. The letter claims that Lucien, in marrying me, is making a business deal. I don't understand that."

Monsieur Lerbier scratched his head. The difficult moment had come.

"A business deal? Oh, God no...I can affirm that from that viewpoint, he's showing a great deal of elegance, even disinterest. Listen, my dear; I have a confession to make to you. I intended to bring you up to date soon, since it's necessary that we're all in accord before the signature of your contract. You've given me the opportunity...

"This is it. You know that before being my son-in-law, Lucian is to become my associate. You also know the value of my invention. I haven't talked to you about my life devoted to that research, the sum of effort that it represents...efforts, and also, alas, tribulations. I've been obliged, in order to reach the goal, to spend a great deal of money...a great deal...and to engage more than half our capital. And if it were necessary for me at this moment to liquidate the money of your dowry, as

I'd hoped to be able to do, I'd be inconvenienced...greatly inconvenienced..."

"Oh, Father, why didn't you tell me?"

"It pained me. It was then that your fiancé, knowing about my embarrassment, spontaneously offered for his part, in spite of the industrial crisis that we're all going through, to renounce the payment of the five hundred thousand francs...provided, of course, that you consent..."

"Of course, Father!"

"...And leave it at my disposal."

She kissed him.

"That's very kind! Why didn't he tell me?"

"He preferred that I do it myself. You understand: this will save me. We'll even be able to see entering into play the other propositions that are beginning to be sketched out: White, Ransom, Plombino. It's only a loan that you're making me, of course, no money lost, be sure of that! The future is magnificent...magnificent.

"You see, my child, that in consenting to take you as you are, at this moment—which is to say, without a sou—Lucien is behaving...as I was certain that you would cause him to do...he's treating me as a son. And with regard to you...do you see? No wife, more than you, can boast of having been married for love!"

After the initial impulse, Monique reflected. The disappointment of her material independence having vanished with Lucien's proposition? Tenderness, regret also, in her native pride, of being married without her bringing anything aside from the assistance of her good will, her ardent thirst for work? She was touched, above all, by the delicacy of the sentiment and the discretion of the gesture...

"It's genteel on his part, isn't it, Maman?" he said.

Aunt Sylvestre, who had been listening attentively, said: "May I put a word in? I'm sure that I'm going to be criticized by everyone, but so much the worse—I say what I think. Isn't it a million that Monsieur Vigneret is to subscribe to the constitution of your partnership?"

Monsieur Lerbier frowned. "Yes. Why?"

"So, in renouncing the five hundred thousand that wouldn't belong to him, since Monique is marrying under the regulation of the separation of wealth, it's that much less that he'll be paying out personally?"

"Obviously."

"That's all I wanted to know..."

"What are you insinuating?" exclaimed Madame Lerbier.

Nothing, nothing...I'm merely observing that the operation is advantageous, in these times of crisis, for everyone..."

"How's that?" asked Monique.

"For your father, in solving his predicament...for your fiancé, who, in forming the partnership at half price, is making that generosity at your expense. For you, finally, since, completely shorn, you can say *amen*..."

Monique burst out laughing.

"Aunt is right! Fundamentally, Father, in your calculations, you're only including me as neither more nor less than a zero. That's vexing!"

But she was so glad to have some sacrifice to make to those she loved—a sacrifice of money to one, of self-respect to the other—that all egotistical preoccupation was effaced. The joy of giving intoxicated her as much as that of receiving. She was in haste for Lucien to arrive, so that she could thank him, while teasing him. How he was making her wait!

The clock struck ten.

"He's late!" At the same time, she shivered. "There it is!"

Before anyone had heard anything, she perceived the magnetic presence. She could sense the approach...

The bell in the antechamber finally rang.

"What did I say?"

She went to open the drawing-room door, and took her fiancé by the hand.

"Come in, Monsieur. This is a fine state of affairs..."

He interrogated her with a vaguely anxious gaze.

"No excuses! First of all, you're late. Then, Monsieur my husband is permitting himself to dispose of me like a simple item of merchandise! You're already counting me as nothing, Monsieur? And what if I want my dowry myself?"

He perceived, beneath the mockery of the reproach, the fortunate submission. He blossomed. It would all go of its own accord…!

There was still that damned Cléo…another matter entirely…

He hid his anxiety by means of tender demonstrations.

Monique abandoned herself without restriction to the delight of loving and admiring. In her eyes, Lucien was all the beauties and all the virtues. She dressed him with the prism of her dreams, confident and spontaneous by nature, launching herself beyond common measures, ready to throw herself with equal violence into the bound and the rebound…

While Monsieur Lerbier, feigning an interest in bezique, sat down between his wife and Aunt Sylvestre, Monique and Lucian chatted, as usual, in the small drawing room, where they isolated themselves every evening.

They were sitting side by side on the large sofa, the sanctuary of blissful hours spent in the intimacy of conversation…and also the ecstatic minutes of the first kisses, in which she had offered herself with all her soul, before the definitive gift…

Monique seized Lucien's hands, and looked into the depths of his eyes.

"My god, I have something to ask of you."

"Granted in advance."

"Don't laugh—it's serious."

"Go on."

"That you never, never lie to me!"

He scented danger, and took the offensive. "Always your obsession! Do you know how annoying that is?"

"Forgive me, Lucien. I've put in you, religiously, all my hope. I would suffer so much if I were ever disappointed. For me, as I've told you, there is only one thing that is unpardonable between a man and a woman who love one another, and that's lying. Deception! And when I say deception, understand me: one can still pardon an error, a fault that one regrets and one confesses, but one can't forgive a lie. That's the true deception, and it's degrading, it's base..."

He acquiesced with a nod of the head. It was necessary to play a tight game.

"I beg your pardon if I'm a little nervous. When I came in, I received an anonymous letter, about which I'll only tell you this: I burned it, and I don't believe a word that it said."

He frowned, and very calmly said: "You were wrong to throw that filth in the fire. Perhaps there were useful indications, which would have permitted the confounding of the author..."

She slapped her forehead. "You think it's a man? Why didn't I think of that?"

She reproached herself for having thought that it was a woman's vengeance, and saw in his attitude, as well as the unexpectedness of the suggestion, the proof of which, being credulous, she had not had any concern.

He added: "Although someone has been able to write to you, I have no need to swear that it's false."

She closed his mouth. "I didn't believe it for a second."

He kissed her trembling fingers one by one. Tranquilized, he assured her: "I'm sure of it. Since you have my word! From the day when you've accorded me your hand, I've given you, in exchange, a faithful heart." He lowered his voice. "And from the day after tomorrow, my darling..."

He contemplated her, his eyes shining. She blushed, inclining her head onto the firm shoulder. She shivered all over at the memory. Then she looked up at him blissfully. Desire extended its mirage between them...

Without any afterthought, without any remorse, the man leaned over the mouth as open as a flower, and sealed the false oath with a long, profound kiss.

With her eyes closed, Monique lost herself in the communion.

IV

Aunt Sylvestre, unaccustomed to the encumbrances of Paris, anxiously watched the smooth velocity of the auto through the tangle of trams, trucks and taxis. A brush with an autobus had just extracted a "Good God!"

Monique took her hand and squeezed it. "Don't be scared. Marius is a good driver."

Since the previous evening's explanation, she smiled at everything. While Lucien had finished the night with his mistress, she had slept with a child-like insouciance. Her morning had been nothing but a song. She was taking delight now, in advance, in the visit that they were about to make to Professor Vignabos.

Comfortably installed in the car lent by Lucien—*her* Vigneret!—Monique experienced a satisfaction in chaperoning in her turn the worthy old lady who had raised her, and whose age as well as her sedentary province had gradually relegated her to the margins of existence.

"Do you remember Elisabeth Meere—Zabeth?" Monique said. "I saw her again last month. Lady Springfield, with two fine children and a Statesman for a husband! She's become a Theosophist and a Spiritualist."

Aunt Sylvestre shrugged her shoulders. "When one gets closer to God, it's because one is distancing oneself from men. It's true that she never liked them much."

Monique smiled at the definition of Elisabeth Springfield's new mysticism, and, by contrast, at the thought of her younger brother, Cecil Meere, a "philanthropist," and, furthermore, an amateur painter.

"Cecil is…the inverse."

Aunt Sylvestre became indignant. "There it is! That's the malady, the aberration! Decidedly…is it because I'm getting old? Is it because everything here is going backwards that your Paris frightens me? Long live my little corner! Ah!

Here's the Rue de Médicis...twenty-three...twenty-nine...we're here."

Monique was rejoicing, almost as much as her Aunt, in seeing Professor Vignabos again: an old bachelor, a celebrated historian, a glory of the Collège de France, with whom the humble schoolmistress had entertained, since the distant days of their studies in the Latin Quarter, an old camaraderie. Mademoiselle Sylvestre loved to re-soak herself, whenever she could, in that environment of sane ideology and free examination.

They both went up joyfully to the fifth floor apartment overlooking the Jardin du Luxembourg.

The antiquated staircase, the entrance door with a single batten, and the antechamber where hats and overcoats already signaled the presence of disciples all spoke of modesty. Monique exchanged a knowing smile with her Aunt. She preferred that dignified poverty to the ostentation of more sumptuous dwellings.

"Ah! My good Sylvestre!" exclaimed Monsieur Vignabos, surprise causing him to push his bonnet too far back on his Socratic cranium. "I'm glad to see you! And you, too, Mademoiselle. Permit me to introduce to you...Monsieur Régis Boisselet, the novelist...Monsieur Georges Blanchet, professor of philosophy at Cahors, one of my old pupils..."

Tugging his beard with a mechanical gesture habitual to him, as if he were extracting the thread of his discourse, he resumed the one that he had interrupted, after the reciprocal politenesses.

"I was in the process of demonstrating that marriage, as we see it practiced in our bourgeois society, is an unnatural state. You'll forgive me, Mesdames! The fault is Monsieur Blanchet's, who was consulting me on the thesis he's preparing, on marriage and polygamy. He knows that I've just finished the final chapter of my *History of Mores* prior to 1914. The evolution of the idea of the family. We were discussing it with regard to this essay..." He designated, on top of a stack of volumes, a few of whose titles Monique read at a glance—*La*

Femme et la question sexuelle by Dr. Toulouse, *De l'amour au marriage* by Ellen Key—a book with a yellow cover. *"Du marriage* by Léon Blum."[7]

"I've read it!" she said. "It's full of true, ingenious and even profound things, but..."

She sensed the gazes of the three men focusing on her; that of Monsieur Vignabos was smiling, that of the novelist hostile, and that of the third visitor, finally, ironic and polite.

"Continue, we beg you!" said Monsieur Vignabos, with his delicate generosity. Turning to Georges Blanchet, he added: "Here's an unexpected documentation! Take advantage of it, my friend."

She was conscious of her ridiculousness, in confrontation with these scholars—psychologists who, not knowing her, armed themselves instinctively against her mundane chatter, with masculine prejudice reinforced by the conviction of their superiority. Then, obstinately, resentful of the professor's guests, she fell silent.

Georges Blanchet perceived her embarrassment, and courteously took the floor: "Mademoiselle's 'but' indicates sentiments that, without bringing a great logician, can be deduced from her hesitation. I claim, with Léon Blum, that humankind is, in fact, polygamous. Understand by polygamy, by an extension of the accepted sense of the word, the instinct

---

[7] The title of the first book cited is actually *La Reforme sociale: la question sexuelle et la femme* (Charpentier, 1918) by Édouard Toulouse, and that of the second *De l'amour et du marriage* (Flammarion, 1907) by Ellen Key. Léon Blum, author of *Du marriage* (Ollendorf, 1907) was the principal theoretician of the French Socialist Party, who became more active therein after the assassination of Jean Jaurès on the eve of the Great War, and eventually served three terms as President of the Council before and after World War II. The text caused something of a scandal, reiterated when it was reprinted in 1937, by virtue of prescribing the equality of the sexes in marriage.

that makes a man seek, simultaneously or successively, several women, and the woman, similarly, several men, before each one finds the individual of definitive selection."

Monique felt an impulse of protest. Let him speak for himself, that man, and even for the majority—Lucien excepted—of his fellows! But to claim that women... She felt humiliated to be taken for some Ginette or Michelle! Hardened by sports and clear in mind, she was as chaste as she was blonde, naturally... And chaste she had remained, until the embrace that had just, before she was a spouse, made her a wife.

Georges Blanchet perceived that he had displeased her, and continued gallantly: "I hasten to add, Mademoiselle, that the majority of women, and all young girls who are not perverted before being nubile, have, on the contrary, an opposite sentiment, not to say a sensibility: that of monogamy. They only ask to become, on condition of being loved, and to remain, the wife of one man."

She approved with a nod of the head.

"It's precisely that age-old discordance between the feminine ideal and masculine bestiality that generated, along with sexual anarchy, the tendency to polygamy—or, to be more exact, to the polyandry toward which woman has evolved in her turn: an anarchy that it doubtless deplorable, but fatal. Your conclusions are there to prove it, my dear master."

"I fear so," sighed Monsieur Vignabos. "At least until a new education..."

Boisselot drew a puff of smoke from his short briar pipe, which, with Monique's permission, he had kept alight, and sniggered. "A cautery on a wooden leg! Education? Without laughing? One could, rigorously, speak about that before the war—but since?"

A malaise hovered: the poignant recollection of charnel houses and ruins.

"In that case," Monique asked, interested by the unexpectedness of that argument, "what hope is there? If man, master of his privileges, finds that everything is perfect in the best of all possible worlds, what do you expect the pupil to do?"

Boisselot shrugged his shoulders evasively. *The pupil*, he thought, *has surpassed the master!* His heart was still burdened by his years of nightmare, at the front, while at the rear, those little awakened individuals had been moving their buttocks... Hospitals, dance halls! And he clenched his teeth on his pipe, grimly.

Blanchet continued: "Mademoiselle is right. Polygamy, from the viewpoint of women, is less an instinct than a reflex, less cause than effect. A disorganizing reflex with an unfortunate effect, but of which, in strict justice, we have no grounds for refusing them the exercise. All the more so as, it's necessary to recognize, marriage is one thing and love—which is to say, the sexual instinct—another. But I don't know if I can..."

"Get on with it, Monsieur!" said Monique. "If I dread certain ideas, I'm not afraid of words."

He nodded his head. "To want to associate marriage and love is to conjugate fire and water, to unite the tempest and the haven. Love and marriage can coincide, certainly—but rarely, and in any case, not for long."

"Thank you very much! And I, whom am marrying in a fortnight's time the man I love...!"

"You, Mademoiselle, will be one of those exceptions that proves the rule. How many counterparts of Daphnis and Chloe end up in wedlock as Philémon and Baucis? So few! And only after a few tribulations."

"What conclusion are you trying to reach?"

"This: that it would be equitable, and prudent, to let young women, before marriage, also lead their bachelor life. They would only be better wives, for having sowed their wild oats."

She burst out laughing. "It's fortunate that all men don't think like you. Otherwise I'd remain unclaimed!"

"That is, however, a step to be accomplished toward a more just society. Not to mention that we'd be rid along the way—on one side and the other—of the monstrous ball and chain of jealousy. All things considered, wouldn't stripping love of its mania of reciprocal possession, its pretended right to eternal property, be entirely beneficial? One would marry in order to conclude one's life happily, and to give birth to children. That would be better than giving birth to stupidities."

Régis Boisselot muttered: "Love without jealousy? Might as well say a body without a soul. That's what your loveless marriage is like: a combination of asphyxiating gases; two interests and two fatigues! That's not what will embellish future society: the fine merit of remaining coupled when one no longer has legs!"

Monique approved vehemently. "Monsieur Blanchet's marriage is a retirement home for cripples."

"Pardon me, Mademoiselle!" the professor objected, swiftly, blushing. "I think, on the contrary, personally, that there is only true marriage—or, to put it better, union—when one is in love, and to the extent that one is in love. What I'm claiming is simply that the union in question will have more chance of duration if the woman and the man embark upon it in full knowledge of the case. For me it's not the formality that counts but the foundation, and free union would please me as much as marriage if our laws protected there, as is the latter, the sacred rights of children."

Monsieur Vignabos raised his voice: "Free union is indeed, theoretically, the finest of contracts. But Blanchet is right: there are the children. Marriage at least protects them. Free union, at present, sacrifices them."

Head down, Boisselot frowned. "Well then, change your laws, since the drop-by-drop calculation of individuals is in inverse proportion to that of the State. As many children as possible, naturally..." He winked. "...For the next war."

"You know very well," Blanchet put in, "that France only changes her laws after changing her mores."

"Then we'll all be dead in the interim."

Monsieur Vignabos tormented his beard. "Remember Renan's image, my boy: the living only advance over the bridge of the dead."

Silence fell.

Aunt Sylvestre was the first to pick up the ball. "One objection that might be raised to Monsieur Blanchet's theory is that it doesn't resolve—on the contrary, it complicates, at least until the State has rejuvenated its Codes—the delicate problem of children. With that license granted to young women, apart from the fact that it would lead straight to the conduct of bitches in heat..."

"Pardon me," objected Monsieur Vignabos, "but it's the present morality—or rather immortality—that leads directly to behavior reminiscent of bitches in heat. If the tendencies in women hadn't been repressed for centuries, there would be more sexual equilibrium in the world..."

"There would, above all, be more illegitimate births, and in consequence, inextricable situations. Don't you think that there are already too many abortions of that sort? And in any case, too many natural children born of adultery?"

Georges Blanchet smiled. "Certainly, Madame. So you can be persuaded that the...let's see, what shall we call the emancipated woman?...the *bacheloress* of tomorrow..."

"Oh, no!" Monique declared. "I'm already something of a bacheloress, and I swear to you that I don't have any of the whims of which you speak..."

"Oh, Mademoiselle, the bacheloress of tomorrow will no more resemble the one of today than you resemble your sisters of twenty years ago. Think what a revolution there has been, in all spheres, in the space of a generation! Well, that bacheloress will be like the bachelor; she will be a little more of the school of Malthus,[8] that's all. Not to mention that she

---

[8] This is a somewhat inapt euphemism, although its usage helps to demonstrate the strength of the taboo that is on the brink of being broken. In spite of its immense pertinence as a solution to the problem of potential overpopulation, Malthus could never bring himself even to mention the possibility of using artificial birth control, and in spite of recognizing its necessity, Blanchet still finds it a little difficult to spit it out—

won't have a great deal to learn. The birth rate will go down, and with reason. By virtue of only having children when they want to, we shall soon have no more idiots. And the seducers will become, by the same token less improvident, and less boorish."

"But that's the end of the world that you're announcing!" protested Aunt Sylvestre, astounded.

"No, Madame, only the end of a certain society. The end of *crimes passionnels*, hypocrisy and prejudice. The return to nature, the order of which contemporary marriage misunderstands and eludes."

"I hope that's not the philosophy you teach to your pupils," Monique said, in jest. "How paradoxical!"

She stood up—but, on hearing Régis Boisselot ask Monsieur Vignabos what he thought, with regard to the sexual interest, of Freud's *Introduction to Psychoanalysis*,[9] she paused to listen, amused.

While the old master, having changed the tilt of his skullcap, embarked on a response, each phrase of which he emphasized with a twist of his beard, she contemplated the three men, so different were they from those she was accustomed to seeing.

---

although the narrative voice will soon clear the hurdle. As the taboo has now been largely discarded, it is difficult for contemporary readers to imagine the force it still had in 1922, and thus to appreciate the contribution that its broaching might have made to the scandal surrounding *La Garçonne* on its publication.

[9] Sigmund Freud's popularization of his theory, *Vorlesungen zur Einfürhung in die Psychoanalyse* (1917), was translated into French almost immediately, with some chapters appearing piecemeal in French even before the full version had been issued in Germany. The complete work was published in French by Payot in 1921, and was widely considered to be indecent, although that is presumably not the reason that Margueritte refrains from spelling out its themes.

Of the three, the most sympathetic was incontestably Monsieur Vignabos, in spite of his slightly hunched back, his short legs with trousers that were too short and twisted, and his face like a sculpted chestnut! He had such a sparkle of clairvoyance and common sense in his gaze, and such in- dulgent delicacy in the pleat of his lips that it seemed that his entire being was illuminated.

As for the others, with regard to Boisselot, one of whose books she remembered having read, the curious, bitter and yet moving *Les Coeurs sincères*, in spite of him having said intel- ligent things about jealousy and love in marriage—she judged them as such because they corresponded to her own senti- ments—she would never be able to get over that total lack of elegance. Very muscular, long-legged, with gnarled hands and a ravaged face with strange eyes opening their cat-like irises in a jaundiced sclerotic, his complexion bilious amid a bristle of red beard, Régis Boisselot gave the impression of a carnivore tormented by a tender heart. A curious fellow, with whom one might sympathize...

As for the fine talker...thin, short, distinguished, with the smooth face of a young bishop...Monique could not abide his professorial attitude, and his affectation of skeptical serenity. A bore to be avoided, that Blanchet! Generous? Perhaps, in theory—but oozing eloquent egotism. In spite of the ideas with which he juggled, and which, whatever she had said, of- ten matched her own, she judged as an impropriety, a personal offense, his opinion about the fate of marriages in general and hers in particular. Yes, she would make an exception, whatev- er that fop thought! Beneath his oratorical concessions, it was evident that he did not understand her. With what a serious, tenacious determination she would able to edify and defend her happiness!

She shivered. Monsieur Vignabos' voice faded away.

"In sum," said Boisselot, "to be documented on Freud, it will be sufficient for me to read the study by Jules Romains?"[10]

"And you will know as much as I do about psychoanalysis," said Monsieur Vignabos. He turned toward Monique and concluded: "Or, to be clearer, about the psychic contents of human beings. What a chamber pot, my friends! At least if one believes Herr Professor Freud, who, in his Austrian sagacity, has invented nothing—as witness the Zurich school.[11] In science as in letters, we are more adaptors than creators."

"You're always the same," said Aunt Sylvestre, admiringly. "Simple, like all true scholars."

"Ta ta ta!"

He was sure that the greatest minds, if they did not specialize, were immediately dispersed in the infinite field of knowledge. "One can only see what one has discovered clearly through a microscope," he was wont to say. "And then...! Talk of *de omni re scibili*—yesterday of Bergsonism and today of Einsteinism—is the business of men of the world and cheapjack critics..." He was, however, curious about the work

---

[10] In his early poetry "Jules Romains" (Louis Farigoule, 1885-1972)—later more famous as a novelist—espoused and illustrated an anti-individualist philosophy he called "unanism," advocating a general sympathy with life and humankind. He visited Freud, and reported on his meeting, but the principal literary result of his enquiry was a satirical play *Knock, ou le triomphe de la medicine*, premiering in 1922, in which the eponymous Dr. Knock is a successful charlatan.

[11] The followers of Wilhelm Wundt (1832-1874), the first scholar to term himself a "psychologist." He was associated for a long time with the University of Heidelberg, but had recently been appointed professor of "Inductive Philosophy" at Zurich when he published his ground-breaking *Principles of Physiological Psychology* in 1874, where his ideas took root before he returned to Germany to renew his studies at the University of Leipzig.

of others, and passionate about the work of the young, and called attention to them on any pretext.

"Well, what do you think of that?" asked Aunt Sylvestre, when they were on the staircase.

"Monsieur Vignabos is charming. But the others..."

"You're difficult to please!" she reproached, forgetting that her detached old age did not see with the same gaze. "Georges Blanchet is charming, too. As for Régis Boisselot, he's an eccentric. Admit, at least, that we spent a pleasant hour? When one thinks that for so many foreigners, and even Parisians, there's nothing but Montmartre!"

"That's true. The butte hides the Collège de France from them."

V

The curtain came down on the first act of *Méné*.

"It's amusing," opined Madame Lerbier, turning to her daughter.

"Pooh!"

"You have the imp of contradiction." She lifted up the shoulder-piece of her dress, which had slipped off, revealing the polished roundness.

"A good audience," said Monsieur Lerbier, parading his opera glasses. "You can tell that it's Christmas Eve."

Recently founded for the performance of international operettas, the Cosmo-Théâtre, with its sloping orchestra stalls and its balcony of open boxes, was resplendent with light. To the celebration of Christmas Eve was added that of a première, with Alex Marly in *Ménélas*. Men in dinner jackets; women in low-cut dresses. There was nothing, on the fresh flesh as on the display of gamy meat, but droplets of pearls and a dew of diamonds. The least desirable bodies, as well as the most harmonious, exhibited the cleavage between the breasts in the cleft of light dresses. One might have thought it a slave market, under the expert eyes of merchants and connoisseurs. They calibrated at a glance the contours of torsos, the arms glad to be naked, the offering of breasts in their niches. The great flag-display of coiffures, blue-black and mahogany blonde, and the heightening of powders gave the exhibition of faces, proudly borne, an appearance of pointed masks. All of it was astir, scintillating and chattering, in the expanding warmth, with the exasperating scent of perfumes, and a bestial reek of human odor.

With small hand gestures and head movements, Madame Lerbier pointed out in the stalls the long-haired Plombino; General Merlin and his wife, the former, deprived of his uniform, looking like a retired bureaucrat; Madame Hutier with the incredibly anonymous former Minister; the de Loths, father and daughter, the insinuations of whose name were doubtless insults.[12] Cecil Meere, plunged in his elegant neurasthenia, deigned to emerge from it in order to address a distant salute to Monique.

"Look!" said Madame Lerbier. "Over there, in the covered box next to the column...Madame Bardinot and Madame Jacquet...Michelle's saying *bonjour* to you. Who's that with them?"

The man turned round. Monique smiled.

"Max de Laume."

"Antinous! What's he doing there? Paying court to Michelle? No—she's going to marry d'Entraygues. To her mother, perhaps, for the Prix George Sand? No, he's sure of winning it. To Ponette, then? *Tee hee.* I can see Ransom in Abraham de Rothschild's box. But I don't see Léo. Is our national *coureuse*[13] really thinking of changing cavalier?"

She smiled at her malevolence. While cultivating her, she did not like "that great Jewess." Pleasant, yes, with her gazelle-like eyes and her inclined stance...the habit of bending her back!...but Madame Lerbier judged as repugnant the platitude and untiring artfulness that La Bardinot applied to pushing her husband by all possible means. A minor functionary at the Finance, he had scaled the heights of the bureaucracy, with

---

[12] The English word *loth*, meaning unwilling, is derived from the Anglo-Saxon, so that is not the inference that a Frenchman would take from the name, the sly reference here is undoubtedly to the Biblical character whose name is rendered Lot in English versions, and who committed incest with his daughters. Alfred de Musset wrote a famous poem, "Les Filles de Loth," reputedly in order to win a challenge posed by George Sand, who had promised to have sex with whichever of two poets produced the most obscene poem (Victor Hugo was the loser).

[13] I have left *coureuse* [literally "runner," in argot "slut"] untranslated, in order to preserve the scabrous pun on Madame Bardinot's equine nickname.

scandalous rapidity, achieving a deputy directorship, and then, without pause, becoming Private Secretary to the Minister, Director of Personnel and Inspector General. There was now a question of him quitting the administration of the State for that of a large bank, the presidency of which was about to fall vacant, and which, with Ransom's support...

"It's frightful," sniggered Madame Lerbier, when speaking between friends about 'that dear Ponette,' "the path that she's been able to clear for her husband simply by getting down on her knees!" Or: "She has a fashion of holding out her hand that men can't resist." But Bardinot had succeeded—a result that softened the worst allusions.

Madame Lerbier recalled the rumor that had run around that when Ponette had first heard mention of "Antinous" she had said "What's that?"

"She must know now."

"What a scandal monger you are, Maman," said Monique. "Anyway, I'm going to see Michelle."

"Remind her mother that I'm expecting her tomorrow, with Hélène Suze, for a tasting at Claridge's."

Monique strode through the corridors at a brisk stride, indifferent to the gazes that were undressing her. She had a distaste for these "very Parisian" gatherings whose surface gleam only hid a sewer. Bodies for sale, consciences going cheap! Fortunately, there were still exceptions—as Georges Blanchet had said that afternoon. But, she, Lucien, Vignabos and Aunt Sylvestre could be counted on the fingers of one hand!

Monique laughed at the face the last-named would have pulled at the double spectacle of the stage and the auditorium if she had listened to her sister, who had done her utmost to drag her to '*Méné.*' What a good idea the aunt had had in going to spend Christmas Eve and Christmas Day tranquilly, with Madame Ambrat at Vaucresson...

Another friend of the Vignabos genre! A feminist and militant, Madame Ambrat, a teacher at the Lycée de Versailles, still found time to direct, after having founded it, the

Oeuvre des Enfants Recueillis—which did not prevent her from being an admirable companion for her husband. Monique imagined all three of them waiting for midnight, chatting under the lamp, washing down stuffed goose and black pudding with a glass of Vouvray—Monsieur Ambrat was from Touraine. She envied them their life of intelligent labor and simple joys. She would have liked, since she was not going to see Lucien, to accompany Aunt Sylvestre, and to finish the day, which had been excellent, with her.

She recapitulated: the visit to the Rue de Médicis; the squirrel coat and ermine cape ordered at the furriers; meeting Lucien in the Boulevard Suchet to choose the furniture recommended by Pierre des Souzaies—a nice filing cabinet and bookshelves—and then, under the luminous gaze of the excellent old lady, tea at the Ritz.

When he parted company with them, Lucien had regretfully repeated his chagrin at not accompanying them to the theater and being obliged to have supper without them...but there was definitely no possibility, the Belgians having telephoned again that same morning. She had promised him, for her part, if she did not see him before the end of the performance, to go straight home. If her parents wanted to go partying, as had been mentioned as a possibility, with Madame Bardinot and, she thought, Ransom and Plombino...well, the band would play on without her; that was all!

"May one come in?"

"Come, quickly!" exclaimed Michelle, on seeing her.

Short, plump, and so palely blonde that one might have thought her colorless, Michelle, in the back of the box, was in the process of telling Max de Laume an exciting story, to judge by their shiny gazes.

"Wait while I salute the ancestor!" said Monique.

Madame Jacquet, lowering in her honor the opera-glasses through which she was passing the audience in review, like a sovereign reviewing troops, agitated her white wig graciously. Madame Bardinot tore herself away momentarily from the saliva with which Ransom's toothless gallantries was persistently peppering her. She had been accustomed for years to receiving it imperturbably.

A just ransom, Monique thought—*why, a pun!—for the banker and his shower of gold.*

Ransom was, along with Bardinot, the only man whose presence endured around Ponette. Every six months she changed her lover. Her other whims, varying by the week or the day, only lasted as long as the time it took to extract what she could in various advantages.

"I won't ask you for news of Monsieur Bardinot. I know that he's at the Conference."

Ponette had obtained from the President of the Council—whose sympathy she had conquered via the intermediary of Plombino—that her husband be included, as an financial expert, in the French delegation to the twenty-seventh meeting of the Supreme Council.

"Well, children," said Monique, returning to the back of the box, "you're obviously not bored! One only has to look at de Laume."

"Indeed!" he confessed, and pointed at Cecil Meere, who was exhibiting himself in the orchestra stalls in a jacket the color of dead leaves, and his splenetic expression, more disgusted than usual. "It's his funereal expression that's making us split our sides."

"He's never been more downcast," Monique observed.

They guffawed. "You can say that again!" said Michelle, triumphantly.

And as Monique looked at her questioningly, she recommenced her story without being asked. "Can you imagine that I was taking tea this afternoon with de Loth's daughter. There were five or six of us, plus the young regulars—the whole gang, in fact, except Ginette, invited, it seems, with Hélène Suze to a concert at Anika Gobrony's. Chamber music—I can see it from here. We'd arranged to meet Cecil, making him believe that he'd find Sacha Volant. That's his latest crush. He came, naturally. Then, to assist his patience, we

started playing the game again...I adore that, the young inno-
cents!"

"If one can call them that," observed Max de Laume.

"You see evil everywhere! What's so shocking about being on a stool, blindfold, with your hands tied behind your
back? You have to guess who's sitting on your knees, and
who's kissing you, that's all. As long as someone's mistaken,
the turn continues.

"So?"

"We arranged to stick Cecil on the stool. When the
handkerchief was knotted we signaled the youngsters to keep
quiet. Men would have given him too much pleasure. And we
commenced kissing him, one by one, as best we could. Simone put oakum under her nose, to make a moustache. When, by
chance, he said the right name, we cried: 'Wrong!' and carried
on...on the neck, on the lips. In the end, he was going mad. We
let him go. And do you know what he had the cheek to say to
us? 'Little sluts—you didn't have me.' But Simone, who's sat
on him after me, was well able to reply to him. Besides, just
by looking at his funny eyes and squashed expression, I was
sure that he was lying. One might have thought he was a bal-
loon into which one blows, and which makes a rude noise as it
deflates!"

The bell for the end of the intermission rang.

"Well, you disgust me!" said Monique. "*Au revoir.*"

She ran away, sickened. What must an intelligent man
like Max de Laume, who had fought in the war and whose
métier, as a literary critic, was the observation of mores, think
of that scatterbrain, and of her? Monique was sure that he en-
compassed them in the same scorn.

Scarcely was her back turned that Michelle, obligingly,
labored the point.

"Go on, prude! There's always some who make a big
deal of it. Because she's going to be married! Well, so what?
Me, too!"

"Excuse me, my dear child," said Ransom, paunch drooping as he headed for the door. "Until later, at the Rignon..."

"That depends on Maman."

Her angelic smile concluded with a lick of the palm, addressed to the fat man.

"Oh, I'll go... Glad that you've accepted!" she said, darting and admiring glance at her companion, who was delicately mopping his brow. "It's true, it's stifling in here. Pretty handkerchief! Show me..."

She breathed in. "Nice!"

It contained an imperceptible puff of powder, with which she powdered her cheeks, and then held it out to him. "Here, coquette!" But she changed her mind, so abruptly that he was astounded. Swiftly, she stuffed the handkerchief into the pocket of his trousers, accompanying it all the way. He could not help grabbing her hand.

"What's the matter?" she demanded, with an expression that was too naïve for him not to perceive the hypocrisy.

"Nothing," he murmured. He sat down beside her, flustered.

The curtain went up on Alex Marly, playing a scene with Hélène, more than half naked, who, in order to soften him up, stripped off even further. Max de Laume darted a glance at the fleshy back of Mère Jacquet and at Ponette's tempting equivalent. To think that it was for her that he had come! Then, darting a glance toward the enigmatic Michelle, sitting to his right, he observed that her legs were crossed so high that the calves and one of the knees were sticking out in their silk stockings.

Then, having advanced his chair between those of the ancestor and Ponette, thus blockaded, he pretended to be listening with the most profound attention to Alex Marly, who was singing, while dancing: "*Je suis Méné, Méné...par le bout de nez*."[14] At the same time, he grabbed one of the slender ankles, encircled the roundness of the calf, and then the knee...

He stopped, uncertain, and then slid, with a light touch, above the hamstring; and, at that precise gesture, as Michelle uncrossed her leg, as if by chance, he followed his path, slowly. After the irritating silk, his fingers brushed a skin so soft that he would have liked to kiss its warmth...

He was troubled to the point that his heart was beating in great leaps. No resistance. Then, boldly, he brushed the lawn, which opened, and palpated the mysterious fruit in its mossy nest. He understood that he was its master, and caressed it expertly. Suddenly, however, the legs came together, like a vice. He let go, and had no need to turn around to be sure that Michelle, who had stiffened, had just experienced as complete a sensation as the one she had inflicted a few hours earlier on Cecil Meere.

When Hélène, finally naked save for a *cache-sexe* and a drape that, lying across her body, veiled one breast and the navel, had reconquered Ménélas to frantic applause, Max de Laume decided to meet the eyes of his partner, he only read there the natural expression of the most innocent camaraderie. Nothing had happened. He had the good taste not to persist, and merely to ask himself, modestly: *What the devil could she have been thinking just now? About d'Entraygues, perhaps? Much good may it do him! He'll have reason to be jealous with that vicious little she-cat!*

And without remorse, he leaned over the nape of Ponette's neck, where the brown curls moved under his breath.

She shivered. Would he be better than Léo? She was searching, with unwearying hopefulness, always disappointed, for an embrace that could shake her jaded senses for good and all.

---

[14] *Méné*, which is a contraction of the name of the character in the comic operetta (Menelaus, in the English spelling), if heard as "*mené*," would allow the line to be construed as "I'm being led, led...by the nose!"

"Let's go," she said, after the second act. "Come on. I have to have a word with Lerbier on Ransom's behalf. Plombino and he are absolutely determined that they must have supper with us. You'll excuse me, my dear friend?"

Madame Jacquet bared her false teeth gracefully, while Michelle addressed her most charming smile to Sacha Volant in the orchestra stalls.

Outside, Madame Bardinot, who was incapable of keeping secrets with which she loved to surprise people, confided to the handsome Max: "I believe there's a conspiracy in progress, with John White, to buy the Lerbier patent."

"What about Vigneret?"

"He'll be in it, naturally. What about you—would it amuse you to get involved in the plot?"

"Do you take me for a boyar?"

She smiled. She was about to find out!

"There are always shares, for friends..."

He balked. "Oh, you know, I don't eat that bread. I'm not Léo."

Ponette did not detest the whip. That rudeness pleased her. Max de Laume earned his living by his talent alone. A superiority over Léo! Furthermore, although both of them wore the Croix de Guerre, at least Max hadn't stolen his...

Outside the Lerbier box, as he was about open the door, she stopped his hand. "You please me."

He received the shock as an accustomed tribute. His curiosity regarding Michelle, sharpened by his initial success, did not prevent him from being sensible to the advances of Madame Bardinot, an enviable mistress. Cuckolding d'Entraygues all the way, before the event, had its charm, but giving the push to his friend Léo had no less.

"What about Mercoeur?" he enquired.

"What about Mercoeur?"

"Disappeared? What have you done with him?"

"I think he's deserted me this evening for Hélène Suze...or for Ginette Morin."

"And that's all the same to you?"

She looked him in the eye with a submissive tenderness. "Beast! I like that."

He responded with a wink.

Pact concluded.

An hour later, the Lerbier auto stopped outside the Rignon. In spite of her declaration and her repugnance, Monique had been obliged to yield to her parents' insistence and, above all, to the supplications of Michelle. Madame Jacquet had only authorized the presence of the latter at the supper offered by Ransom if her daughter's friend was also there; as for herself, she was past the age of such amusements... Madame Lerbier would drop the child off on her way home, since she had kindly offered to take charge of her.

Max de Laume and Madame Bardinot had already arrived, with Ransom and Plombino, whose twelve-cylinder Voisin was just pulling away to leave room under the awning.

"You know," Monique said to Michelle, "it's only because of you that I've come."

She held that against her after the promise she had given Lucien. She would never have broken it if she had not feared annoying her father by being obstinate. She still had his bitter invective ringing in her ears: "Do it for me! No? Well then, go to bed, since you're devoid of family spirit to that extent!" Poor Father! Were his money worries really that serious?

Michelle took her friend's arm. "Let it go! We'll have fun. First of all, I'm going to dance!"

She was already humming, as her entire body swayed to the tune of the tango, whose strains reached them in gusts through the rotating glass doors. Before going in, Monique cast a hostile glance over the crowd flooding in. Doors clicking, they were piling out of autos, the men with their top hats titled backwards and their silk mufflers open over their fur coats, the women draped in chinchilla or mink, waving their feathery hats or sparkling torsades.

She was about to join the queue when she thought she recognized Lucien's auto. But instead of pulling up under the awning, the car turned the corner of the street and stopped twenty meters further on at the private entrance to the reception rooms.

"Go on," she said to Michelle. "I've just seen something."

She said to herself: *He might have lent his auto to a friend just as he sent it to me this afternoon.*

She stood there, astounded. Lucien opened the door, got out, and extended is hand to a young woman draped in an ermine cape similar to the one she had just ordered or herself at the furrier's.

Quickly, like secret lovers who want to avoid being seen, the couple was engulfed under the porch.

She wanted to clear up any confusion. The memory of a recent lunch with Lady Springfield reminded her that the restaurant had an internal staircase leading to the first floor. She ran back in to Michelle. In front of then, Monsieur and Madame Lerbier were hastening, between the bows of the head waiters, toward the large oval table where the standing bankers were beckoning to them. Sitting side by side, Max de Laume and Ponette were already flirting tranquilly.

Monique vaguely herd Ransom declare: "We'll be better off in a private room—it's more cheerful," and her mother say to her: "What's the matter with you? Aren't you going to take your coat off?"

"In a minute," she murmured. "I'll be back..."

Like an arrow, she fled, and ran up the staircase. She arrived just in time to see Lucien, from the landing, in front of an open door that a waiter was indicating to him. He took off his companion's cape. Her dress was split to the waist. She was brunette, with a malicious expression behind the feline smile. Cléo, evidently.

Monique clung to the banister rail; her legs buckled. Hallucination? No! A reality, which, in striking her with bewilderment, filled her with horror. The waiter, who had just closed the door of the private room on the terrible vision, approached her obsequiously.

"Madame desires…?"

"Monsieur Plombino's table," she stammered. And thought: *In that case, the anonymous letter…*

At the famous name, the waiter bowed. "It's downstairs, Madame. If Madame would like me to show her…"

"No, thank you!"

Like a madwoman, she turned her back, and, fuming, descended the stairway by which Lucien had come up so rapidly that the waiter could not help crying out: "Not that way, Madame! Not that way!"

She was already in the street, going along the file of autos. The chauffeurs were chatting among themselves. She went past the Vigneret. Marius saw her and, surprised, mechanically took off his cap.

"Mademoiselle!"

Only then, as if she had needed that final proof, did she realize the full extent of her revolt and her pain. She turned back, and walked past Marius again. Better prepared this time, he pretended not to see her. She went back up the staircase to the private rooms, and had the presence of mind to say to the waiter, suspicious that something odd was going on: "I forgot something in the auto."

And, with the tread of an automaton, she went back down into the restaurant. The table welcomed her with enthusiastic *ahs!* Plombino indicated her place, "Beside me!"

Without sitting down, however, she leaned over her mother and whispered in her ear: "I'm not feeling well. I'm going home."

She was visibly shivering, her features so distressed that Madame Lerbier was alarmed. "What's the matter? I'll come with you."

"No, no! Stay!" she ordered, imperiously. "I'll send the auto back for you. You can take Michelle home after supper. I'm going to bed." She added: "It's nothing, I assure you. A slight fever. Don't worry about me."

And without another word, without looking at anyone, she buttoned up her coat and left, head held high.

VI

Outside, she went straight ahead, into the darkness.

Frost was hardening the asphalt. A starry sky was vaguely visible. The luminous halo of the city—the radiation of the streets with all their lamps illuminated—extended a long way, very far, into a catafalque of shadow. Crowds were still frittering away time on the boulevard, as busy as in broad daylight, with people emerging from theaters and heading for midnight feasts: floods of people overlapping and intersecting their currents; a desert through which she advanced without seeing or hearing anything, at a mechanical pace, in complete solitude. The interior tumult to which she was prey absorbed her to the point that nothing else existed. She was the overturned center of the world.

At times, she tried to reason to get a grip on herself. Immediately, the vision surged forth, implacable; she could no longer experience anything but blind distress and muted incomprehension. Everything in her had tottered and collapsed. Along with her crushed dream of love, her faith was gasping under the ruins. She was not yet suffering in her pride, so overwhelming was her stupor. She was nothing but a single bruise. She would have liked to be able to sob, to cry.

Then, with consciousness half awakened, she was imperiously invaded by a child-like surprise that she had been struck without cause, and revolted in consequence. Was it possible? Why? How? She heard once again Lucien's intonation at the Ritz. He had attested his regret, cursed the Belgians, their telephone call, that very morning... He had smiled as he said *au revoir* to her, tranquil after the promise she had made to him to go home after the theater, and not to go on anywhere for supper!

She asked herself, in the ingenuousness of her lamentation: *After having taken me? Why has he left me? Why?* An inexplicable treason, an incomprehensible lie, which, after having confounded her, brought back the repercussion of fury. More even than the dolor of her slain passion, perhaps, she was enraged by such falseness, as the worst outrage of all.

Certainly she was bleeding throughout her being, torn abruptly from a sentiment that she had thought to incarnate her life itself. She was bleeding all the more cruelly because the gentle wound of her abandonment had scarcely scarred over. But in her instinct of the absolute, she wanted to detach herself, instantly and forever, from what had been, a little while before, her reason for existence. A part of herself had been amputated: an illusion rotted; dead flesh.

Love Lucien, her? No. She detested him, and despised him. A judgment, if not without chagrin, at least without appeal, because it had been rendered by an inflexible thought. A virgin only yesterday, having not yet tasted all the physical intoxication of love, Monique was ignorant of the most powerful of bonds, the Gordian knot of sensuality. The mind alone, at that moment, had deliberated within her, and had decided.

She walked for more than an hour, insensible to murmured invitations, jesting cries, and even gestures. When a little calm descended, and her double torture was attenuated momentarily—the ignoble insult to her love as well as to her virile sense of honor—she saw once again, at the table that they had probably already quit in favor of the bed, Lucien hastening around his companion.

He had never loved her, then! He had been playing with her, in passing, like a whore—like that whore! He preferred that one to her! She suffered less from that idea than the humiliation and the rancor of having been nothing but a plaything. Worse! A steppingstone in business! Of what mud could such a soul be made? How had she been blind to that degree?

And tomorrow, it would be necessary to see him again, to hear him lie again? For there was no doubt that he would lie. Not to deny the fact, for it was there, but to color it with some excuse. There was none for such actions. And if such boorishness could be found in Lucien's eyes as in those of other men, it was the case, then, that there was no more love, no more honor. There was nothing left but to live like the animals, unconsciously, with impunity...

Tomorrow! And the inevitable explanation, and the justifications that he would attempt, the final deceptions that he was preparing at that very moment, with his head on the breast of that whore, before proceeding with their filthiness, as they were jeering together! At that image, Monique started to laugh so nervously that a *sergent de ville* approached her curiously.

She was afraid, and, crossing the road, hailed a taxi.

Just as she opened the door a white-gloved hand reached out toward her wrist.

"Oh, pardon me, Madame!"

The man, elegant, with delicate features whose sinewy contours she perceived vaguely, looked at her with amused surprise. *A whore? A socialite? Pretty, anyway. What is she doing out alone at this hour, on a day like this?*

She hesitated before giving her address and climbing in. He perceived her disturbance, sniffed the miraculous hazard of an adventure, and without losing a second, installed himself authoritatively beside her.

"You're mad," she said. "Get out, or I'll call...!"

An imperceptible dissonance which, with his instinct of a hunting male, the stranger seized upon as an involuntary indication, signaled the disturbance of the sentiment beneath the clarity of the words.

"Oh, Madame," he replied, "I beg you...at least permit me to drop you at your door; we're going in the same direction. I'd never console myself for losing, at the predestined moment when I encountered it, a company such as yours..."

She had retreated into the opposite corner. She remained obstinately silent. What could happen to her, after all? Nothing that she did not want...

He talked, not stupidly, ended up introducing himself, was gallant, then insistent...

She was not listening. The phrases died at her feet like the murmur of waves. She was floating, soullessly, on a mysterious sea. He took her hand; she did not pull it away. He tried to kiss her; she slapped him.

"None of that!" he said. He seized her wrists and drew her toward him by force, searching her lips with a brutal kiss. Surprised, she had been unable to defend herself. An almost sweet nausea invaded her beneath the violence; a light, as yet obscure, dawned in the shadow of her flesh in accord with the sudden, irresistible commandment of pride.

The man that she loved had betrayed her. She would take her revenge against him: a revenge of liberty, and above all of frankness. Tomorrow, when she saw Lucien again, she would tell him everything. She, too, would put the irreparable between them. And he would have nothing, absolutely nothing, to say about it. Had he not, at the instant of the perjury, returned her to herself?

The rest unrolled like a cinematic nightmare. The change of address given to the driver; the bottle of champagne drunk in the frantic din of a Montmartre dive, the mechanical entry into a hotel room....

She had no shame and no remorse. She was accomplishing a logical action, a just action. She had neither attraction nor repulsion for or against her temporary companion. He had promised nothing, He had not lied. He was some passing traveler or an officer on leave...an anonymous form of hazard. She did not even think of identifying him, of reading the address on his valise, and allowed him to undress her without responding to the questions he asked.

Before the contracted features animated by a double and contradictory expression, of absence and determination, he thought of some drama of the heart—unless it was a simple confusion of the mind. The vengeance of a deceived woman or a perversion of curiosity, what did it matter? She had come, without being begged. He told himself that it would have been very stupid not to take advantage of the windfall.

He gazed, drunk with joy, at the magnificent, abandoned body...the long legs, the roundness of the hips beneath the transparency of the short chemise, the arms folded over the naked bosom. With the freshness and the slenderness of a girl, the she-devil had the plenitude of a woman. What was she doing in life, that passerby of whom he did not know the thoughts or the name, and whom he drew, without resistance, to the bed?

Lying down, with her arms outstretched, Monique let him have his way like a beast, an inert beast. Her eyes were closed, her hands so tightly clenched that her fingernails dug into the palms. Beneath the caresses than ran over her entire body, or suddenly lingered, over the taut breasts or the secret furrow, she sometimes shivered with nervous reflexes. Then she clenched her teeth, in order to surrender nothing of herself but her flesh. A bitter pleasure of vengeance transported her, so plenary that all modesty was abolished in the depths of her being. Anguish only tormented her at the approach of the painful contact.

At first savant and gentle, the man's kisses became exasperated. And as she refused her lips, grimly, he lost control. Instinct took over. Under the burning sting that penetrated her, she uttered a cry so shrill that he stopped. But when she shut up, he wrapped his arms around her more tightly, and although making them less brutal, he accelerated his thrusts. The head buried in the perfume of her hair, he did not see the large tears that were running down the tortured face.

Suddenly, when the pain became too intense, she threw him off with an effort so abrupt that he let go, cursing. *Just at the crucial moment!*

He was standing next to the bed, not knowing what to do. His conceit, the desire, both satisfied and spoiled, gave way to an obscure anxiety. Monique had stood up, with an irresistible movement. Before that haggard face, he could only babble inconsequential phrases.

She got dressed with mechanical haste. A tragic silence weighed between them, which neither his efforts at conversation nor his offers to take her home could succeed in dispelling. Abruptly, as if a storm were bursting she began to weep, convulsively.

The tears stirred and moved the man. They ran incessantly, with great sobs. When the sobs calmed down, they were still flowing over the mute face.

He became frantic, but only obtained a "Leave me alone" and an "*Adieu*." She had closed the door behind her with such a glacial expression, such formal decision, that he made no attempt to follow her.

Tiredly, he sketched an "After all!" and lit a cigarette, pensively, dispersing the smoke philosophically.

One memory more.

When she got home, Monique found the light on in the antechamber. Her mother had just arrived, and, finding the apartment empty, was tormenting herself with anxiety. She came running when she heard the sound.

"What! There you are! Where have you been? I thought you were in bed! You can boast of having scared me. I've just taken Michelle home. I left your father at the restaurant with those Messieurs. They're talking business. But what's the matter with you? You're terrifying me with your crazy eyes."

Madame Lerbier took Monique's hands. She was sincerely frightened.

"Where have you been? Your skin is burning!"

What could the child possibly have been doing for two hours?

"Are you going to tell me?"

In halting phrases, Monique related her encounter at the entrance to the Rignon.

"You must have made a mistake. It's impossible."

She gave her confirmations...the auto…Lucien lifting the ermine cape from the woman's shoulders—"the same one he advised me to buy"—and Marius' embarrassed greeting.

"I understand now. My poor child..."

She saw Monique wandering the streets, in despair. What a stupid adventure! Men must be stupid. Stupid and maladroit...

82

She took hold of her and stroked her. "Put your head on my shoulder...are you in pain?"

She wanted to soothe her, but did not know what to say. She was simultaneously furious with her future son-in-law and animated by a desire for conciliation. What advantage was there in pushing it to the tragic end? None.

"Your chagrin and your surprise are quite natural," she affirmed, "But after all, perhaps it's nothing but a misunderstanding. I don't know, myself. Wait for an explanation, and don't form an idea in advance that might be disproportionate. In your place, I wouldn't torment myself as much."

Monique looked at her, stupefied. At first she had had a desire to proclaim, after what she had seen, what she had done. Her despair and disgust had reached out to maternal comprehension, with the need to be understood, to be pitied...but before the banal compassion that she read in the eyes that were dear to her, before the almost indulgent tone of the voice in which she had expected indignation as a comfort, her heart was as taut as it had been sat the moment when she emerged from the hotel room...

The impression of solitude and despondency that had crushed her then was doubled by a further distress. She sensed that she was distant, to a degree that she could not believe, from that being who was smiling at her softly, and in whom, a little while ago, she had seen a confidant and a consoler.

"In sum," Madame Lerbier went on, "what Lucien has done is very bad, evidently. It's not common sense to go sneaking around with his mistress under the eyes of his fiancée. It's inappropriate, silly, anything you wish...but from there to making yourself ill, as you're doing...! Be reasonable, then! He's a fellow who certainly loves you. That supper, you can be certain, is a rupture with his past. A definitive rupture. When you're married, he'll be the most faithful of fellows. On condition that you know how to hang onto him, of course......"

Monique shook her head. "No, it's finished."

"Ta ta ta! Excitation, before the marriage, as much as you wish! Afterwards, it's necessary to do one's share. To live together without making one another suffer isn't easy. It's the great affair of life! One succeeds in it by means of reciprocal concessions..."

Monique felt each sentence penetrate, into the revolt of her suffering, like a fiery dagger. A gap between their souls? No, an abyss. She discovered, under the brushwood of quotidian affection, the depths of a precipice. And at the same time, she retreated into mutism as if into a refuge.

She extended her forehead. "We'll talk tomorrow. I can't do any more."

"Try to sleep!"

Alone, she ran into her bathroom and plunged, for a long time, into water so hot that she ended up cooling it down. The shock of the cold water completed the relaxation of her nerves. Although she was still suffering in her torn flesh, she experienced no regret for her action. Her initial sensation of being soiled had been effaced by the benefit of the lustral water. All she experienced, along with an indistinct horror for the savagery of the man, was a collective hatred of everything— mores, people and laws—that had just tortured her so cruelly. Lucien, her love, and the completely modified future, fell to the rank of contingencies.

A kind of moral curvature cast her down. She ended up going to sleep...

When she woke up again, everything was dancing in her brain. If only she still had, in order to think aloud, the good aunt, her pity and her active tenderness! She would have been able to vomit at least part of what there was in her heart, since, at the end of the evening, she had decided to say nothing to her mother before having had it out with Lucien.

"He's desolate; he's coming," were the first words that Madame Lerbier pronounced, on entering her bedroom and embracing her.

She had telephoned Vigneret as soon as it was light to tell him about the consequences of his exploit. She had also alerted her husband at the factory, to which Monsieur Lerbier—who had a bedroom there and a change of clothes—had gone directly after the supper. He had uttered loud cries. Above all, Monique must not send anyone packing! She had to wait until she had seen him!

Madame Lerbier, concerned for the material future, had more on her mind than her daughter's chagrin.

"How you're tormenting yourself, darling! He was wrong, yes...but it appears that the woman is like a dog with a bone. She demanded an enormous sum to keep quiet. An authentic blackmail! Hence the supper. At least, that's what Lucien told me in a few words on the telephone. It was necessary to bargain, to convince her..."

Monique shook her head. "No. He dared not confess everything to me frankly before..."

She hesitated. What was the point of revealing the full extent of her grief? Her mother would never understand what touching motive she had obeyed in giving herself to Lucien before the social stamp of approval. An imprudence, yes, but of which only she was aware, since she alone was its victim.

"Don't believe, above all, that it's my jealousy that's making me suffer. I'm not jealous, because I no longer love him."

"Then you didn't love him!"

Madame Lerbier looked at her daughter with a doctoral authority, and also the hope that in these conditions, perhaps all was not yet lost. From the moment that love was not in play, one did not break official agreements, out of self-respect.

"It's necessary never to have loved to believe a veritable sentiment could disappear at the first deception, like a match going out."

"You're wrong, Maman. My distress arises from the fact that I had vowed to Lucien a love so confident, so great, that you can't even imagine..."

"In that case, when the imbroglio is elucidated, I hope that..."

"No, Maman, it's finished. Nothing can any longer be arranged."

"Why? Because your fiancé has lied to you? But it was to spare you needless torment! A chagrin that, without this deplorable hazard, you would never have had. You're reproaching him for what was probably only a delicate attention...a maneuver that shows him, perhaps, to be more careful of your peace of mind than his own..."

"You don't understand," sighed Monique, with a bitter sadness. "For you, Lucien's lie is trivial. Yes, it's even a good, if not a fine, action. For me, it's an unpardonable fault. Worse than a fraud—a murder! The murder of my love, of everything I contained of the pure, the ardent and the noble! I astonish you, yes? That's because between the fashion in which you envisage the world, and that in which I conceive the idea, there's the Great Wall of China! We live alongside one another, but I've woken up a thousand leagues away... Know that, since what we're debating here is my life, not yours."

"You're suffering...and you're exaggerating..."

"I haven't yet told you all that I think."

Madame Lerbier shrugged her shoulders. "You're exaggerating, in any case, the extent of Lucien's *faux-pas*. Believe me, if all women approached marriage with the intransigent spirit that you're attaching to it, there'd hardly be any bans published! On the other hand, there wouldn't be enough ledgers for the recording of divorces! Not one marriage, my girl—not one—would survive it. It's necessary to be reasonable, with a little common sense. Yes, Romanticism, the comedies of de Musset—*Of what young women dream!*...and you think you're awake? Well, open your eyes, look around you; be modern."

"The dream of Ginette and Michele isn't mine."

"The dream of all young women is marriage: an association without any obligatory relationship with love. And marriage is...what it is. Do you intend to reform society at a stroke?"

"Certainly not! Any more that you should intend to make me see marriage as anything but a need for absolute union, a placing in common of the entire being, without restriction of any sort. Marriage without love is, for me, nothing but a form of prostitution. I no longer love Lucien, and I shall never marry him!"

Madame Lerbier's eyes widened. "What!"

"As soon as calculation is involved with it, your association is no more than a coupling of interests, a reciprocal contract of sale and purchase: a prostitution, I tell you; a prostitution!"

She suddenly thought about the stranger, saw once again the hotel room, the hour of vertigo, and blushed to the neck— but a certain pride made her reject any analogy between her action and the syllables she had emphasized, like a branding-iron. Feverishly, she continued:

"All the benedictions of the Nuncio and the Pope won't prevent the Marquis d'Entraygues, in marrying Michele's millions, from being what Ponette has called Mercoeur, and what we think of Bardinot...and Ginette, with all her skill, doesn't seem to me to be any more praiseworthy, in fishing for a husband, than the least of the anglers in the mire of the gutter!"

Madame Lerbier, taken aback, heard the thunder rumbling. She pulled herself together and said, volubly: "It's unimaginable! Oh, the aunt and you are just alike! I recognize all the nonsense with which she's stuffed your skull..."

"If you'd brought me up yourself..."

"I've always regretted not having done so! Your health..."

"Or your convenience?"

"And this is my recompense! A daughter fit for Charenton, with her revolutionary principles! Do you realize that you're trampling over all social conventions? With your truth, since it's only yours that counts, it's not just marriage but life that would become impossible! Come on! Let's get back to reality. A little tolerance, a little broad-mindedness..."

Monique looked at her mother. The ground of habitude beneath her feet was shifting, like a sea of mud. She was stamping her feet, but only sinking deeper. She wanted to cling to the appearance, to suspend herself from the image that she had formulated, during her exile and since her return from Hyères, in spite of temporary dissonances, of the woman who had given birth to her, and, in spite of their separation, spoiled her after her fashion.

As if appealing for help, she cried: "But Maman, you love Papa! You married when you were poor, before his discoveries had made the factory what it has become. You can't think differently from me. You're scornful of Ponette. In spite of her money and her salon you don't truly admire Mère Jacquet. You have no esteem for Hélène Suze, who's only given herself to a dirty old bandit like her ex-husband in order to barter, by divorcing him, her label of Mademoiselle for the stamp of Madame. And I'm citing those at random—there are hundreds like that. You don't behave like them and you don't approve of them."

Madame Lerbier was evasive. "You always go from one extreme to the other! No, obviously, I don't regard my friends as saints. But what do you expect? When one lives in a society—and not only do we live in it but on it—it's necessary to accept…oh, not vices, no, but certain customs, certain necessities. That's the way it is. We can't change anything. Oh, if you had my experience, you'd see that there are certain actions that might seem incomprehensible today, even revolting, but which have their extenuating circumstances, their excuses, their fatality. Come on! Everything can still be sorted out between Lucien and you."

"Renounce that hope. There's one thing that you'll never make me admit: lies, between people who love one another. I've never lied to Lucien. I had the right to reciprocity."

Madame Lerbier smiled, with superiority. "The right! The rights of women! A familiar tune…Aunt Sylvestre, Madame Ambrat! But my child, there are instances in which lying itself can become a duty. Don't look at me like that! You had those eyes yesterday evening—you're scaring me."

"Lying, a duty!"

"Calm down."

"No and no! Duty, Maman, is to tell the truth. And since I shall say it in a little while to Lucien, you might as well know it too, and immediately! Nothing can any longer be arranged—nothing—because yesterday, when I left you, I slept...do your hear, *had sex*...with someone."

"Oh!"

This time, the thunderbolt had fallen. Madame Lerbier, astounded, looked at her daughter, trembling. Suddenly, beside herself, menacingly, she said: "You did that? You did that?"

"Yes, and I'd do it again if it had to be redone."

"Little imbecile—that's too stupid. With whom? May one know?"

"No."

"Because?"

"Because I don't know myself."

"You don't know? You're making fun of me? Tell me...one of our friends? No? A passerby, then—just anyone?"

"Yes."

"That's not true! Or else you're mad."

"It's true, and I'm not mad."

Madame Lerbier folded up, collapsing. Catastrophe! She was crimson, with fury more than indignation. Rage was racking her to such an extent that she was stammering.

"S...slut! What if you have a child?"

Monique went pale. A child...with which father? She wished, if the supposition were realized, that it would not be the wretch in whom she had believed... A child?

She thought, aloud: "Well, I'll bring it up, that's all."

"Your unconsciousness surpasses all limits! You're nothing but an idiot, a..."

She stopped short; an issue had opened up in the cul-de-sac. She saw a distinct glimmer of light—the turning point. No proof, in sum! No sign to fear, for some time. If Monique consented not to boast about her dementia, it would be as if nothing had happened. In any case, violence, with a nature like that, would not get her anywhere. She softened.

"I won't waste time with criticisms that are doubtless superfluous, since you tell me that your conscious of yourself! The harm is done; what remains is the remedy. You think that you acted well? So be it—you judge according to your own morality. Good. Would you like me to give you, as the old Maman who loves you, in spite of all the chagrin you've caused her, some wise advice? Keep the secret of this escapade to yourself. When I told you there were cases in which lying is a duty, I didn't think that you'd give me such a complete justification, and so soon! To talk, as you want to do, would be to degrade and disqualify yourself, and us with you…not to mention the ridicule! On the contrary, if you keep quiet, the harm, neither seen nor known, is reparable."

"Oh, Maman…!"

"What? Scruples, with regard to Lucien? A man who deceived you first? You've had your revenge…aren't you satisfied? Tell yourself that, my child. In society, and, in consequence, in life, what's important is less what one does than what one says—and, above all, what is said about one."

"Maman! Maman!"

"As one makes one's reputation, one makes one's road. You've done something stupid. That's your affair. On the other hand, the day when I'm no longer alone, with you, in knowing about it, your honorability and ours are thrown as fodder to public malevolence. Is that what you want? Certainly not. Anyway, reassure your fine conscience! If, even married, it were necessary after each slight injury one inflicts, to make it known, all households would be at daggers drawn—all of them! You don't keep your eyes in your pocket, damn it! Do you think that your father and I would be living in such fine harmony if, every time there might have been a misunderstanding between us, we'd cried it from the rooftops? I've been deceived, too, and you're doubtless the only one who doesn't know that your father's mistress is little Rinette in the Rue des Capucines. I console myself for that as best I can...but no one hears the slightest echo of my deceptions and my chagrins..."

"You, Maman! You!"

Madame Lerbier suddenly dreaded having said too much. Then, turning her eyes away from the interrogation that Monique's distressed gaze was darting at her, she added: "But all that is only a matter of general consideration. I'll get back to what concerns you. More than ever, you must keep quiet.— and marry Lucien, without delay."

"Even bringing him another man's child?"

"First of all, that's only a supposition."

"And if it were to become a reality?"

"He won't know. So..."

"Shut up. It's ignoble..."

"You're going to give me orders now? To judge me? You! Look at me: either you keep quiet, and marry Lucien..."

"Never."

"Or I'll tell your father everything, and he'll throw you out."

"Agreed."

"Monique, come on, you..."

She did not finish. Her child was before her, as before a stranger. A pallor frosted the anguished face. The lowered eyes testified to a frightful distress. Madame Lerbier wanted to embrace her, to draw her to her poor, corrupted, but nevertheless maternal, heart.

"Monique," she repeated.

"Leave me alone."

Rejected, and not knowing what to do, Madame Lerbier adopted the course of draping herself in her dignity.

"Think about it," she said.

And without persisting, she beat a retreat, nobly.

Monique, her head in her hands, did not see her go out. A second collapse had just taken place within her.

Affection and filial respect were lying among the rubble.

VII

"Monsieur Lerbier informs Mademoiselle that he is waiting for her in the drawing room and asks her to come to meet him there."

"I'm coming."

Alone, Monique cast a glance in her mirror.

"I look frightful!"

She put on some powder, looked at herself again and sighed. Another Monique, so different from yesterday's, was looking back at her. Yes, a new Monique! She thought of the old one, so near and so distant, as someone dead.

"Let's go!" she said.

She had had lunch in her room rather than confront the presence of her mother and the curiosity of the domestics in the ostentation of the dining room. Monsieur Lerbier had telephoned to say that he would not be home for lunch—always business—but that he would call in immediately afterwards.

On the threshold, she searched with her gaze, but only saw a preoccupied back. Monsieur Lerbier, while waiting for her, was pacing back and forth.

"Sit down," he said, indicating a chair facing him.

The dock! she thought.

He took an armchair himself and, drawing himself upright, pronounced, severely: "Your mother has told me everything. I shan't waste time telling you about the imbecility and ignominy of your conduct. I know that we're addressing ourselves to an obstinate character. Let's set commentaries aside. All the more so as Lucien's fault is nothing compared to yours."

"If you've condemned me, Father, why bother entering more pleas?"

"I'm not pleading," he observed, dryly. "As for your sentencing, since, in fact, remind yourself, I'm your judge, without appeal—it isn't yet pronounced. The future depends on you...on your intelligence, and on your heart. It's to those that I'm making an appeal, to that which might remain healthy and normal within you. You're reckless, but you're not wicked. You proved that to me yesterday with regard to your dowry..."

"That money is yours, Father, and you were under no obligation to give it to me."

"That's true—but I love you! And on the other hand, being honest, I ought to add that not to endow you, in my business situation, would be impossible. The marriage of a daughter, for a great industrialist, is, in every sense of the word, an investment. It must correspond to the size of the account, and reinforce its credit. A dowry, in our society, is not merely a custom that makes law; it's a criterion of opinion, the share price of a fortune. By agreeing, as you have with Lucien, only to receive a fictitious dowry, you've obliged me more than you think. And I thank you again for it."

She did not flinch The surge of her affection in accepting being deprived had been succeeded by the disgust of having been, within the negotiation, an item of trade with a price tag. She was being passed from hand to hand, not for her own worth, but a mere market evaluation.

"I had lunch this morning with Lucien. I wanted to get his side of the story, to know what was behind this story of Christmas Eve. All right, all right! I won't repeat it all, but it's necessary that you know: that woman..."

"Mother's already told me. Blackmail, avoidance of scandal, etc. Don't repeat it; there's no need."

"Because he's coming to tell you himself! Your mother only revealed your fine coup just now...and I no longer know whether to tell him on the telephone..."

"I'm expecting him."

"Let me speak! Either you're reasonable, and there's no inconvenience—on the contrary, that you'll settle the matter—or you're irreducible, in which case you won't see him. I'll arrange things as best I can. Decide."

"I'll see him."

Monsieur Lerbier's face cleared. "I was sure of it. Fundamentally, I didn't doubt you! Pride, when it isn't a fecund virtue, is a deadly sin. You're reflected, you've done well. Above trivia and petty things, there's only one thing that really counts: affection, tenderness...and the family!"

He stopped, because the phrases were falling into an embarrassed silence, and also because he was choked by his own eloquence. He sincerely believed that he was putting himself at the service of Monique's interests, when he was only defending his own.

She finally stood up. "The family! no, Papa, don't hope that Lucien Vigneret will ever be part of it."

"Be careful, if it's not your own exclusion that you're looking for..."

"You won't have to throw me out of the house."

"Because you'll leave of your own free will?"

They challenged one another with their gazes, confronting one another as enemies.

"Yes."

"That's madness!" Monsieur Lerbier exclaimed. "Madness!"

Bitten in the entrails by the dread of the compromised deal, of seeing Vigneret and his partnership lost, payments perhaps suspended at the factory, the quest of buyers of bankrupt stock for the shreds of his patent, he moaned with such utter sincerity that it became poignant:

"Listen! You know how hard I've worked devoting my life to the research of the invention that I've finally completed! An invention that won't only make us rich, but which might, which will, you hear, ensure the prosperity of the country! Thanks to my nitrogenous fertilizer, the soil of France might render ten times as much as it does at present. Just two fine harvests and the equilibrium will be changed, the ruins of the war renewed! It's a prodigious leap for our entire people...only, as I told you yesterday, I've run out of cash. Tomorrow, if I'm not refloated, I'll sink within sight of port..."

"Oh," said Monique, "there's no shortage of sharks to take the boat in tow: White, Ransom, Plombino..."

"Exactly! The sharks would already have devoured me, if I hadn't found in Vigneret the partner who, spontaneously, had confidence in me. They'll devour me tomorrow, if you refuse to marry Vigneret and he lets me go..."

"Either your invention is valuable," said Monique, "and he won't let you go, or it isn't, in which case..."

He shrugged his shoulders. "It's valuable! And not just one, but ten, twenty fortunes!"

"Then you can be tranquil," said Monique.

He did not like the irony. Doubtless the prospect of keeping Vigneret, if not as a son-in-law, at least as a partner, was not absurd, and would even permit, if the little fool persisted in her refusal, a new overture...

He reflected, remembering a remark made the previous evening at supper by Plombino after the sixth bottle of champagne...

Yes, perhaps! A scheme that, while establishing the business on a broader base, might save face, without any help from Monique...

With dignity, he resumed the tone of prosecutor in order to return, almost immediately, to the complaint.

"I don't know what's gotten into you—unconsciousness or ingratitude! You're refusing to marry Lucien? It's irrevocable? All right. Let's admit that. Let's even assume that, after the gravest worries, caused by your recklessness, and afterwards, but your incomprehensible obstinacy, that I succeed in putting my affairs in order. What will happen? You'll emerge dishonored..."

She shrugged her shoulders.

"Dishonored!" he cried. "And you'll drag us through the mud! Us, who have only ever treated you well! It's frightful! Think about that! Spare a thought for your old father, for your Maman, who loves you in spite of everything. Monique, my daughter, think about us instead of only thinking about yourself! You don't have the same ideas as us, I know. Yes, you

95

have your petty conception of the world, and we have ours. Have we ever opposed you, though? Today, when you can, by saving yourself, make us so happy, you're only thinking of completing your ruination, without caring about completing ours. If you wanted, however, there might still be a means..."

She bowed her head. Poor people! Distant as they were, and vain as the reasons for their difficulty seemed, she would have liked, after having suffered so much, to appease their distress, if it were possible. How?

"A means?" she repeated. "What means?"

"Well, here it is! Let's not talk any more about Lucien. You see, I'm not insisting—I'm conceding... There remains the situation, which must at all costs remain strictly between us, in which you've put us and its...possible consequences. Have you measured the risks of a pregnancy such as the one to which you're exposed? For here, whether you like it or not, the family is united. It's not only a matter of its interests, but its honor..."

With an emphatic gesture he filled the entire room.

She murmured: "Honor..."

"Exactly. We're doomed, if you don't seize the recourse that I'm offering you. A magnificent, unexpected opportunity to get us out of this…"

"Go on."

He coughed. "Ahem! Baron Plombino has always had a very keen sentiment for you. When he first mentioned it to me, you were already engaged to Lucien. But just yesterday evening, he returned to the fray... 'If ever that fellow doesn't make your daughter happy, I'll reserve his place… Number One...' That's as serious as can be. What do you say?"

"Have you finished?"

Her stomach rising, Monique evoked the image of the banker lying in wait, with the maw of a hippopotamus. She felt that heavy paw descending upon her, soft and moist...

"No! I remind you that if, in certain respect, the Baron doesn't represent...the ideal...you don't have the right, you hear—*you don't have the right*—to be difficult. Married, a

Baronne, with an income of more than a million, is better than being an unmarried mother, or having an abortion. It reconciles everything: advantages and morality."

Monique was petrified. Her father, that filthy tradesman! He was waiting, complacently, with the conviction of having enunciated an undeniable truth.

Finally, in a low voice, but while looking him in the face, she said: "You disgust me."

He jumped, and advance toward her: "What did you say?"

"That I've had enough. *That*, for marriage! *That*, for morality! Adieu. We're not speaking the same language."

"You're nothing but a monster! I disown you! You're no longer our daughter..."

"Let me go, then."

He had seized her by the wrist and was shaking her brutally. He was the master: the man, the father, the head of the family...

"And to begin with, you'll do as you're told. You aren't of age! You owe us obedience!"

She shook her head, crying: "Let me go! You're nothing but a brute! I'll go with Aunt Sylvestre. Here, I'm nothing to my mother but a doll, to be played with and then put in a box. And for you—for you!—even less: livestock to be sold. The family! That's rich! I don't need you, or anyone. I'll work, I'll earn my bread."

Transported by rage, he sniggered. "With your painted flowers, perhaps? Or as a whore, eh? That would suit you... As you please. *Bonsoir!* Don't let me find you here at dinner time!"

"Don't worry!"

A bell rang. They stopped.

"That's Lucien," said Monique.

Monsieur Lerbier ran to the drawing room door, but she got there ahead of him, and opened it without him having time to stop her.

"Damn it!" he swore. "I forbid you..."

97

Already, humbly, with an expression both supplicant and taut, Lucien had come in. Disconcerted, Monsieur Lerbier looked at him, looked at his daughter, and, seeing that all was lost, cried: "She's mad, my dear! Mad! Don't listen to a word that she says. I'll see you afterwards—come to my study. We'll talk..."

Monique had taken Lucien by the arm. Her father left, and as soon as they were alone, she let go. A little of her excitement had suddenly disappeared. The cruelest part was over. There remained the painful explanation. But with her hopeless lassitude, a kind of somber satisfaction was mingled.

Apparently calm, beneath the tumult, she said: "Listen to me."

In haste to justify himself—for he believed that he loved her, less in the measure of his desire than that of his projects, to which she was linked—he exclaimed: "You have to forgive me, Monique. I'm not guilty, in spite of all the appearances that are against me...all of them, including the care I've taken to spare you any suspicion! Doesn't that prove to you, though, the lengths I went to in order not to torment you, especially so needlessly. It's liquidated now! You'll never again hear mention of that whore! Only know that we've been under the threat of a terrible scandal, revolver shots, etc..."

She let him go on, ironically, as if she had not penetrated those final lies, divined the understanding concluded between his mistress and him. He had appeased her easily enough, with the gift of a pearl necklace and the offer of a monthly payment, with the promise of frequent rendezvous...

He fell silent and raised his eyes: the insolent face disturbed him, with its expression of contained distress.

Monique summoned up all her will power. "I admit the sincerity of your intentions. I even admit the sincerity of your love."

"Oh, Monique!" he protested, "Me, who...."

She cut him off. "What? Your disinterest? My dowry? That's what you're thinking about? Yes, yesterday, I took your renunciation for proof that you did, indeed, love me for my-self. Today..."

She made an infinitely weary gesture.

"Can you doubt that...?"

"I doubt everything, now."

He cried, sincerely: "Except me, Monique, and you!"

The idea of losing her, and with her the imminent reali-zation of the good deal, brought him back to the fundamental: self-interest. She was looking at him gravely. The voice had washed over her, without moving her—the voice that only yesterday had penetrated her, exorcised her.

Summoning up his courage, he continued: "I swear to you that I'm only making one calculation. In a fortnight, we'll be married. We'll be leaving for Cannes. It will be the great aviation week. Or, if you prefer some nest lost in Hyères, we'll have an embarrassment of choice. The Maures are full of delightful auto excursions. When we come back, a nice little life, very cheerful, in our apartment in the Champs-Élysées. Pierre des Souzaies told me this morning, at Maxim's, where we were having lunch with your father, about a little Louis XV table for the bedroom. We'll put it beside our bed, of amour and repose, on which we'll be so comfortable..."

He smiled conceitedly at the allusion, at the same time as she shuddered with horror at the memory. The minute of di-vine disturbance, the faith and hope sullied! She tore herself away from the derisory embrace.

Just as she was another Monique, a new Lucien was be-fore her, who was speaking in vain with the phrases of old. For she was sure of it: he lied; they all lied—all of them! An-ger gripped her. She could no longer suppress her feelings.

Harshly, she said: "Our amour! Never talk about that again!"

"Frankly..."

She burst out laughing. "Frankly! Do you even know what the word means? Well, so be it: frankly, everything be-tween us is finished. No, no, it's futile. Don't think that it's some kick of a young animal that can be appeased with a caress. I shall never marry. Not you, nor anyone else. Yesterday, when I left the restaurant, I left behind me forever, in your hands, the Monique that I was...may her remains not weigh you down. Now, it's no longer a girl but a woman who is speaking to you. Do you hear? A woman!"

He looked at her without divining her meaning. Then she cried: "I've given myself to someone else! Yes, before coming back here, where my mother was waiting for me..."

"Monique!"

"Don't interrupt me, or I'll leave. Why did I do it? Because we no longer have anything in common. Why am I telling you? In order that there will be, henceforth, an insurmountable barrier between us."

He sketched a gesture. She cut him off:

"The past, you have rotted, like everything else. My abandonment of a credulous child? What does it matter? Especially to you! You never loved me. Me? I don't even hate you—but if you knew how I despise you! No, let me finish. This is what you were going to say, isn't it? The consequences? I don't care about them. Society? I renounce it. I'm breaking with it, in order to live independently, in accordance with my conscience. To live, as a woman, as...well, what you'll never be...an honest human being! *Adieu.*"

She moved toward the door. He blocked her way.

"I don't want us to part like this. I'm fond of you, and I'm ready to dispute you with yourself. There's too much vehemence in your explosion for it not to be hiding some...deformation. Fortunately!"

"None."

"Two questions then..."

"Speak."

"Swear that what you say you did yesterday evening, you really did."

"I swear." She read a doubt in his eyes. She added: "I swear on the head of my Aunt Sylvestre. And you know how much I love her."

Gripped by rage, he cried: "May one know the name of your accomplice?"

Amazement and indignant self-esteem angered him less than the failed scheme.

"My accomplice? That's certainly the bourgeois word that you ought to use. The accomplice to my sin, isn't it? A duel? You can re-sheath your fury. First of all, I'm not yours; I only belong to myself. And then...I don't know."

"You don't know?"

She would have smiled, had she been able to, at his bewilderment, but everything within her rebelled.

He shrugged his shoulders: she was inventing!

Then, pitilessly, with a kind of grim appeasement, she gave him details. She enjoyed seeing him curl up and go pale in his turn: the man from whom she had expected the happiness of her life, and who had, in the space of a minute, precipitated her into the unknown...

Lucien Vigneret was suffering without understanding. Character, education: everything within him raised an obstacle between the fact and his appreciation. He hated her, and yet he regretted her. For a moment, he even balanced the possibility, if he could silence his rancor, of proposing the continuation of their projects: marriage compensated with reciprocal liberty. But with such an individual! Better simply to renegotiate the deal, in some other form, with the father. Perhaps, all things considered, he had had a lucky escape! He retained a troubled sentiment nevertheless. Ruined—and in such a manner—she still seemed to him to be desirable. Differently, and perhaps even more so...

She took account of that, sickened by the strange gleam in his gaze, and wanted her entire revenge.

"Look at me! Oh, it's not your judgment that I care about! I only want the lesson to be of use to you. I might perhaps have forgiven you an error, but the conception you have of life, of men, of women, your ideas...all your ideas! The scorn that they testify for me...that misconception of the heat and the intelligence, that's what's unpardonable. That's what

101

makes us as foreign to one another as if we were of different races, and even different colors. That's why it's better, believe me, to have laid bare immediately. The suffering of a day will spare us years of misery."

"What should I have done?"

"Tell me everything—before!"

"You wouldn't have admitted..."

"Who knows, if you'd explained it to me? I loved you; I would have tried to understand."

He saw, from the depths of his fall, the collapsed bridge—but he continued to defend himself.

"Perhaps! I ought to have sensed that you don't resemble the others...that you're a unique creature!"

"Don't believe it. We all have a thirst for frankness and honesty."

He reflected. "There are cases, however—including mine!—in which lying is a pious intention...and others in which it's a necessary precaution."

"With regard to women?" she mocked.

"And men," he completed.

"Get away! You'd lie to one of your associates in business?"

"It's not the same thing."

She forgot her own suffering. She rose as far as the comprehension of the immense drama that had opposed, for centuries, the slavery of some to the despotism of others. All feminine revolt became indignant within her.

"That's it!" she exclaimed. "Your two moralities! One for the use of the masters, the other for the servants."

"There's a difference..."

"There's the difference that for us, marriage and love are more important than the biggest business deal is for you. It's our whole life."

"There's a different mentality, if you prefer..."

"Our poverty of intellect? Our futility? If it's so, isn't that your work? No! It's not inevitable and forever. Only you continue to live in the same eternal prejudice, without perceiving that everything changes."

He sniggered. "Progress?"

"Simply the conditions of existence, which force us to evolve."

"Towards equality, it's said! Bring on the big words!"

With a profound conviction, she repeated: "Yes, toward equality. The equality that perhaps we wouldn't have wanted if you hadn't imposed it yourselves, and which we need today like bread...like sunlight! Do you understand now? Do you understand?"

They confronted one another, lifted above themselves.

He looked at her without replying, troubled in spite of himself. She had never been so beautiful! He felt his rage of a few moments ago give way to a sadness so great that he could have cried. He refrained, however. In his distress there was a little of the despair of a child who suddenly sees his toy broken, and also a little of the fear of the Catholic brutally invaded by doubt. The entire framework of his education cracked under the impact.

Before that tragic revelation of a soul driven to despair, and the fact that the order of things, of which he had been the executor, had just been condemned to anarchy, he descended into himself with a certain amount of trepidation. He perceived, confusedly, all that might be dangerous and iniquitous in the exercise of the privileges with which a man has been inculcated since infancy by the instinct of sovereignty. Immediately, however, the pride of his humiliated sensibility and wounded vanity blinded him to that faint light.

He picked up the hat that he had placed on a side table.

"I understand that, without wanting to, I've made a mess of my life and yours. The lesson will be useful to me. *Adieu*, Monique."

"*Adieu*."

He went out without looking at her, not proudly.

She remained sitting there for a long time. She ached all over. She dreamed that she had become very small again, and that she had just fallen from the top of the big rock at the boarding school, from which she had overlooked the world. She was lying on reefs, which the water was battering furiously under a black sky. And she was calling out in a faint voice: "Aunt Sylvestre!"

How much time had she spent like that? She wondered, suddenly, as she started. There was a noise of unfamiliar voices and footsteps coming from the antechamber.

"Monique!" her mother shouted. "Monique, come quickly! It's frightful...and your father has gone out with Vigneret."

An old woman, whom she did not know, and whom she would always remember with the expression of a fearful puppet, under a feathery hat, was telling Madame Lerbier, breathlessly:

"When I heard that scream my blood ran cold...I saw it as I'm seeing you. I was on the sidewalk in front of the pharmacy at the intersection of the Rue de Havre, at the Gare Saint-Lazare. Poor lady! She was running across in front of an autobus; she stumbled, and then...the driver did everything he could to stop. She was already under the wheels... They found an envelope with your name and address in her handbag—here it is, intact... When they took her into the pharmacy, she was still breathing. She asked to be brought...the municipal ambulance is downstairs. I came with her, in order to warn you..."

At the last words, Monique had started running. The stretcher was at the foot of the staircase in the vestibule. With a sacred terror, she lifted the veil covering the face.

She thought she would go mad.

Death, while lacerating the abdomen and the legs, had respected the beloved face. She seemed to be asleep, still alive.

"Dear Aunt!" Monique appealed, shaken by sobs. "Aunt!"

An atrocious anguish penetrated her. Cold sweat moistened her brow. She felt that her entire youth had now completed dying. And, bending over the cadaver to kiss it, she fainted under the supreme blow.

PART TWO

I

Monique Lerbier to Madame Ambrat
Route des Acacias, Vaucresson
24 Rue Chaptal, Paris, 1 March

Thank you, Madame, for your exceedingly kind offer, but I cannot accept a position as your secretary at the moment. I have the sensation of walking an empty body through life. It seems to me that I shall never be able to laugh again. My parents gone, my aunt dead—all this has been such an abrupt upheaval.

I would have liked to die, since everything is lost to me. This afternoon, on coming out of the notary's office after the reading of the will, I thought, in the tea-rooms where I took refuge, of my poor, dear aunt, and was envious of her fate...

At the table next to mine there was a grandmother with two children dressed in mourning: a girl of fourteen, already a young woman, and her brother, a six-year-old boy. I thought that I would never be a mother, that I would remain useless. I would grow old, like Aunt Sylvestre, alone...

I am alone, from now on! Alone in my house, alone in my heart, without social attachments, without a hearth.

Thanks you again for having thought of welcoming me to yours, but I sense that it will be a long time before I shall be able to live among children. I'm too grave for their young souls; they would be two joyful for mine.

I embrace you very affectionately.

Monique.

Monique Lerbier to Madame Ambrat
Paris, 15 July
Dear Madame,

It has been a long time since I sent you my news. I was confused by my silence after your kind letter. Today, I'm suffering less, and I can write to you...

It seems to me that my dolor has numbed somewhat. I gaze, without any sentiment dictating either pain or joy to me. I see this morning's pale sun and the profound garden beneath my windows, and priests passing by. I'm simply vegetating.

Have I told you that after the settlement of my poor aunt's inheritance, I left the Rue Chaptal, which was so dark? I live on the left bank now, in the Rue Vaneau. My three windows overlook the grounds of the Missions Étrangeres.

I still always wake up to suffering, though. It takes so little to bring my despair back. Oh, to be able to stop thinking... It appears that one is consoled, or at least accustomed to one's injury, to all injury. To be happy again, one day? Is that possible? I can't imagine it...

> Your grateful
> Monique

Monique Lerbier to Madame Ambrat
22 November
Dear Madame,

What have I become? A very poor thing, ill-resigned to my lot. Thank you for your kind words. Alas, I'll never be consoled. I set my ideal so high as to be unable to attain it; there is nothing for me to do now but descend low enough never to be able to perceive it again. Perhaps then I shall get used to no longer thinking about it. I live, in the meantime, like an invalid caring for herself, without any inclination to undertake anything, or to hope...

However, I sense that it is in work, and in work alone, that I might find a lightening of the ball and chain that I'm dragging around! Perhaps, therefore, I shall attempt to return, with more continuity, to my old essays. Perhaps you remember the little compositions with which I amused myself in the days when I had nothing to do? I've taken up my sketchbook again, and my paintbrushes. I'm even producing some designs for furniture, painting fabrics...

I've been advised to take up interior design, as a métier not yet overly encumbered. I also have a desire to combine it, thanks to my aunt's money, with a shop selling antiques. I believe that I might find in that, at the same time as a means of earning a living, an occupation, and—who can tell?—a distraction.

If I continue ruminating my chagrin, I shall go mad.

I hope, in the first days of spring, to take advantage of your kind invitation and come to dinner one Sunday.

Monique.

II

The jazz band spread its savage rhythms through the frenetic dance hall. Couples were swaying under the blue light.

Michelle d'Entraygues nudged Hélène Suze's elbow as the latter was sipping an ice cream sherry cocktail through a long straw.

"Oh! look!"

"What?"

Leaning over the edge of the booth, Michelle pointed. "There, beside the professor and the young Englishwoman...those two women passing under the chandelier."

"But for the short hair and the mahogany color, one might think it were Monique."

"It is her—isn't it, my dear Max?"

Having adjusted his monocle, the critic declared: "It's really her. It changes her, of course, that hair. Today, for the woman, that's the symbol of independence, if not strength.[15] Once, Delilah emasculated Samson by cutting off his hair. Today, she imagines she's virilizing herself by cutting her own!"

"She's ten years older!" exclaimed Hélène Suze, generously.

"Say five! And as she looked nineteen when she was nearly twenty-one, that only indicates her real age, since it's at least two years since she took the plunge!"

"Twenty-three? She looks thirty!"

"Get away! She's never looked so good. Still the same glamour, with a little something mysterious, bruised. Personally, I think she looks splendid. Ouch!" He turned round, furi-

---

[15] De Laume is referring to the symbolism of the "bob," which became enormously fashionable in the 1920s even before it was adopted by the iconic actress who gave it the name it retains nowadays: the "Louise Brooks bob".

ous, toward Michelle, and threatened her: "If you do that again, it's a thrashing!"

But with the expression of a greedy she-cat, she declared: "I adore that!"

Since the evening of the *Méné*, she had attached Max to her person for particular cares. Quickly dropped by Ponette, who had become smitten with Sacha Volant after his triumph at the Isère circuit, Max had, for his part, acquired a taste for joint ownership with d'Entraygues. Absorbed by his racing stables and the education of young jockeys, the Marquis enjoyed the dowry, and he enjoyed the wife. Since the Prix George Sand, Madame Jacquet had adopted him and was incubating the Académie Française's Grand Prix du Roman, worth thirty thousand francs—a reply to the competition of the twenty-thousand-franc Grand Prix Balzac founded by Z. Makarof—at her Thursdays.[16]

The final measures of the shimmy faded away. The coupled separated. Michelle aimed her opera glasses.

"It's true, though. Monique has an astonishing character. The cavalière, for example. What a type!"

Max de Laume recognized her. "But that's Niquette!"

"No! How it changes her, the hair color."

Are they always together, then?" Hélène Suze marveled.

They stared at Monique Lerbier, the interior designer, curiously, and her famous friend Niquette, the Music Hall star, celebrated for thirty years. Paris went mad over her high-pitched voice and her perfect legs; she was as witty as her tongue was agile, always fluttering at the corners of her heavy lips. Ugly, with her turned-up nose, but for her carbuncle eyes...

"There's no doubt about it, they've got guts," observed Max de Laume.

Niquette and Monique had just sat down at their table. One would have thought them an amorous couple. Niquette

---

[16] The Prix Balzac was actually endowed by the arms dealer Basil Zaharoff.

leaned over tenderly, and wrapped her fur stole around Monique's neck.

"That's touching," joked Hélène Suze.

"Don't get excited, Suzon," said Michelle. "The place is taken."

Hélène Suze, whose lesbian inclinations were becoming increasingly pronounced, shrugged her shoulders. She had always borne a grudge against Monique for having once rejected the advances she had made via Ginette Morin before the latter—replacing Madame Hutier, carried away by an embolism—had become Vice President of the Oeuvre des Mutilés, and soon thereafter, the wife of a Minister in the Pertout cabinet.

Ginette! Hélène Suze remembered how she had cooed like a dove when kissed on the mouth. That was in the times of fine evenings at Ainka Gobrony's. Not a prude, anyway, Gi, like that Saint Touch-me-Not Monique!

Hélène Suze was one of those who had welcomed without qualification all the horrors that had run around at first: Vigneret had surprised his fiancée in a hotel room with a Rumanian businessman by whom she was pregnant. The parents had thrown her out. The aunt had committed suicide out of grief...

Today, finding their old friend relaunched, with a bang, into Parisian circulation, Max de Laume and Michelle d'Entraygues, forgetful of their recent disdain, smiled at her indulgently. Even Hélène Suze went so far as to declare: "After all, she's free. With talent and money, everything is permissible."

Coldly cut off by everyone between one day and the next, Monique had reappeared a year after her disappearance, opening a shop in the Rue de La Boëtie: ancient and modern art. Pierre des Souzaies, whom she had met shortly before, when she had just realized her aunt's petty fortune—a hundred and fifty thousand francs in savings and as much again from the sale of the boarding school—had oriented her toward the profession from which he made his own living.

In her disgust for existence, she had found in him, as well as a devoted associate, an indicator and guide, all the more precious because he was, outside of the commercial viewpoint, disinterested. Elegant invitation cards had notified the connections of old of the resurrection: Monique Lerbier, *Au Chardon Bleu*.[17] But everyone had stayed away.

Monique, who never saw anyone any longer—except for Madame Ambrat on Sundays—had then spent black days. The general slump in business added to her neurasthenia. She spent weeks languishing, only seeing occasional passersby, who haggled a great deal and spent very little. Her resources, almost all invested in buying stock, diminished so rapidly that she was beginning to despair.

The worldly authority of Pierre des Souzaies, however, doubly reputed as an antique lover and a homosexual, was considerable. His usual clientele refusing, one day, he had sent Niquette to Monique—and all of a sudden, the Rue de La Boëtie had found an artistic and cosmopolitan clientele. Mademoiselle Lerbier's interior designs became fashionable.

A new personality had then surged forth, which, different and surrounded by an atmosphere of success, caused the "outcast" of yore to be forgotten. Driven by the seething of new waves, the purulent ripples of the old rumors had been erased from the great pond.

Niquette sensed the attention of Hélène Suze posed upon Monique and on her, like the sting of an insect. She stared at her.

"Who's that woman making eyes at us? Do you know her? Look...in the booth to the left."

Monique immediately looked, and said, disdainfully: "Old friends."

She named them. At the same time, Hélène Suze mimed *Bonjour* and an expression of joyous surprise. Monique responded with a vague wave. She measured, with her total in-

---

[17] The name translates as "The Blue Thistle." It is, of course, a pun on *cordon bleu*.

111

difference, the road traveled in the distance of the past. It was the first time she had encountered those revenants. Witnesses to her anterior existence, they did not move her any more than if she had said *au revoir* to them the previous evening.

She sensed, by that sign, that the wound was in the process of scarring over. Had she not, a month earlier, already seen her old rival Cléo in a general performance, without experiencing anything but platonic curiosity?

The only individuals the sight of whom would still have been capable of making her suffer—as her memory suffered every time that, with increasing rarity, she reviewed the abominable days—were her parents and Vigneret. She had never encountered the latter in her path, and had obstinately refused any contact with her parents, in spite of the invitations that Madame Lerbier had sent her several times during the last few months. Monique, being someone, was beginning to be worth something again...

The orchestra, attacking a "Spanish schottische," cut Niquette's ill humor short. She growled, wrapping her arms around her dancing partner, who let her do it, like an upright dormouse: "Hélène Suze? Hang on, I've heard talk of her from someone who used to smoke at Anika's. It appears that one Christmas Eve, two years ago, they had one of those blowouts in the studio. Yes, your Suze was a virgin with a taste for the finger, who was due to marry a Minister soon after—but that day was strictly for the ladies. However, there was also a journalist there who saw...hang on! You might know him. The one who did the dressmakers' shops...a blond with a heart-shaped mouth...."

"Mercoeur?"

"That's the one! I know that there was a heart in it somewhere, if one can put it like that. A fine society!"

"And ours?"

"At least, if there's vice, it doesn't hide. Rotten on top, healthy inside. That's neater. In contrast to that one: Hypocrisy & Co."

112

While talking, she modeled Monique's docile body on her supple carcass. In a kind of unconsciousness, Monique abandoned herself to the imperious rhythm of Niquette's movements.

An inextinguishable fire was burning in the bones of the quinquegenarian, so prodigiously well preserved by gymnastics and hydrotherapy that she did not appear, in the city as well as on the stage, to be more than thirty-five beneath the secrecy of make-up. Fur and feather, all was good for her celebrated ardor. She had nevertheless kept a singer-dancer for five years, elevated by her to the big screen, and had dropped him six months ago for Monique: a titular amour, which did not prevent either infatuations with different sexes, nor affairs.

Careless of the publicity, Monique allowed herself to be steered by the dominating arms. Good, evil? Words empty of meaning. They rang in the ears like cracked bells. She was here because her métier and hazard had led her here, and her insensibility had accommodated her to it. With the appearance of healing, she remained an invalid of sorts, still anesthetized by the chloroform and on the operating table. It was thus that she savored, with half-closed eyes, the intoxication of silent rotation.

Niquette's first caresses, while awakening in her a sensuality bruised at the moment of birth, had left the sentimentality of old sealed in the depths of her heart. Completely dead, she believed. She loved, for that analogy, the verses of poor profound Seurat, one of the young poets scythed down by the war; a tender soul that she cherished:

A heart of lead in which love rots with pride
Under stiff shrouds of yellow wood and ebony...

But she was, at the same time, rich in too much sap, for that which could not bud in one fashion would still spring forth in another. Thus, pleasure had led her, little by little, to a semi-revelation of sensuality: brief moments, and fundamentally deceptive. Those kisses, however, in which compassion-

113

ate tenderness was mingled with disturbance, led to a discovery that was not repugnant to her. Beneath the visage of consolation, that of enjoyment had appeared confusedly. Monique retained for Niquette the gratitude of only having brought her the one after the other, and only revealing little by little, beneath the delicacy of the friend, the ardor of the lover...

She whirled, her gaze lost. She was so tightly held that, squeezing one of Niquette's legs between hers, she felt the movement of the dance undulating within her. An Argentine who crossed their path applauded them mockingly: "Oh, well!"

Niquette burst out laughing: "One can easily do without them!"

Monique approved, with a lowering of the eyelashes. However, while still experiencing the same pleasure in the hours of their abandon, she was beginning to open on the world of the senses a less restricted thought. Men! After having first held them in grim disgust, and then disdain, she was beginning to take them into consideration again—but she saw them from exactly the same angle as bachelors saw girls: without any stirring of the soul. It as a curiosity that she had not yet confessed, in the inertia of the soul in which she was floating like a wreck—but she did not look away when she caught sight of someone who was not, *a priori*, displeasing.

"*Zut!*" said Niquette, consulting her wristwatch as they sat down again. "It's ten o'clock, and my sketch starts at eleven. Shall we go?"

"You have time, Beauty!" said Monique.

The Casino was next door to the dance hall.

"The time to change, yes. Are you coming?"

But Monique was not in a mood that evening to drag herself, as she usually did, into the asphyxia of the narrow dressing room and the promiscuity of the dresser. All of Niquette's perfumes could not succeed in drowning out the odor of the nearby toilets in the corridor.

"I'll catch up with you."

"You! You have a aim to cuckold me..."

114

Menacingly, Niquette's eyes searched for Hélène Suze in her booth. It was empty. A sham, to meet up elsewhere? Suspiciously, she said: "You have a rendezvous, eh?"

Monique found the supposition so absurd that she exclaimed, laughing: "I'll tell you about it!"

"What's got into you? Why, *bonjour*, Briscot."

"*Bonjour*, my Queen."

Niquette shook the hand of the famous comedian. They had known one another for a long time, having gained their stardom on the same stages, step by step. Monique detested Briscot's whimsy and, beneath his street urchin appearance, his jolly round face."

"You aren't playing, then?" asked Niquette. "What about the Revue?"

"Rehearsal for the lights."

"You can look after this little girl for me, then, who wants to carry on dancing. And both of you, come and collect me at the Casino after my sketch, won't you? We'll go have supper somewhere."

Briscot made a military salute, and Niquette left, tranquilly. Having ordered an Irish whiskey and soda, he sat down on the warm seat. He winked. "By the way, as I was passing through the Rue de La Boëtie this afternoon, I saw the decoration of your studio, turquoise and mandarin. Nice!"

"Really? Why didn't you come in?"

"Impossible. I was after one of those Americans. One of your sort—Rose, mahogany hair. And one of those saltires...pearls hanging down to her knees."

"You've done as much."

"Funny," he appreciated. "Oh, Niquette's not stupid..."

"And you?"

"Me, neither. To get carried away in this low society, you'd have to be crazy. Short and sweet..." He sketched an allusive grin. "At your service!"

"Thanks, but I don't use them. Keep it for the American..."

"Ancient history. On to another!"

"No! Just like that? At first glance?"

"She recognized me," he confided.

"That explains it."

Monique had never understood the strange prestige of clowns, including the ugliest. To what desires were those who chose them yielding? She studied Briscot attentively, and was surprised to do so without repulsion. He had an air of rustic health, and lurking behind the slightly lazy eyebrows was a gleam of tender malice.

"That's right," he muttered. "Laugh at me. I was just about to tell you something nice. An idea occurred to me regarding your turquoise thingamabob. My friend Edgard Lair..."

"The actor?"

"Yes. He's going to do a play by Perfeuil—stage sets and everything. Two sets, both interiors. If it would amuse you to furnish them, I can have a word with him..."

"No joke?"

"If it pleases you, it's done."

"Thanks."

"Bah! Between mates!"

He studied her in his turn, and ordered another whiskey and soda.

"It's true, you're not like the others. More appetizing, for a start...one could fall! And then, you have fashions of speaking, acting...squarely. Properly. Even though you lost your head once, eh? But with you, it's not the same as with the American? One has to remain comrades?"

A tango started up, unfurling its first measures. He stood up.

"Let's go! To make Niquette green!"

"But Briscot, if ever it gave me pleasure to imitate the American—oh, hands down! I didn't say with you—why shouldn't Niquette know about it? We're not married, for a start. And if we were, all the more reason to be frank!"

Mechanically, she put one hand in Briscot's and the other on his shoulder. Discreetly, he put his arm round her rounded waist. She swayed to the undulation of the rhythm. He felt, pressing against his chest, the firm warmth of young breasts.

Often, since she had been playing house, and more, with Niquette, Monique had danced with men. They were the only partners permitted to her, except for a few proven female friends, by a jealousy that amused her, as a mark of affection. Exclusive tenderness only exists within sincere affection. She had not thought of offending a vigilance that might be wounded, given their convention of reciprocal confession, whatever motivated it...

The sole eventuality that Niquette's tolerance, reassured with regard to masculine danger, had not foreseen was that some combination of unexpected electricity might be born from those repeat frictions. A hundred times, Monique had turned in the arms of charming cavaliers, without thinking of taking any other pleasure than that of a child agitating innocently. It was inevitable that one day, in the vertigo of movement, sound and light, in the particular intoxication carried even in the most sluggish veins, in the acrid and overheated atmosphere, that a moment would come when contact with instinct would be established.

It was Briscot, without even wanting to, who triggered the current. He had not attached any importance to his jokes a few minutes before. But in the sway of the beat, in which, after the march of twin bodies, came the inclined coming-and-going on the spot of the *corte*, that crudely evocative simulation of the sexual act, Monique felt against her flesh—imperceptibly at first, and then with a precision such that she nearly stopped and broke the grip—her dancing partner's erection. Beneath the light fabrics, the warmth of the blood was burning within them. A numbness invaded her. She closed her eyes, and tightened her grip. Arms taut, they snaked, knotted...their joined fingers interlaced, palm to palm, and suddenly, the imagination of their nude bodies...

At first, he had affected an air of detachment. Then, seeing that, far from defending herself, she was abandoning herself, he grasped the muscular rump more tightly to his stance.

117

He was excited to feel rising toward his shoulder the unconscious caress of a clenched hand. They rolled, one over the other, and then pitched, in a mechanical flux and reflux, slowly accomplishing the repetition of the hereditary gesture...

The tango stopped, abruptly. Their arms came apart. They contemplated one another with a kind of amazement, as if, having returned from a distant voyage, they were meeting one another face to face after a long absence, without recognizing one another...

He had the intelligence not to make any allusion to the surge of madness that had just shaken them. Accustomed to feigning sentiments that he did not feel, he was nevertheless carried away by the adventure, the pretense of which was worth more than the reality. The idea to having deceived Niquette made his eyes gleam, joyfully...

Monique's simplicity, disconcerting him, returned him to common sense and enticed him definitely.

"You dance very well," she observed. "We must do it again some time."

Still red-faced, her eyes shining, she did not give evidence in her satisfaction to any false modesty. And she said to herself: *After all, it's only a gymnastic exercise...but very agreeable, even so. I wouldn't have believed it.*

The next day, at the *Chardon Bleu*, where, alongside the turquoise and mandarin studio, an eggplant boudoir had been installed that morning, with speckled maple-wood. She listened deferentially to Edgard Lair. Brought by Briscot, he proffered definitive speeches, to the amazement of Mademoiselle Claire.

The latter was Monique's first sales assistant, Mademoiselle Tcherbalief, a young woman of the Russian aristocracy, uprooted by the revolutionary torment, who, after having worked in the cinema to make a living, was happy in her temporary shelter.

"For the one, where love will be born, I see hangings in crushed hanneton, with large pleats. Nothing else—limbo! For

furniture, just a Récamier sofa and a side table in black lacquer. And cushions, cushions, cushions..."

Niquette, modern in style, approved. The disinterested
Briscot tapped out a march with the tip of his cane on the belly
of a Hindu bronze.

"Aah!" roared Edgard Lair, with a sudden fury. "Stop it!
You're exasperating me..."

The windows trembled. He got up, through the vast felt
hat with which he was shading his forehead of genius onto an
armchair, and then mopped it with a minuscule green silk
handkerchief that was hanging from his jacket pocket. Beneath
the cranial cupola, his bulldog face creased into a small
crushed nose above a slack lip.

The fellow's mad! Monique thought.

The actor resumed in a serene voice: "In the second, love
has been born. A *coup* of passion. Red. Red and gold. Blood,
blood! All the reds. The most violent. A mouth agape! There."

Monique suppressed her desire to laugh.

"The indication is excellent. I see. And for the furniture?"

"No machines—carpets. And cushions, cushions, cushions..."

Madame Claire, who was taking notes, pencil in hand,
exclaimed: "Magnificent!"

Edgard Lair bowed with dignity, and turned to Monique:
"Understood, Mademoiselle? The mock-ups in three days."

"I'll do my best."

After a circular scan, he let fall, condescendingly: "You
have talent. And when you've worked with me..." He opened
the limitless future with a round sweep of his arm and put his
hat on with the flourish of a Spanish grandee. Then he turned
to Briscot. "Are you coming, old man? Mesdames!" He made
his exist, majestically.

Monique raised her eyes to the heavens and Niquette
cried: "Isn't he handsome, the animal?"

"In his genre."

Dexterously, Niquette tore him to shreds: "Pride to that point...wait till I announce: 'Messieurs, the Emperor!' He enters, and takes off his muffler; one would think that he were removing the great sash! He strides across the stage. *Bang*— all the actors prostrate themselves! For according to him, Antoine, Gémier, Guitry are worthless! *Aah!* he roars. The scenery trembles, and the author has fainted. With that clowning, if he were playing the Music Hall... But Briscot would still put him in his pocket..."

"He's nice, Briscot!" Monique murmured.

She was grateful to him for his intervention. The Perfeuil play, well presented, would be useful publicity. Interesting work, at any rate. Amused, she thought about their evening, which concluded around a few dozen oysters and a bottle of champagne at Le Prieuré...

The two stars, by popular request, had performed one of their old waltzes. The restaurant had never known such enthusiasm. The foreigners, standing on their chairs, had frantically acclaimed the glory of Paris. Monique had jokingly confessed her infidelity to Niquette, who had taken it in good humor. With a few drops from Briscot's glass she had even baptized them behind the ear with her moist finger, and, with an I-don't-care flourish, she had given them her blessing, adding: "But if you sleep with Madame Suze, I'll strangle you..."

"No danger, with Hélène or with Briscot!"

Monique was confident about that. However, on thinking back to her numbness of the previous evening, of the quasi-anonymous pleasure taken in the whirl of the dance, a less somber perspective extended... The repose of letting herself live, without thinking, in complete torpor. The obscure birth, too, of a new sensation...

She looked at Niquette, who was studying herself in a hand mirror. It was one of those Persian trinkets: flat rectangles whose burnished silvering retains, beneath a lid of delicate mosaic, a profundity of still water. Monique thought about the distant visages that had peered into it. She told herself that a day might also come when, in her memory,

Niquette's would fade away like the shadowy images in the antique mirror...

One could not be more closely linked than they were, and yet she suddenly sensed the actress as foreign to her thoughts as those unknowns whose interrogative eyes had once posed upon a vanished reflection...

"Ah!" said Niquette, in a melancholy tone, closing the rust-colored lid over the forgotten rectangle. "It doesn't embellish, your mirror! Anyway, I must go... Until this evening... Where?"

"At the dance hall, if you wish," Monique replied, without hesitation. "Like yesterday."

III

For an entire season, once her day's intelligent labor was accomplished, Monique had given evenings and part of her nights to dancing.

Alone or with the acquaintances, in which her métier had put her in communication, and having visited gradually the milieux of art and the theater, the numbing vertigo was unleashed for her.

She had been one of the thousand swooning faces that, to the shrill sound of the orchestras, beneath the blinding midnight suns, quiver in a turbulence of lights and sound. She had been one of the poor little human appearances, agitated, at the impulse of instinct, by an irresistible pendulum motion, a wavelet of the universal tide, whose ebb and flow have the same unconscious rhythm as amour.

To that incessant representation of the sexual act, to which the deregulation of mores invited an ever-increasing crowd, in music halls, dance halls, tea rooms, salons and even restaurants, Monique had become fatally infatuated. Niquette's passion and the kind of docile accommodation with which she had responded to it had gradually relented as the months went by...

Of that temporary intersection, they retained a comradeship, astonished when they ran into one another to have been able to be more than friends. For want of any other hunger than physical pleasure, the violence of their past sensations had quickly been entirely consumed. Nothing remained of it but a warmth, still gentle beneath the ashes. And already, when Monique encountered her former mistress escorted by some new companion, Monique felt, in the depths of her indifference, that the memory of it had almost completely cooled: a mirror in which were resolved, before vanishing—dissipated even in memory—all the temporary fires that desire had illuminated in her, since the voluptuous revelation that Briscot had brought her.

By the rapid simplicity with which she had passed on and put an end to the passing fancy, Monique had astonished the comedian. Blasé as he was with regard to the inconstancy of women, it was the first time that, having become infatuated himself, he had seen himself tossed aside in that fashion. On finding his conquest at the dance hall the very next day, abandoned to the arms of a handsome American, he had been unable to believe his eyes.

Beneath the violent-tinted moonlight, however, and then the orange blaze, with which the changing lights enveloped her rhythmic sway, the tango slowly brought back in front of him, with the chain of couples, the ring of the two enlaced bodies. Monique, raising her eyes, perceived Briscot as she passed by, and gave him an amicable wave.

When the dance finished she went past him, returning to the booth where Pierre des Souzaies, with whom she had come, was holding court. With a vexed expression, Briscot shook the hand that she extended to him in comradely fashion.

"My compliments," he said, mockingly, indicating the American, who was lost in the crowd. "You don't hang around!"

"No, indeed," she admitted, with tranquility. And, laughing at the spectacle of the grimace, simultaneously ironic and pinched: "Come on, Briscot! Is it so extraordinary, then, that in matters of...amour"—she had hesitated, unable to find another word—"a woman can think and act like a man? You have to get used to that idea, and take me for what I am: a bachelor."

He had the term *slut* on the tip of his tongue, but for politeness' sake, completed the word.[18] "A bacheloress, I know. *The* bacheloress."

---

[18] In French, the word that Briscot has on the tip of his tongue is *garce* [slut], which is why he seems to be completing it when he adjusts it to *garçonne*.

In spite of his indulgence to everything, however, his vanity recoiled. Nevertheless, he risked: "Shall I find you at the exit?"

"Impossible, regrettably. My associate is going to introduce me shortly to Lucienne Marnier, with whom I've arrange a meeting."

"Aha!"

She shrugged her shoulders at the insinuating smile. "You introduced me to Edgard Lair for the Perfeuil play, and I haven't slept with him. Lucienne Marnier...do you know her?"

Of course! Who had not heard talk of that eccentric? Beautiful and rich with millions—possessed by her official keeper, a Belgian banker—she prided herself on being an art-lover.

"She's going to talk to me about decorations for the Hindu festival she's giving in honor of her latest discovery, Peer Rys, the naked dancer..."

"Everything indicated for a tango," Briscot concluded. "Enjoy yourself!"

That astonishment of masculine self-esteem before instantaneous detachment had amused Monique greatly, in the three or four experiments she had attempted since—without searching them out, but not hesitating to push them to a conclusion each time she had found them.

Although now familiar with the most normal and healthiest of actions, she felt—at least when her partner knew how to give it to her—all the pleasure that Briscot had so furiously desired. She never went beyond her own satisfaction, almost always experienced before the other had concluded. Then, with the same brutal instinct that, on the first occasion, in the hotel room in which she had given herself to a passing stranger, had caused her to break the embrace prematurely, she shoved away the discountenanced man. She did not want to submit to hazardous maternities, but only to have children with the father that she had chosen. Even when she would willingly have continued the game, it was sufficient for her to perceive the approach on the creative spasm for her to remove herself from it voluntarily with a skillful maneuver.

Thus far—once those encounters, the peril of which had been an additional spice, began to disappoint her—she had only retained a somewhat mocking indifference for those who had been less a subject than an object so far as she was concerned. She smiled at the ill humor, with which, thanked without return, they had greeted their dismissal.

That reversal of the habitual roles—for Monique left them in no doubt of their secondary utility—caused them a humiliation or irritation that they could not disguise. It was necessary for them, before their fleeing adversary, to confess themselves beaten and regret the prey that had escaped: petty revenges that, at first, had flattered her tenacious rancor.

She had, resolutely, divided her existence into two parts: that of distractions—the shorter and less absorbing—and that of work, her true life. No matter how late or early it was, she always went home alone to the Rue de La Boëtie. She had never allowed anyone but true friends—like Madame Ambrat or Professor Vignabos, whom she invited from time to time—to cross the threshold of her personal dwelling. Every morning, even when, occasionally, she had not been to bed, she went down at ten o'clock from the entresol where she lived to the shop, which Mademoiselle Claire had already put in order and prettified for the quotidian sale.

Since the dazzling success of the Perfeuil play, the *Chardon Bleu* was launched. Five hundred performances and the publicity in the program had multiplied the merit of the décor designed by Monique in accordance with Edgard Lair's summary indications. Her renown had been definitively consecrated at a stroke.

Monique Lerbier: on the green marble entablement extended above the spacious window displays, framed in ebony, her sumptuous sign, the name henceforth adopted by Parisian high society, stood out in isolation in slender gold letters, instead of the original inscription. After the difficult months of the debut, when she had seen her capital disappear without any clientele becoming manifest, in less than a year, with the aid of the vogue, fortune was beginning to arrive.

That day—it was the third spring after her departure from the Avenue Henri-Martin—the weather promised to be magnificent.

Her body fresh, reposed by the cold shower with which she punctiliously accompanied her quarter-hour of physical culture, Monique was enjoying, without any afterthought, the happy equilibrium of her strength.

Aided by Mademoiselle Claire, a vigilant and precious lieutenant, she deployed lamé fabrics, showing off the luminous pleats in the morning splendor. At the last moment, Lucienne Marnier had wanted to change the backcloth against which Peer Rys' dances would show off their sculptural nudity that same evening. Instead of the uniform velvet, whose lavender blue, in the frame of coral curtains embroidered with gold, made a slightly insipid contrast, she wanted a more sumptuous fabric to set off the living jewel.

"No, not pink or red," Monique declared. "Let's stick to complementaries. This, perhaps?" She tried out a royal blue lampas, trimmed with silver—"Not bad"—and then pointed to a roll of empire green brocade, with a vermilion palm leaf design. Authoritatively, she said: "That ought to go. Show!"

Mademoiselle Claire displayed the princely fabric. Simultaneously bright and dark, it retained a flexibility in its heavy fractures. With her eyes closed, Monique imagined the movements of the pale beautiful body against it. She had come back from one of the recent rehearsals wonderstruck.

"That's it!" she concluded. Using a sample of the coral, she compared the two fabrics in the little room reserved for nocturnal illumination in order to be certain.

"The green is perfect!" Mademoiselle Claire exclaimed. "Mademoiselle Marnier will be pleased."

"Take a taxi and go yourself with Monsieur Angibault to show both of them to her. She can choose…do we have enough of both? Good. Take them in hand immediately. Ready for six o'clock."

Militarily, Mademoiselle Claire and Monsieur Angibault—the trusted factotum, who had hastened in response to the summons—bowed and departed.

A smiling but firm discipline reigned at the *Chardon Bleu*. It was sufficient for "the boss" to appear and to give orders. The eight employees that the establishment now had pronounced the word "Mademoiselle" with a religious respect. They held her in high esteem because, although severe, she was fair.

Monique, with her back to the entrance door, examined a few antique faiences and iridescent glasses that had just arrived: purchases made the day before at the Auction Rooms, from the Monestier collection. An oil lamp, with a thicket neck on three intact goose feet, shone in the midst of the lot like a giant turquoise. What an item! She was combining it with an apricot and flax-blue muslin shade when a guttural voice beside her made her shiver.

"My dear child..."

She turned round. Plombino! He inclined his thick shock of hair, turned gray, and his broad shoulders, and, raising and embarrassed face, said: "Yes, it's me. I beg you to accept my respects."

She contemplated him insolently.

"They've aged...in four years!"

He dissimulated his grimace behind a smile, and replied: "One can't say the same for your beauty."

"I don't suppose, however, that it's simply to the need for that madrigal that I owe your visit?"

"But yes, in large measure! It's for the sake of discretion, knowing your pride, that I've abstained until now...in the...difficult times you've been though. I wouldn't have wanted you to be able to see, in a possibly importunate step, the slightest... interested motive."

He was lying. She knew that full well, having brutally rejected the offers of money that he had made on several occasions after she had quit the Avenue Henri-Martin. Undoubted-

ly, for him to present himself in person after that long efface-
ment, he must have some pressing reason.

He took her silence as an invitation, and continued in a
penetrating tone: "Today, when you have no more need of
anyone, I feel more at ease in assuring you that my affection
has not varied and that my admiration has grown."

She read in his hippopotamus eyes the same slimy sincerity as in the distant days when she had still been a mar-
riageable young woman. What news had brought him, and
what bargain did he want to propose to her?

"Indeed, Monsieur le Baron," she said, politely haughty.
"What do you want?"

Plombino, on seeing her again, had felt his infatuation
reawakening, more vividly than ever. The manner in which he
had been dismissed, the preoccupation with his enterprises,
incessantly broadened to the point of now encompassing both
worlds, and long absences, had been able to deflect him temporarily from his pursuit. Monique, glimpsed at a supper celebrating a hundredth performance, had taken possession of the
millionaire again, against his will. The obsession of seeing her
again, and of having her, at no matter what price, had haunted
him ever since.

He declared, unctuously: "Well, this is it. You're aware
of the relationship of quotidian affection that I've entertained
with your father, since..."

He hesitated, hoping that she would come to his aid, but
she stared at him, with a mocking expression. Yes, she knew!
The association concluded, initially between her father and
Vigneret, once she had gone, as if nothing had happened...
Then the augmentation of the capital, transforming with
Plombino's millions and those of Ransom and White, the
small primitive company into a formidable international business. She even knew that she would one day be a rich heiress,
and that the fortune in question, which she did not want,
would become that of the Enfants Recueillis, answering, by an
unexpected donation, the humble dreams of Madame Amblat.

128

That way, the gold of an evil deed would become the lever of a noble work.

"Pass on," she said.

Plombino made a gesture of approval. What was the point, in fact, of raking over painful memories?

"You're right—let's not talk about all that. This is what I have to say to you. Your mother's health, tested last winter, is giving rise to some anxieties...yes, serious. The heart... Lerbier told me, yesterday, that it would be a great joy for her to see you again, and that they would both be very happy if you would consent to go to dinner, one evening soon, at the Avenue Henri-Martin. What response shall I give them?"

Monique went pale, nonplussed. She evoked the tragic moment in the vestibule, and her vision of horror: the cadaver of Aunt Sylvestre lying on the stretcher... The face of her mother, ill, mingled in the distance with that of the kindly old lady. She drove away the phantoms.

No! She would never return to the Avenue Henri-Martin!

And yet, at the memory of the affection that, in spite of everything, the two sisters had had for one another, the confused mirage of hours of old, when she had still been a child...Monique questioned herself, not without disturbance. What if Plombino's step was not only, as she supposed, a blackmail aimed toward reconciliation. What if her mother's condition really...?

No! In spite of the rupture that had made her parents strangers to her, she experienced, instinctively, some emotion instead of that insurmountable suspicion.

"I'll think about it," she said, finally.

She looked at Plombino without seeing him. Her thoughts wandered from the garden in Hyères to the villa at Trouville. The days lived abruptly wove their delicate spider web in the shadows of her memory.

Under the distracted gaze that warmed him like a ray of sunlight, he dilated, happily. He persisted, effusively:

"You won't refuse them that joy!"

"My mother is confined to bed?"

"She's been up for a fortnight. She even goes out sometimes in the afternoons."

"Well, then," she said, reassured, but shaken nevertheless. "Tell her to telephone me. We'll see."

Plombino seized her hands so suddenly that she did not have time to defend herself, and planted his heavy lips on them devotionally. She recoiled violently. But the fat man, excited by the fresh flesh, was not at all deterred. He stammered: "Thank you, my child. And permit me to congratulate you. What marvels!"

He turned, breathing heavily, in the midst of the ancient trinkets, and pointed at the gracefully-contoured lacquer chairs.

"The Lerbier style! You must do me the kindness of re-furnishing the ground floor of my house on the Parc Monceau. I only want the modern."

He did not let go. She had to employ the pretext of work to do, and only breathed when, back in his auto, she saw him draw away, still waving from the window.

Work for that resident alien? The idea! She shrugged her shoulders, ill-humoredly. Plombino had spoiled her entire day.

At the same time, a cloud passed over the sun. Within her and around her, everything darkened abruptly.

She had not yet returned from her melancholy voyage to the land of past suffering when, after an afternoon enclosed in her apartment with her memories, and then a solitary cup of tea and toast, the wall clock in her bedroom, chiming nine o'clock, recalled her to reality. Lucienne Marnier's soirée, and then, at midnight, Peer Rys' exhibition! She only just had time...

She had recourse to the habitual remedy for her fatigue and neurasthenia: good cold water, and her whiplash. Naked in her bathroom, all white ceramic and mirrors, she stretched, after the friction of the horsehair strip.

The salubrious reaction calmed her down. Her fit of languid savagery yielded to a need to forget. As usual, she emerged from her reverie with an urgent need for action of any kind. There were crises whose acuity was spaced out, but in which the wound, which she believed every time to be scarred over, reopened entirely and more profoundly...

She gave the image that the full-length mirror sent back to her a glance that satisfied her. What was the point of tormenting herself like that? She resented that weakness, and chided herself: there was nothing to be done about accomplished facts except to draw lessons from them, courageously!

Mechanically, she caressed her firm breasts, the rose-pink areolas of which, upon the veined roundness, had deepened to carmine. Then, descending along the muscular torso and the flat abdomen to the curve of the hips, the amphora of which was extended by the long legs, she followed, as if she were designing it, the contour of the thighs. She evoked, with a smiling comparison, the pure lines of the naked dancer.

Did she not have, like him, the body of a hymnist in which Beauty was born with a natural rhythm? She did not know, any more than him, the vain complications of modesty... Masked by ugliness or hypocrisy... But, superior to him, she bore in her beautiful animal flesh a soul that he did not have...

A proud joy uplifted her at the idea of her duality.

Men! She smiled, disdainfully. By virtue of having wished it, she had become, physically and morally, their equal. And yet, she could not help admitting, there was, in the bitterness of her revenge, an unformulated sentiment...

Solitude? Sterility? She did not feel its affliction precisely, as yet, but the invisible worm was nascent in the magnificence of the fruit.

A slow, scrupulous toilette, and at eleven o'clock—clad solely in a silver lamé chemise-dress from which the arms and upper body emerged, while the heavy fabric clung to the rest of the body—she was ready. Pierre des Souzaies' auto blew its horn just then, beneath her windows.

They made a sensational entrance: he tall and slim, in a puce jacket, with his face delicately made up, with hair styled à la Clouet;[19] she immediately surrounded by a veritable court. Lucienne Marnier came to meet her, regal in the bright red of a dogaress. A turban of diamonds and pearls, the emblem of the Hindu feast, evoked the splendors of Asia in her Venetian tresses. She politely associated Monique with her triumph.

The drawing rooms were packed. Mademoiselle Mariner had only invited close friends, but she went from Belgian finance to Parisian upper crust, passing through all the notorieties of cosmopolitan art and letters. Monique advanced through the crowd and the commotion, claimed in passing by her admirers.

There were none warmer than her old friends. The gang, which seemed to have arranged a rendezvous, made itself recognized with loud protestations. It seemed that Ginette Hutier and Michelle d'Entraygues had never ceased to cherish her. There was only one voice with regard to her talent, her grace, her glamour...

"Etcetera," she said, shaking the insistent hand of Madame Merlin, without warmth.

But the lights went out abruptly. All the noise died away as if by enchantment, after a prolonged *ah!* At the far end of the suite, the sanctuary was illuminated: the coral and gold curtains parted slowly. The desert of verdure and vermilion palms appeared. A large black carpet with trimmed velvet was spread over the entire stage.

Then a strange music rose up. The invisible orchestra launched its nostalgic tune. The Orient unfurled, mysteriously. Then the curtains fell back at the same time as the music faded...

Suddenly, at the last sigh of the soft and high-pitched flutes, the curtains rose again in the midst of the pregnant silence.

---

[19] The painter Francois Clouet (c1510-1572) painted numerous portraits of the French royal family, several of which are in the Louvre, and which became significant stylistic models

On his knees, his arms outstretched and his back motionless, the naked dancer, prostrate, was touching his forehead to the night-black floor. His paleness stood out, pure, against the dream-like backcloth. Suddenly, as if resuming the cadence of the arpeggios, the marble was animated; the beautiful, harmonious body stood up. With the gravity of invocation, his entire being hoisted in an endless leap, Peer Rys extended toward an imaginary sky in the splendor of a young god. He was so beautiful that he seemed chaste.

The orchestra rolled out the eternal theme: murmurs of desire and the cries of unchained passion. Across the sands, the forest, water and fore, the multiform Dance bounded, from the freshness of morning to starry nights. To the monotonous appeal of the flutes and lyres, however, the implacable azure finally imposed itself.

Monique, hanging on the dancer's movements, wound herself around the Indian Bacchus and the entire procession of ancient corteges. The room, in turn, surged with its sacred intoxication from the depths of all souls at an intense moment when Peer Rys incarnated, in himself, all orgiastic delirium.

When he collapsed, exhausted, a tumult of applause and cheers rang out. The curtains, immediately fallen back, parted, and the triumphant performer appeared, completely self-controlled, giving no sign of fatigue. The frenzy of the bravos was such that Monique's enthusiasm was irritated by it. The women, standing up, were shouting: "Encore! Encore!" It was no longer the naked dancer, nor even the gymnast, but the naked man, the complete athlete, that they were visibly acclaiming. But Peer Rys slipped away from the ovation, modestly.

How, three hours later, did Monique find herself in Anika Gobrony's studio, having supper, sitting between Peer Rys and Ginette Hutier, while opposite the violinist, the Minister of Transport was enthroned, flanked by Hélène Suze and Michelle d'Entraygues? Max de Laume, Pierre des Souzaies and Cecil Meere completed the unexpected ensemble.

She did not ask herself, entirely given over to discovering in her neighbor, who had become once again the most correct and elegant of Argentines, a companion of child-like gaiety and simplicity.

While Monsieur Hutier silently removed the cork from another bottle of champagne with the gravity of a *maître d'hôtel*, Anika had gotten up in order to switch off the central chandelier and play a Czech march on the piano. Her hair cut short, with her ardent bronzed face and her flat throat, in her immutable incarnadine velvet smock, she was reminiscent of some demonic angel.

Hélène Suze and Michelle d'Entraygues, having demanded a shimmy, immediately enlaced one another. Pierre des Souzaies and Cecil Meere, following their example, spun and leapt. Max de Laume, his mouth close to Ginette's ear, was relating such horrors to her that she was gurgling with pleasure, while His Excellency, left to himself, was drinking glass after glass with a blissful expression. Monsieur Hutier, while sympathetically considering the suggestive couple formed by Antinous and his wife, smiled at the memory of the fustigation that he had administered the previous evening by a solid wench at Irène's. Birch-rods, alternating with knotted cords—there was nothing like it!

Monique, slumped in her chair, was listening with pleasure to the gallantries with which Peer Rys, a trifle drunk, was showering her. She had a thick head and could only hear the brassy sound of his voice. She did not care about the meaning of the words; she did not desire him to have wit; she preferred, for what she wanted, that he be no more than what he was: a beautiful machine of pleasure.

He had his arm around her waist. The unconscious labor that had been going on within her for several days had abruptly materialized in a project that was gradually becoming more precise...

The piano had fallen silent. In a dark corner of the studio, Hélène Suze, Michelle and Anika Gobrony were lying full length on a heap of cushions. A Turkish lamp illuminated the interlacement of this indistinct group with a vague red glow. With the same indifferent gaze, Monique observed that Cecil Meere and Pierre des Souzaies had disappeared, and that Ginette and Max de Laume had left the table, followed by Monsieur Hutier. She perceived him, adrift in the tumbril of an English armchair, his eyes oblique, not far from the divan on which his wife had just laid down, drawing her cavalier down with her.

Aware as she was of the corruption of that milieu, through which she had once moved like a salamander through flame, Monique found her former friends "a little excessive." Peer Rys, with a profile of an antique medallion, appeared to her even fresher by contrast, and restful. She responded with a long pressure of the hand to his pleading.

After all, why only enjoy the ephemeral moment by halves? Why that absurd dread of a risk, given that, independent from every point of view, she had no need to count on anyone? Yes, why not a child? A child that she would keep to herself, and whose soul she would fashion, along with a robust body, by means of education. A child from whose father, forgotten tomorrow, he would only inherit the magnificent gifts of health and strength...

Love? She no longer believed in it. Art, such as her skill practiced it, what was that? A distraction...yes, the illusion of not being completely futile... Whereas a child! To create action and thought—life!

Proudly, she saluted the dawning light, the redemptive idea... A child! A companion and an objective of every hour!

Monique darted a final glance over the vast room, in which the cold light of dawn was mingling with the glimmer of veiled lamps. A gray shadow enveloped the immobility of the semi-naked groups that were agitated, from time to time, by an undulation or a sigh.

She stood up abruptly, dragging her companion.

"Come!"

IV

There were a few weeks of entire happiness. Proudly, Monique enjoyed her full liberty, finally conquered. The unrestricted pleasure that she was beginning to experience gave her youthful thirst for sensuality an appeasement that never wearied.

Until then, a confused sentiment of inferiority, a rancor of submission, had, in the arms that believed they possessed her, spoiled the violence of her sensations, no matter how sharp they had been. Of the men whose embrace she had accepted or desired, she had always felt herself, in the supreme moment of abandonment, to be the subject, since the creative possibility that she still refused depended more on them than on her. They were intoxicating but precarious moments, to which her determination to withdraw, sometimes even before the moment of their perfection, not only diminished their value, but also added an unsatisfied bitterness. She felt profoundly humiliated by the idea that her entire person, including its future, depended on those fleeting dominators for a second...

And it was not only her own life, which, if she had not taken precautions, they would have remained, even after disappearing, the durable masters—that which for nine months she would have to knead with her flesh and animate with her breath—it was the prolongation, the survivor of herself...!

Was not such a risk, out of all feminine servitudes, the worst, the most mortifying of all? Maternity only had a reason for being, and a grandeur, if it was consensual—more than that, desired.

Certainly, she could, like many others, have eluded that law of nature by some prophylactic artifice...the school of Malthus—as Georges Blanchet, the man who had displeased her so much, had once put it—was open to all. But she could not see herself asking someone like Briscot to put on, before approaching her, one of the hoods that Michelle, before becoming the Marquise d'Entraygues, had always taken the precaution of carrying in her handbag. Monique had smiled at that idea, which had once only made her indignant. The ridiculous spectacle only further underlined the hypocrisy and, in her eyes, the debasement. As for equipping herself with some such protection, along with her lipstick and powder puff, really, no! That disgusted her...

The choice voluntarily made of Peer Rys to collaborate in the great work of which she would thus remain the principal artisan relegated such pretty preoccupations to negligibility, along with any sentiment of dependency. She was returning to natural law, joyfully accepted. She would thus recover equality.

To the delight of abandoning herself entirely to physical enjoyment was added that of self-esteem, sweetly caressed. For the first time, Monique's personality blossomed completely. To have selected the most handsome man of all for the carnal Wedding, and to be, by virtue of that Elevation, a truly incarnate woman, gave her pride, flattered by making use of a man in her turn, a divine exaltation.

The gratitude of pleasure received, which completes the transformation of many others into bewildered slaves, softened into a pleasantly mischievous, involuntary but constant manifestation of her superiority. She was extremely conscious of it, and, in spite of herself—for she had never been vain—she allowed it to pierce her so frequently that, soon fatigued with being reduced to the role ordinarily assigned to women, Peer Rys, spoiled by innumerable successes, quickly gave evidence of his discontentment.

His saracen blood—which, fused with that of all the European races, predominates in spite the composite amalgam in the veins of the Argentine people—further inclined his native conceit, swollen along the way, to rebel against a mistress who wanted things her own way. Beneath his Scandinavian pseudonym and his Latin hereditary, Peer Rys was fundamentally just a Spanish Moor.

After a month, Peer—a translation of Pietro—had had enough. A naked dancer, he could only cope with a sedentary and veiled companion. Monique, devoid of pretention, would have seemed to him the most delightful of comrades. Authoritarian and, in the desire that she had for him to give her a child, confining him to the role of stallion, she became unbearable. A son? He had had others without so much fuss!

A respite, however, brightened the last fortnight of their affair. Easter fell at the end of April. On the other hand, Peer found himself devoid of any engagement until mid-May, when he was due to leave for London. The aristocratic salons there were demanding him—on condition, however, that he wear a *cache-sexe*. For her part, Monique, after the laborious winter, was yearning for repose and solitude. He allowed himself to be abducted for an escape to the sun—off to Clairvallon!

The marvelous Provençal spring welcomed them. They loved the tranquil palace overlooking the Golfe Sambracitain. The great black umbrellas of the parasol pines stood out against the azure. The rosemary had extended its robe of pale blue flowers, and embalmed the keen air. Facing them, the sea was displayed like a resplendent lake. One might have thought it a single sapphire, embedded in the emerald of the hills, at whose center, shielded by its ancient ramparts, Saint-Tropez seemed to be a red-gold clasp.

That was, in their dying torch, the ultimate flicker of flame.

Monique then began to dread that her wish might not come true: she had not avoided the monthly return that she dreaded. Passionately desirous of becoming a mother, an instinctive calculation of her entire being caused her to rediscover, in the ardor of her need, the secret of pleasing. The gentle seduction of the lover, flattering "her Pietre" reignited his appetite for the act that he had ended up only practicing as a function.

The illusion of being loved for himself rendered him the naivety and spontaneity of sentiments. They allowed themselves to live, in the great saline air, without afterthought.

Their youth dilated, magnificently, with animal bounds or the vegetable torpor. Trivia of all kinds amused them: the thousand petty remarks of everyday existence, and their comic simplicity. Their naked nights were one long embrace in which desire was incessantly reborn of its own accord, until the heavy sleep and the light awakenings of the morning.

Monique experienced an insatiable thirst for caresses. Pietre's love-making had completed, by awakening a complete sensuality within her, her progressive initiation. She was entirely open, with the ingenuity of a rose blooming in the sunlight. Abrupt impulses drove her, suddenly, into his muscular arms. The boat in which they floated alone on the marine plain—at the whim of the fixed tiller and the motor—the warm sand of the inlets, and the odorous paths of the mountain served as beds of hazard for the caprices of their desire.

She cried out, during the ardent minutes, the intoxication that his furious thrusts gave her, teeth-clenched. Or, beneath the savant slowness of penetration, she sighed in a whisper the glad plaint of doves. She believed then that she loved him— and even more violently, at the moment of the shared effusion, she wanted a son to be born from their confounded flesh.

One day, when, without her expecting it, he had taken her abruptly in the wild mountains, she had tried to convince herself that her dream had been realized. She was in the process of collecting dark violet lavender under the pines. Unexpectedly, he had taken advantage of her lowered rump, lifted up her skirt, and she had felt the burning god possess her. She had uttered an animal moan, and then had given herself, actively. Beneath the open sky, the energy of nature, the blind surge of age-old forces, which, without any regard for learned chastity, works instinctively for the perpetuation of the species, had been freely unleashed.

Subsequently, she remembered for a long time, with a regret mingled with tenderness, that moment in which she thought she was in communion with the soul of the earth...

"My bouquet!" she had exclaimed, before resuming their route...

She picked up the perfumed sprigs. Then she put her arm round Pietro's bronzed neck. He was contemplating the landscape, with a satisfied expression. She was resentful of that. He ought not to be thinking about anything but her! And she put the tuft of lavender under his nose, saying: "Smell!"

Tickled, he sneezed. Then she started to laugh...

"I'll keep these flowers! They'll never fade in my memory."

Two months later, in Paris, with amused detachment, Monique found one of the stems, dried between two poems by Samain, which she had taken to Clairvallon, and whose pages she had renounced reading aloud to her companion as soon as the first evening.

The end of her sojourn had been soiled by a painful disappointment. The inexorable periodic apparition had convinced her, for a second time, that she had nothing more to expect from her partner beyond an exchange of sensations that any other gymnastics, decent and healthy, was capable of procuring.

Peer Rys immediately appeared to her in his true nudity: he was an ignorant and vain beast. The pride with which she had previously exhibited him, like a beautiful domestic animal, before the admiring gazes with which the entire palace continued to surround them, changed into an insurmountable irritation. Everywhere, at the restaurant, on the terrace, in the corridors, and even in the pathways of their promenades, women followed with a pronounced or shameful leer "the naked dancer." He preened himself, conceitedly...

Or, taking out a minuscule repair kit, which contained, along with a pocket mirror, a comb, and make-up brushes, he took minute care of his face while she was talking. She shrugged her shoulders, pityingly.

Piqued, he had since sought any and all opportunities to quarrel. The letters with which his admirers pursued him furnished many. In the beginning, Monique had been interested in their provenance, less out of jealousy than the curiosity of observation. It was the great distraction of an hour in the café.

Together, they opened his correspondence, commenting on it—a habit that, in recent days, she had renounced disdainfully.

On the eve of their departure, as she pretended to be absorbed in reading *L'Éclaireur de Nice*, Peer, galled, coughed as he placed a perfumed envelope on the table, ostentatiously.

Silence. Monique did not blink. Then he exploded. "I don't see what I'm doing here, now that you no longer take any notice of me! Fortunately, if you scorn me, others do me justice!"

"But so do I, my dear. You're the most handsome of dancers, that's understood."

"And the stupidest of men, no—as you're the most intelligent of women?"

"If you say so."

He got up, very pale. "In any case, of the two of us, it's the more stupid who's the less futile. I'm capable of making children!" He showed her the letters: "Look—as many as you like! There's no lack of opportunities."

She looked him up and down, haughtily, but the sarcasm had hit home. Useless, yes! And the sentiment of her sterility suddenly grew within her into the desert of her solitude.

Wounded, she replied: "Don't worry. It's not me who'll hold you back." Then, on reflection, she added, with a melancholy smile: "You're wrong. Why squabble? As comrades we met; as comrades we'll part..."

Peer Rys! He was in Rome now. She thought of him amicably, in spite of his faults. From the start, of course, none had escaped her, but it was not for his intellectual ascendancy that she had loved him. Could she really hold it against him that he had not fulfilled all her desires, all her hopes?

By virtue of a tenacious determination not to despair yet, it was him, not her, she rendered responsible for the failure. Given that, setting mediocrity aside, having only spent with him good, then delightful, and then less good moments, what reproach did she have the right to address to him?

141

She did not linger long over the idea that she and she alone might be the cause of her disillusionment. No more did she ask herself why she had so quickly become blasé about the amorous qualities with which she had been momentarily smitten.

She was convinced of her moral superiority over the men who surrounded her, retaining, from her scarred wound, a horror of amour such as it was understood by those around her, and also a fear of suffering if she allowed herself to be taken in again, Those blinkers limited the fertile field of life to the prideful furrow of her research.

Peer Rys went back into the circle. Monique had continued, confidently, along her own route. That which one had been unable to do, another might be capable of doing. It was thus that she distinguished, successively, several reproducers.

First there was a député from the Midi, whose resemblance to the Mistral has seduced her. Encountered at a grand dinner party at the Hutiers, she had noticed his proud and delicate features, and then listened with amusement to his sonorous speech. But, pressed amorously, the pipe-and-drum man turned out, like Chanticleer, only to have the deceptive appearance of crest and spurs. Her ambition and his sufficiency had quickly been disappointed.

Then there had been an engineer with a Roman nose and broad shoulders, a great builder of bridges and railway tracks. Possessed of clear ideas and undertaking bold enterprises, he had pleased her with his frankness, and a broad intelligence with a horizon of travels and overseas endeavors. After three months, however, the hopes founded on his taurean member had vanished. The engineer was no more prolific than an ox.

A doubt ended up troubling Monique. What if she were the faulty one? She made a resolution to consult a physician, and then put the project off, week after week. The hours passed with an increasingly bustling brevity as business, one thing leading to another, augmented her income and, simultaneously, the necessary sum of efforts.

It had been necessary to extend over neighboring shops, the leases of which she had been able to afford, the long green marble plaque, and include mention on the triumphant sign of *Interior Design* and *Curiosities*, affirmed in somber golden letters.

Without regret, Monique had put an end to mundane evening excursions. She was no longer seen in dance halls and music halls. Always at work at ten o'clock in the morning, she stayed up late, designing and coloring mock-ups, and every time that she had not dined in the city or with the friend from whom, after the député and the engineer, she was still hoping, but no longer expecting, to obtain the child, vain notions began to color her initial experiment.

The worldly victory, in fact, she only enjoyed inasmuch as it realized, by consecrating it, her material existence. Society accepted in Monique Lerbier, once she was famous and earning her living brilliantly, that which it had reproached in her when she was obscure and poor. That consent, made of latitude and servility, brought her only one satisfaction: that of the power, without the stamp of a companion and a respondent, freely to bring into the world a free being, and to raise him in scorn for the customs and laws that had made her suffer so cruelly.

A natural child—and then? Head held high, he would bear his mother's name. She would liberate him, from the very beginning, from the social prison. She would teach him to love, without hypocrisy, everything that was worth the trouble, and not to love anything unworthy. She would thus spare him, along with superfluous words, unnecessary evils.

Yes, that alone, in her eyes, remained the reason for living: a child, who would belong only to her, and of whom she would be proud; the center of solitary days and the empty hours that neither work nor sensuality, ultimately sated, could succeed in filling.

That, she had not yet confessed to herself, was not the profound motive, which was an unslaked need for tenderness and love, all the distress of a woman abandoned, even in the solitude *à deux* of all her attempts. Monique launched toward her dream of pregnancy the same frenzy for complementarity, the sentimental substitution that so many unhappy spouses seek in maternity.

It was at the moment at which her hope had faded away that the sentiment of a new failure had infiltrated her without her being aware of it. She retained, from her fourth trial, a sadness that gradually turned to neurasthenia. She soon broke it off, to the enraged despair of her lover.

He was a painter of her own age, intelligent and hearty, who built landscapes out of roundels and portraits in cubes. The whole had a grenadine tonality, dotted with white. Not that he judged these conceptions logically, but he was obsessed with an appetite for evolutionary splendor appropriate to his youth. There was never between them any question of esthetics...

Fortunately, the vacations arrived. Monique was obliged, in order to cut short his pursuit to depart, to send him on a false trail. While he looked for her in Switzerland, she went to the coast, to a little Breton beach: Rosmenidec, a gap between two high cliffs. The trees descended all the way to the sea; it was a fishing village where there were only half a dozen villas and a down-and-out hotel.

She lived there alone for a month, refusing all company. She was outside at dawn, with her drawing pad and pencils, and only came back at noon to hasten through lunch at the proprietor's table, and then went out again to muse amid the rocks until bath time. And in the evening, late into the night, she dreamed, lying on the sand or wandering in the countryside.

It was a salubrious return to herself, in which she was immersed in solitude, but stayed in contact with indifferent nature as well as her neighbors—relationships reduced to the inevitable. She soon felt even more alone than she had in Paris, in the agitation of her work and the crowd of ever-appearing and ever-disappearing faces.

The spectacle of human mediocrity seemed all the more afflicting to her amid the splendor of the serene décor—the land, the sea and the sky through which her intimate distress tried in vain to spread its wings like a bird. Her impotence then had a desire to sob, before the infinity that she had embraced the day before, animating it with her faith, whose impassivity now overwhelmed her.

Then, for the first time since her escape, she materialized the evidence in her tormented heart. She had conquered nothing with her liberty. Her work? What good was it, if it only amplified her desolation? She had only found the pleasure of a false semblance of love. If she could not have a child, what remained to her?

To entice herself any longer served no purpose; such was, in its cruel clarity, the balance sheet of the past: a ruin from which nothing could be saved—not even the link that attached her, in misfortune, to the hours of old, to the mirage of the familial nest.

Her mother? She had seen her again two or three times after Plombino's approach. Her father? She had also consented to receive him in the Rue de La Boëtie. At first, after the initial embarrassment, she had experienced an emotion that was almost pleasurable in those encounters. The tenacious bond of memories had seemed to her to be stretched, rather than broken, but very quickly she had sensed that she had nothing before her but strangers, hostile beneath the reproach of their smiles.

She found nothing to say to them but banalities. Otherwise, she immediately collided with the rock of incomprehension. All three of them became weary; they were too old to take the steps necessary to catch up with her; she was too categorical for superfluous affectation. On recognizing that they were still anchored in their beaten track, merely more puerile beneath their wrinkles and white hair, she had sadly sensed the definitive detachment. There was no longer anything in common between them, not even their suffering, so differently felt and supported...

Sitting in a corner of the beach with her back to a rock, Monique mechanically picked up handfuls of sand and then let it filter through her fingers as a fine dry rain. Thus the hours went by, flowing incessantly as the hourglass was inverted: the annihilation of the past.

She watched the seagulls flying over the noise of the incoming tide. Their white wings skimmed the water, and then, at full extent, an abrupt surge carried them away like an arrow. The setting sun heaped up palaces of clouds out at sea; they crumbled by degrees.

The future! she said to herself—and, discouraged, she let her hand fall back. She could not see anything around her but solitude, and then old age.

A distant song resounded. It was some fisherman mending his nets. The ballad strung out its deep notes like a rosary of resignation. All the misery and all the courage of the lives of seamen, struggling against the elements...

Monique felt ashamed, and shook herself.

I'm insane, she thought, as she got to her feet. *Only thinking of oneself is like being blind. First of all, I'm not sure that I'll never be a mother, and even if that's the case...Madame Ambrat lives well, for the children of others...*

The next day, she went back to Paris, September, and the necessity of preparing for a winter season absorbing to the point that she would only find in the first days of autumn the time to have herself examined, as she had resolved to do. Mademoiselle Tcherbalief, one of whose relatives had suffered the previous year from a female malady, had recommended Dr. Hilbour.

She went there with simplicity, confident in his science and the authority of his priesthood. She expected to see an aged, bald gentleman with spectacles, but found a young man with a neatly-trimmed beard and smiling eyes. Having told him the reason for the consultation, aware as she was of the obligations required by such an investigation, she looked twice at the table bed on which, having covered it with a ripolin sheet, the doctor invited her to lie down. But whatever the cost, she wanted to know...

She closed her eyes, and only opened them again when, in his musical voice, Hilbour had declared: "Thank you."

"Well, Doctor?" she asked, anxiously, readjusting her clothing.

"Well, Mademoiselle...but it might be more convenient, in order for me to explain it to you more clearly..." He pointed to a blackboard and picked up a piece of chalk.

"No need—I have a sufficient knowledge of anatomy."

He looked at her, without thinking of hiding his surprise, and said, straightforwardly: "Well then, here it is: unless you have recourse to an indispensable intervention—which, I hasten to assure you, isn't serious...a trifle painful, at the most, you understand—the conformation of your womb presently renders any conception impossible. You have a particularity that many women would envy you: a virginal neck. With that, no danger of pregnancy, or no hope, depending on the point of view one adopts," He added, with a little smile: "The most malign spermatozoa break their noses on it. They can't get through!"

"And the remedy?"

He indicated, on a crystal tabletop, alongside the speculum of which he had just made use, a small arsenal of graduated forceps and laminar probes.

"Clear the path by means of a progressive dilatation. There's also—that's the radical means—surgical intervention: anesthesia, curetage and, again, dilatation. Your choice."

She made her decision instantly.

"Let's try your method. I'll trust myself to you. When do we start?"

"Whenever you wish. Today, if you have time."

"I have time. Go on!"

And, decisively, she lay down again, not without being put at her ease by an invitation.

147

Prudently—and he had a discretion for which she was able to be grateful, the doctor proceeded with the initiation of the treatment.

Although he was one of those doctors who was not insensible to the attractiveness of his clients, Hilbour worked on the principle of not alarming them to begin with. He reserved his surprises for subsequent visits, made to the domicile.

Courageously, in spite of the sharp pain, Monique was determined to follow the course of treatment. She would doubtless have continued if, on the third visit, her charm had not operated on the operator. Taking for effrontery what was merely an indifferent simplicity, the doctor had permitted himself a certain gesture that left no doubt as to the consequence of his intentions.

At that abrupt assault, Monique had felt an irresistible disgust rise up within her. Angrily, she had thrown the boor out.

"A fine Monsieur, your Dr. Hilbour," she had simply said a few days afterwards to Mademoiselle Claire. "After all, perhaps he has clients who like that!"

The coarse salacity of the majority of men, incessantly excited, revolted her. At least some animals were only prey to rut periodically. What idea could that maniac have of women, and herself in particular? She was not a bitch in heat! The procedure humiliated her, as the basest of insults.

Thus, to her chagrin in knowing that she was sterile, a new discouragement was added: that in the eyes of that brute, similar in that respect to almost all those who courted her at a greater or lesser distance, she represented flesh for pleasure. What did anyone care about the best of what she thought and felt? What had she to expect, henceforth, for a life in which not disinterested affection awaited her? For want of the ever-present company that a son or daughter would have given her, and the absorbing task of a little soul to mold, to whom or what could she attach herself? What man was worth the trouble? What task could fill in the abyss of her life?

The idea that all physicians did not resemble that one, and that, on the contrary, that exception proved the rule of professional honesty, and also the idea that, with a little endurance to physical pain, she might acquire the aptitude that she was temporarily lacking—reasonings that, at another time, might have been differently determined—she set aside, so strong was the reaction of the period of depression through which she was going. As for the surgical intervention, what reason did she have to attempt it, since no one loved her, and she did not love anyone?

From then on, she found herself without the strength to swim against the current. She realized that every abdication of will multiplied her weakness, but she surrendered, closing her eyes, to the fatality that was drawing her away.

An incident that, on reflection, was not at all astonishing, but whose unexpectedness surprised her, completed the exacerbation of her misanthropy to the point of morbidity.

Plombino, who had not ceased pursuing her since taking his unfruitful step, found himself, as if by chance, seated next to her one day at a dinner party hosted by Madame Bardinot, the pretext for which was the appointment of her husband to the Presidency of the United Petroleum Bank, but the motive for which was to facilitate a conversation on which on which the Baron was counting for a happy solution to his enterprise. His thwarted passion had turned to obsession.

He had the strength to contain himself until the end of the meal, but as they were finishing dessert, he could not hold on any longer, and rubbed Monique's leg with an insistent knee.

She turned a resolute face toward the pachyderm. "Are you ill?"

His eyes staring at the low cut dress from which the roundness of the shoulders, the arms of a living statue, and the velvety back protruded, he sniffed. They got up from the table; she was obliged to accept to place her hand on the crook of the elbow that he offered, awkwardly. Then, in his soft voice, he had blurted out, with sincere emotion:

"Listen to me. I love you. You've refused to furnish my house on the Parc Monceau. Why? I would have paid an honorarium of two hundred thousand francs for that honor, and a million in credit! More, if you had wanted it. I'd give you everything I have—everything—to please you…"

She laughed, insolently. "I was mistaken. You're not ill, you're insane."

They went into the drawing room. She immediately let go of the Baron's arm, but he had grabbed her hand, and, drawing her into a corner of palms, closed by an awning, he said: "I know that money doesn't count for you. You're rich, and in time, you won't know what to do with…"

"You're mistaken. There are poor people in France, and there are millions starving in Russia. First give them what you offered me. We'll see after that if I'll do you the honor of working for you."

The famine on the Volga, piling up the cadavers of children at the gates of cemeteries, and poverty pushing people to the extreme of cannibalism—that vision of the atrocities ravaging a people whose fraternal blood had flowed for two years in the communal butchery made Monique pale. Eyes lowered, she thought of the galas of old, of the Tsar acclaimed by Paris and the Presidents of the Republic fêted in the Imperial Palaces…

The millions extracted by the Plombinos and the Ransoms and the Bardinots, from peasant stockings and bourgeois strongboxes—the millions on which those bandits had grown fat in passing, and the credit of which had sunk into the double abyss of the war and the revolution—were the gangrene that had rotted all solidarity.

Over that overflow of catastrophes, Monique floated in complete confusion. That, humanity and life? Lies and oppression everywhere! And there were still people who dared to speak of principles? To attest to Order, Right and Justice! When they thought of nothing but filling the belly or relieving their genitals!

Plombino suddenly personified that avaricious band. He was the entire race of financiers, gorged on the misery of peoples. At the spectacle of that majestically displayed paunch, she admired the patience required by all the hollow-faced, starving workers in their hovels, that host piled up like livestock in holes infested with lice and tuberculosis...

It was the bankruptcy of the blind and slow democratic process, the dupery of which had been able to permit such things! She almost understood, at that moment, the anarchist's bomb and its explosion of rage...

She reasoned: *The bomb is no less blind than the lightning! Futile noise-harmful, even! Reprisals met with more reprisals. Nothing to hope for, as long as the machine-gunners, as long as the greasy hands, don't change masters...*

More than once already, on coming out of late-night restaurants to which puppets and marionettes, wearing treasures in diamonds and pearls came to squander in an hour what could nourish all the poor folk shivering in the vicinity for a month, the pale specter and the revolutionary vision had appeared to her. They haunted her this evening more insistently. They excited her revolt when, raising her eyelids, she looked around the Bardinot drawing room.

The Minister of Finance delegated by the National Bloc was there, under the colors of the republican label, at the service of the great International Banks. There were businessmen there with the beaks of crows, in black suits, or with the heavy jowls of stuffed and dressed-up hogs. There were politicians sweating I-don't-care-ism, women undressed as if for bed. Finally, in front of her, there was Plombino, whose eyes were shining.

"That's a promise," he croaked. "And since you don't want anything from me, I'll open an account of two million for the interior designer..."

The idea of helping, if only with a few drops of gold, evils so great that they surpassed the imagination, softened her.

"Perhaps," she murmured. "But outside of the money, nothing of the woman!"

He groaned. "Yes, yes…oh, if you wanted…don't worry…just to be a Baronne, to live with me…you could do anything…" He became emphatic. "Anything you might want… I'd never come into your bedroom… Never…!"

She read, in his plea, the full extent of the offer. Lovers? Yes, he would bring them in, if necessary! And he would watch through the keyhole, like Hutier! She was invaded by a nausea. She turned her back on him without any response, with a slight shrug of her shoulders.

He followed her, obstinately.

Then, she hurled at him, imitating his accent: "I will never—you understand, *never*—work for you, if you ever speak to me about this again."

The fat man took on a jaundiced pallor, and repeated: "Just to be closer to you…to be able to breathe your perfume…you'd be free…totally free…"

Then, dully, in a low and precipitate voice, she declared: "You're ignoble! Can't you see, then, the extent to which everything you say, and everything you don't say, degrades you and soils me? No, shut up! What you represent to me, you and your money, is everything vile that there is in the world, all the baseness and ferocity of men. Your desire soils me, your lust horrifies me. You're…" She stopped. "No, it's futile; you wouldn't understand."

He sighed. "How hard you are!"

She looked at him, obese and lamentable.

"Yes, you can't understand. Let's leave it there. I'm in a bad mood this evening. There are days like that. It only takes one drop of mud, the last, for the heart to overflow."

He swallowed the insult, and bowed humbly.

"I beg your pardon. I don't hold it against you. I didn't know. Unhappy, you? How could I suspect it? Don't worry, I'll never speak of it again…of anything. To make you my apologies, simply let me occupy you…when you wish, when you can…in having my house refurnished…by Mademoiselle

Claire, if it upsets you to think about it yourself. Let me at least have something in my house that comes from you...no, no, I'm not saying anything!...I'll send you a check for three hundred thousand francs for your poor people tomorrow. As long as we aren't at odds...that I can see you from time to time... Thank you...thank you..."

She considered him, pitilessly. He was drooling the fear of being rebuked, and beneath his servility was the multimillionaire's hope, sly and persistent, in spite of everything, that in the end, everything could be bought. Madame Bardinot came over, smiling, attentive to her duties as intermediary. Monique took advantage of it to take her leave, abruptly.

"Come on, stay!" cried Ponette. "Marthe Renal is going to sing after the Opéra."

But Monique shook her head grimly. "No, no! I have work to do...for the Baron."

Madame Bardinot's face cleared, delightedly. She sniffed a fat commission, failing to distinguish any sarcasm or irony in the "*Au revoir*" thrown at her.

To work! Monique repeated to herself, as she fled. *To collaborate in the wellbeing and vanity of those boors! Oh, if it weren't serving to bandage other ills, even worse than mine...!*

She judged her own métier no less severely: superfluous work in itself. Idle distraction. To work at that—what a joke!

She went home, crushed by blackness.

153

V

She was no more, thereafter, but a careless instinct.

The hours went by, all equally bleak in their variety. Monique was moving in a kind of mental night. The energy that impelled her to live was not powerful enough to guide her as she drifted. After having succeeded in pulling herself together, there had been a new collapse—and this time, she thought, it was irredeemable. React? With what aim? She no longer believed in anything.

The obscure sentiment of light that is deep down in all beings, and which subsisted in her amid the darkness of the unconscious, sometimes still rose, however, without her being aware of it, above the mud into which, without regret and without remorse, she believed that she had sunk definitively.

In spite of herself, Monique remained one of those natures so fundamentally straight that a thrust of the tiller can bring them upright again, at the very moment that they seem to be capsizing. But that conviction only penetrated the two people who knew her well and had retained, in her, a little of the affection that she had had for Aunt Sylvestre.

Madame Ambrat and Professor Vignabos had been pained to see Monique draw away from them, spacing out the opportunities to meet. But after one final lunch in the Rue de La Boëtie, in which she had, in a sudden surge of expansion, vented her spleen, they had ended up sadly taking their leave.

Since then, she had felt a need herself to avoid their faces, saddened because they were clear-sighted. The judgment of those old friends had no need to be spelled out. She divined the reproach, all the more sensitive in her self-esteem because they reminded her, along with the memory of the dead woman, of the good and the bad days of the past.

She never returned any longer to that cemetery. She lived entirely in the present—a change appreciated elsewhere, for the most part. She had brought herself into unison, falling to the level of their baseness. Drinking, eating, sleeping and, to complete the program of enjoyments, all that men and women have imagined in the possibility of pleasure and vice. "She's becoming a good girl," her old friends said of her.

"You're better than this!" Madame Ambrat had said to her, one day when she had reluctantly decided to go past the sumptuous window displays, now delivered solely to the refined tastes of Mademoiselle Claire. The latter had effectively taken over the artistic side of the operation. Monique involved herself to the extent of supervising the establishment in terms of summary indications of all the major decorations. Monsieur Angibault, the head of the commercial division, dealt with estimates and receipts.

Standing in front of Madame Ambrat in the small reception room, Monique, who had only just gotten up at two o'clock in the afternoon, repeated, with a sigh: "No, I assure you. It's amusing, fundamentally, that existence. I've taken it tragically, and then seriously...I was wrong. It's a farce. By adopting the comical point of view, and especially not exaggerating anything—for nothing is really important—one can adapt to it quite well. It's wisdom. You can do it!"

Madame Ambrat contemplated sadly the leaden complexion and the dangling arms.

"What wisdom!" she murmured

"It's the best."

"And it's a woman who's talking! It's you, Monique."

"Of course. Why shouldn't a woman, who has neither a husband nor a child—who doesn't even have parents, because mine...!—discard the scruples that men don't have? It's necessary to bring yourself to that fact, Madame. Each to her own life! And then death for everyone. And above all, don't pity me because, in the meantime, I'm living the life of a bachelor."

Madame Ambrat sketched a gesture of impotence. There would have been too much to say! She had embraced Monique tenderly, because, in spite of everything, she had faith in her and then had left, still in a hurry. She was one of those thin quadragenarian women, ageless and almost sexless, who, never having been mothers, devoted themselves, with all their unsatisfied feminine impetus, to the substitute of education. The habits of a teacher had given her a slightly stern authority, under which an ardent sensibility brooded.

Yawning, Monique listened to the reports that Mademoiselle Claire gave her. Baron Plombino was delighted with his new smoking room in veined maple and ash velvet. He presented his compliments to "Mademoiselle." The mock-ups of the sets for the new play by Fernand Dussol would be ready that evening. Madame Hutier had already telephoned twice; she would try again later...

"That's fine. Thanks, Claire."

Monique stifled another yawn. Nothing interested her any longer. The day extended monotonously in the gaze of her ennui. As she paused in front of a mirror that reflected a savant landslide of fabrics collapsing and cascading in a violet and gold flute, she darted a discontented glance...

What eyes! Not surprising, after such a night!

She had spent the whole of it smoking, alone with Anika Gobrony. Delightful hours with numbed senses, but which left one with a sensation of emptiness the following day, and a disgust for everything that was not the pacifying forgetfulness of the drug. Hours of nirvana in which both of them, fraternally lying to either side of the tray, evoked interminable stories devoid of any kind of interest. Miserable gossip, reflecting the agony of the circle into which, along with the talent of the great violinist that Anika Gobrony had been, Monique's gifts were slowly sinking.

She shuddered. The imperious appeal of the telephone resounded. She now had a phobia of those brutal sounds, as an importunate intrusion into her stagnation.

Monsieur Angibault showed the square face of a methodical Lorrain. "Madame Hutier."

"I'm coming."

156

Monique sighed. The distractions that Ginette usually proposed to her were rarely diverting. But after all, it might as well be that as anything else.

She had gradually allowed herself to take up the old camaraderies. Hélène Suze and Michelle d'Entraygues had become her intimates again, along with Madame Hutier and Ponette. She even found, in seeing them again on a daily basis, a pleasure that she had not previously known. In the past she had reproved their apathy and corruption of which she herself presently possessed.

A slight melancholy, irrational but gentle, was added to those amities, which adhered to her like sticky mud: an unconscious reminder of the past, the image of the Monique of old, in the days of illusion, when she had been preparing for a beautiful future...

She listened, with the receiver to her ear, and suddenly smiled ambiguously.

"No, impossible this evening. I'm dining with Zabeth, and I'm taking her to Anika's afterwards...

...

"Yes, she's never smoked. It'll amuse her."

...

"Exactly! The lucidity, the mental detachment it provides...it goes very well with Theosophy."

...

"Yes, and with Spiritualism, too. One sees double."

...

"Oh well, darling, since you're so busy, that's all we can do. Come and pick us up after dinner... Where? The Indian restaurant—do you know it? In Montmartre... Yes, that's the one. Afterwards, we'll see. After all, she'll probably be delighted. Education can be completed at any age... That's right!.... *Au revoir*, darling."

She hung up. The spark that the proposition had illuminated in her weary eyes went out. Monique paraded a gloomy gaze around the small reception room, where she had once loved to work between visits. Unfinished designs lay there

157

under the lid of the closed Louis XV desk. The room appeared empty: as empty as the day in prospect; as empty as existence.

Then, yawning more deeply, she rang. Mademoiselle Tcherbalief showed her face, that of a willing slave with eyes of steel.

"I'm going back upstairs, Claire. Don't ask for me. I'll be out until dinner."

"But what about the meeting with Mademoiselle Marnier?"

The amateur dogaress, having traded her Belgian moneybag and her apartment in the Rue de Lisbonne for an American businessman and a house in the Avenue Friedland, was replacing all her furniture.

"You talk to her…whatever you want. I'll approve everything in advance. *Bonsoir*."

She went back at a leaden pace to her entresol, into which, since Peer Rys, the député and the engineer, no man had penetrated. The consultation with Dr. Hilbour had cured her of futile liaisons. Leading, as she had said to Madame Ambrat, the life of a bachelor—bachelor pad included—she bedded down at the hazards of adventure, most frequently in two small rooms that she had fitted out for a dual purpose in Montmartre. On emerging from music halls or late-night restaurants, where she once again appeared assiduously, it was comfortable, that bathroom and drawing room, furnished solely with an immense divan: a trampoline propitious to the evermore frequent dreams of smoking and occasional sexual exercises. Her interminable sessions at Anika's had given her the need, as a true opium addict, for her own installation, and for her improvised frequentations—generally involving three or four people—it was a sufficiently vast field of maneuvers.

She stretched, idly. Then, having closed the shutters to the daylight, she lay down again on her unmade bed. Eyes closed, she sought sleep for a long time. She thought, with a disgust compounded with remorse, about the noisy street, the shops in which Claire and Angibault were working hard, the sun whose splendor was floating over the ant hill of the city in the full activity of labor…and, as if in a coma, she felt herself descending voluptuously into oblivion.

She did not wake up until dusk was falling, with the sentiment of another day wasted. But what did it matter? Nowadays, the day only commenced for her at nightfall… Night, yes: with the aid of the intoxication of stupefaction and the unexpectedness of encounters slightly stirring her eternal *what's the point?* she imagined that she was living intensely.

She used up, with the mechanical rituals of her toilette, interminable instants, lingering over the choice of combinations of garments, whereas she had once dressed so rapidly in anything…futilities that took her until nine o'clock, when she generally dined.

It was eight when, hearing the bell at the entrance door, she suspended the movement of the finger dipped in pink powder with which she was enlivening her cheeks. *Zabeth already! Zut, I'm late!*

"Come in!" she cried, when the chambermaid announced Lady Springfield.

With a fugitive emotion, she saw in her mirror, like the sudden resuscitation of her youth in its depths, the appearance of her great friend of old. Tall and lithe, like a brunette vine, Lady Springfield, in spite of a generously low-cut dress, had changed so little that Monique thought that she was seeing Elisabeth Meere again. The mat face retained the willful expression, also a trifle enigmatic, that had caused Aunt Sylvestre to say: "Elisabeth is a stone slab on top of a secret."

Without turning round, Monique extended her neck. "Kiss me, but don't leave any lipstick."

Zabeth laughed. "Mine's dry, it doesn't stain. Have you no shame? Still in your chemise!"

Monique applied the last touches slowly—a hint of blue at the corners of her eyelids.

"There—I'm ready. I have my stockings."

She stood up, clad only in scanty underwear beneath the kimono. Lady Springfield contemplated her, marveling.

"How beautiful you've become!" Blushing, she added: "You already were..."

Her gaze, posed on Monique's breasts, evoked the troubled evening when, in a stormy atmosphere, breasts bare, they had compared their nascent rotundities to apples and pears. Instinctively, the Englishwoman extended her hand and caressed the beautiful fruits in their baskets of black, and felt them tremble. At the same time, Monique—while the vanished moment was reinstalled in her own memory—saw two points surge forth beneath Zabeth's corsage, stretching the light silk. Then she blushed in her turn, her cheeks turning crimson with the same fire as her friend.

A vague shame troubled her. The sensation had been agreeable, however, and it was in a soft voice that she murmured, instinctively, the same words that she had proffered before, but with a different intonation. "Stop it! What's got into you?"

Zabeth smiled, so clearly that this time, there was no longer anything enigmatic about her willful visage.

Amused, Monique said, in her turn: "Have you no shame?"

Lady Springfield shook her head, deliberately. No, she had no shame. And why should she be ashamed? Her husband was too busy with affairs of State to pay any heed to sentiments. He had given him two children, as if planting two trees. Their education? The nursery would provide that for the moment; then there would be school. As for Spiritualism, not to mention Theosophy, that was doubtless sufficient for the curiosities of the mind. Lady Springfield did not detest the joys that had finished up taking substance. And what body was more pleasing than that of a young woman? Of all of them, Monique's, long desired, occupied the first place in her memory: the place reserved for the most precious.

Cheerfully, the two friends dined alone in the small restaurant indicated to Ginette Hutier. It was only known to a few initiates for its exotic cuisine. Spiced with curry and red peppers, it made them appreciate the impact of dry champagne even more: a whiplash, which accelerated their abandon...

They let themselves dissolve into hectic laughter, which shook them like two naughty girls. Lady Springfield, gripped by her hobby-horse, attempted to convert the rebellious Monique to her supernatural beliefs, but the latter protested, between two mouthfuls: "No, no...and no! You're speaking in vain. We're nothing but an aggregate of cells, matter that has at length produced, after millennia of improvement, a soul, as a flower produces perfume. But the soul and the perfume die entirely when the matter is disaggregated..."

"Oh! That's sacrilege!"

"No, it's rational. I don't believe in the survival of the spirit—except in the forms that the art and science of the living are able to create. Survival is so ephemeral! As for spirits! Oh, no, if there were even a very few of them, they wouldn't expose themselves to coming back to take a turn in this dirty life. They'd stay where they are!"

She pointed to a succulent dish that the waiter—a Sinhalese with a braided chignon—was bringing. "Look! Cabbages. But there are no spirits. There are unknown forces that might perhaps influence our intelligence as they influence our sensibility."

"Yes, supernatural forces!"

"No, natural forces. We don't know them yet. Perhaps they'll be analyzed one day. We're only just beginning to penetrate the mysteries of heat and electricity."

"But what about telepathy? And premonitions? And the prophecy of events impossible to foresee? They're scientifically demonstrated realities. And the photographs of fluidic bodies? How do you explain all that, except by spiritual intervention, simultaneously human and divine?"

Indignantly, Lady Springfield struck the table with her knife, so sharply that the Sinhalese came running.

"Oh—the spirit!" Monique mocked. "The table has spoken."

For the sake of appearances she ordered a second bottle of champagne. "We're drinking heartily, aren't we?"

"Yes," said the spiritualist, smiling. "And that way, afterwards, the table will turn of its own accord. No, I'm not naïve enough to believe just anything—but I truly think that our souls don't die at the same time as our bodies. Their astral essence is scattered in infinity until it's reincarnated in other forms. Thus, there's a rhythm of universal life whose harmony is in conformity with God's justice."

The conviction made her voice tremble, and suddenly returned a slight accent to it.

"God!" exclaimed Monique, who was such a determined materialist that the word amused her. "Which God? The God of armies, perhaps? What skin, then, would he judge soft enough to embrace...a Wilhelm II, for example? You make me laugh, with your immortality and your metempsychosis!"

She became animated in her turn. The vanity of living resonated dully under the veil of words.

"Around and above us, before and after us, there's night and matter! Our momentary sparks thrown into it, before disappearing, their fire-follet flashes. That's all. In the meantime, my nose is getting shiny."

She powdered herself swiftly. But Lady Springfield, weary of philosophizing, had taken an oriental cigarette from a large silver case. The attentive Sinhalese held out the flame of a lighter.

"Thanks..."

She gazed at Monique with tender attention. "You're making me feel bad, darling. Underneath your gaiety, I sense that there's more sadness...yes? I was sure of it. Discouraged...why? That isn't rational."

Monique shrugged her shoulders, holding out her glass.

"Life...! Let's not talk about that...there are people who drown in a spittoon. I prefer champagne." She emptied the glass in a single draught.

Moving her chair forward, Zabeth imprisoned the extended legs between her knees, and said, in a seductive voice:

"Men don't understand anything about the happiness of women. They're only ever interested in their own..."

"That depends," said Monique. "Yesterday, Ginette said the opposite to me, talking about her husband."

The Englishwoman exclaimed, sincerely: "Oh, that one's a pig!"

Monsieur Hutier's reputation—a common theme of jokes in the satirical papers—had surpassed, along with the frontiers of Maxim's and Irène's, those of the Channel. Lord Springfield, deceived by the fox-faced appearance of the Minister, whom he had met at the last international conference of the Allies, could not believe it, but Milady, better documented, had no doubt about it, having been surprised by Monsieur Hutier one day during her own effusions with Ginette. By way of reparation, he had demanded that they continue for his solitary satisfaction.

"You'll see her, anyway," said Monique. "She's coming to look for us...in fact, here she is!"

The bold and cunning face of the Minister's wife appeared in the crack of the door. The two friends waved to her. Imposing in her evening coat, Ginette swept through the restaurant authoritatively. There was no longer anyone there but the anachronistic Sinhalese, apart from the proprietress, playing cards with a friend with a lap dog.

Without the slightest astonishment, the waiter recognized Madame Hutier as the "demoiselle" who, accompanied by another young woman and an elegant gentleman, had once, on a day when he was on leave, picked him up at the Thé Daunou where he was serving. At the same time, the equivocal gaze and mute laughter of the Sinhalese reminded Ginette of the scene that had followed—in Cecil Meere's studio! The tall black fellow had sodomized the latter, while she and Michelle d'Entraygues had served them as witnesses and aides...

Without flinching, she addressed a reproachful wink to the man, and rapidly proposed that they go—the others were waiting in the auto.

"Who?" asked Lady Springfield.

"Max de Laume and Michelle."

"Where are we going?"

Ginette put a finger to her lips. "You'll see!" She had an engaging smile. She evoked, after an hour at the music hall, a new grouping: Zabeth replacing her brother and Max, the Sinhalese. She did not go as far as the distribution of roles, leaving scope for the unexpected that was all the broader because she had resolved—in agreement with her husband, her own liberty being at that price—to inaugurate a new theater of exploits that evening.

The ex-Minister—for since the supper at Anika's, the Pertout cabinet had been toppled—sometimes witnessed those little feasts and sometimes did not, but in the latter case he demanded a faithful report. For lack of visual excitement, a detailed verbal account had become necessary to put him in a state to be fruitfully flagellated thereafter at the worthy Irène's. Monsieur Hutier, a luminary of progressivism, thus merited his reputation as an intellectual...

"In the back," ordered Ginette, shoving Lady Springfield, as Max de Laume got up to greet her. Sit down, Max! Michelle on your knees, and Monique on Zabeth's. Me in the middle...there!"

She gave the address, and, as Lady Springfield observed: "What about Anika? She's expecting us," Michelle declared: "You think so? Anika? For her, nothing counts any longer but the pipe."

"That's a pity," said Max de Laume. "She had talent."

He judged, severely, the lack of constraint with which the great artist had gradually become a human wreck. Pleasure, in his eyes, as a calculator regulating his life methodically, did not exclude will-power. Every hour to its employment. Thus, at thirty, he was president of the Cercle de la Critique Littéraire, and was already designated by the Jacquet salon as the future Benjamin of the Académie.

Monique was not thinking about anything. She was numbed by a sense of wellbeing, compounded on the one hand from the intervention of drunkenness and on the other from the tender embrace of Zabeth, on whose lap she was sitting. There was, in her abandonment, the comfort of a tenderness similar to that of a big sister, mingled with all the memories of adolescence, and also the stew of a new sensation, like a slightly incestuous curiosity...

At the Olympia, where their entrance into a box by the stage caused a sensation, the band quickly wearied of being the focus of the audience's attention. Distracted momentarily by the appearance of a talking seal, and then by a singer imitating Damia,[20] everyone rallied to Ginette's suggestion that they leave.

Lady Springfield was rather surprised at the exit to be shoved into a taxi, the driver of which, after a supplementary payment by Max de Laume, agreed to take all of them. Ginette explained: I've send back my car, saying that Madame d'Entraygues will bring us back. You wouldn't want our drivers to know that we're going to a brothel."

Zabeth repeated, uncomprehendingly: "To a..." But Ginette cut her off with a burst of laughter, redoubling her amazement.

"Yes, to a whorehouse."

"A whorehouse?"

" A bordello, if the terms more familiar."

"Oh!" cried Lady Springfield, in a tone of indignation so sincere that all four of them writhed with laughter.

"Well, what?" riposted Ginette. "It's the last salon in which one can amuse oneself. No need of introduction, nor any messing about. The natural at liberty. And then, at least, one isn't deceived by the merchandise there!"

Zabeth turned to Monique, and said, curtly: "Let's go home."

---

[20] Damia (Marie-Louise Damien, 1889-1978) had her own establishment in Montmartre, Le Concert Damia, in the early 1920s, where she remained the most famous exponent of *chanson réaliste* until the advent of Edith Piaf in the late 1930s.

But the latter murmured, "Stay, silly!"

On observing the extent to which the sense of respectability and the religion of Theosophy were allied in the Englishwoman with her depravity, carefully hidden beneath religious and worldly hypocrisy, Monique smiled, amused. She squeezed her friend's hand.

"Come on! It'll be fun."

Lady Springfield sketched one last defense: "But what if we're recognized?"

"Impossible," Max de Laume cut in, having brought Michelle into the conspiracy that morning. "First of all, no one there can recognize us, because no one knows us. Secondly, no one will see us. And finally"—he made a noble gesture—"there's professional discretion."

Zabeth made her decision. "I hope, at least," she said, menacing Ginette, "that your husband..."

"Don't worry! He won't arrive for another hour. He's due to pick me up when he leaves the banquet of the Association of I-Don't-Know-Who..."

"I'll leave!"

"Bah! He doesn't get in the way. We're here."

The taxi had stopped a few numbers before the red lantern that indicated, with relative discretion, the house of ill repute. Max de Laume rang and negotiated. The housekeeper gave orders. A stampede was heard on the staircase. Doors slammed as they closed. Preceded by the simpering fat woman, the four friends went up, with a slight embarrassment at the idea that the walls might have ears. With a detached attitude, Max formed the rearguard.

They only breathed easily again when they were installed in the Turkish room, for want of the mirrored room, which was occupied. It was a vast room, in the Constantinople/Place Clichy style, whose lamps with colored glass projected a mysterious gleam on the thick curtains. Masses of cushions prolonged the immense divan, so broad that several people could lie there side by side.

Once the inevitable champagne had been ordered, the housekeeper enquired as to the remainder of the requirements: Brunettes? Blondes? She even offered, classically, a Negress. Max recusing himself, Ginette opted, on the advice of the matron, for Irma, a Fleming, and Michele for Carmen—"A genuine Spaniard, from Seville!"

Zabeth and Monique, disinterested in the choice, were already lying down, their hands crossed behind their heads as spectators. Lady Springfield, her elbow buried in the cushions, hoisting her upper body over Monique's shoulder, watched every gesture while pretending otherwise.

The plump beauty of Irma and the nervous elegance of Carmen—who entered bowing, casually clad in peignoirs, which immediately fell away—were immediately sympathetic to her connoisseur's eye. Naked, the whores stripped off all the livery of social conditioning. They reverted to animal simplicity, to primitive unconsciousness.

There was no longer anything in the Turkish room but pale beasts —except for Zabeth and Monique, who were still wearing their dresses. At the same time as Carmen and Irma, Ginette, Michelle and the handsome Max had sent their superfluous garments flying across the room.

During their games, Zabeth caught fire.

Already, under the kisses that the Fleming was lavishing on her body, Ginette, her hands over her eyes, was uttering her habitual cooing, while beside them, Carmen and Michele, tightly coiled in a circle with Max, mouths applied to sex organs, were an undulating garland.

All of Monique's drunkenness had dissipated. Bleakly, she contemplated Zabeth, riveted by the quivering of all that flesh. The excitement of a novice! How many times, in similar places, in hours of the same aberration, had Monique caressed them herself? Michelle, Ginette, another Carmen or another Irma—familiar, almost anonymous forms—in the ever-sickening embrace, never attaining oblivion...

In the stifling heat of the padded room, a vertigo of fatigue, along with an immense sloth, nailed her to the couch in a stupor, although she would have liked to have been able to leap up, to flee...

But a face leaned over her. Resignedly, she saw the irresistible desire shining in Zabeth's eyes. The gluttonous lips took possession of hers. Their breasts touched. A long body under the crumpled fabrics entwined itself around her weary limbs, like a burning vine. She sighed, defeated.

It was a faint in which Monique experienced, along with her pleasure, the degrading, abominable consciousness that the moment was completing. It was the prostitution of her life, all the way to the last image of herself in her memory, which had until then preserved intact: the Monique of Hyères...all the purity, all the so-far-immaculate whiteness of her youth.

VI

A few days later—Zabeth had gone back to London the following day to attend the great ball held at Buckingham Palace to celebrate the engagement of Princess Mary[21]--Monique had an unexpected encounter in the Louvre in the rooms of the Dieulafoy collection. She had gone there in the hope of shaking off her increasing neurasthenia, looking for an ornamental motif for *Sardanapale*, the Babylonian play by Fernand Dussol. The set for the third act, a terrace overlooking the Euphrates, required a backcloth between two columns. The embroideries imagined by Mademoiselle Claire had satisfied the old master, but had not immediately pleased Edgard Lair, who was directing everything...

Monique was thinking, dispiritedly, before the winged bulls and giant friezes, about dead civilizations and the vanity of her work, when a visitor came to stand a few paces in front of her in order to contemplate the detail of the architecture more intently. He turned round. Their eyes met. She recognized, after he had bowed to her, Georges Blanchet. There was no longer any means of avoiding him.

---

[21] Princess Mary, the only daughter of King George V and Queen Mary, married Viscount Lascelles in February 1922. The engagement had been announced on 21 November 1921. This seems blatantly anachronistic, with regard to the chronology of the novel as established by other references in the text, but that chronology is problematic with reference to the timespan of the entire trilogy, so it might be worth noting, for future reference, that chapter one established that Monique was 17 in mid-1917, 19 in 1919 and 20 when the catastrophe happened—which must, therefore, have been 24-25 December 1920. It will shortly be established—and the timescale of narrated events supports the supposition—that it is now 1924

She had seen him a couple of times since the famous encounter at Vignabos' apartment, first in the Rue de Médicis, when, hostile, she had scarcely addressed a word to him, and then at Vaucresson, at Madame Ambrat's, when they had sympathized vaguely. Blanchet, appointed as a professor at the Lycée de Versailles to which he had leapt from Cahors after a remarkable book on pedagogy, had come to the Vert-Logis to seek information for an article on the Oeuvre des Enfants Recueillis. Evidently, he was a good and intelligent man, but she had not pardoned him, for once having being too perspicaciously prophetic.

He still had his discreet courtesy and his smiling face of a bishop. The hairless visage had thickened slightly, but that was all, He enquired politely about her work, and congratulated her on her success. She demurred, with a modesty so unfeigned that he manifested his surprise and, piqued by curiosity, looked at her a little harder. The complexion, once so dazzling, had lost its freshness. Profound rings emphasized the darkness of the disenchanted eyes. A pleat gave the mouth, still ravishing, a harsh expression.

She perceived the observation—and, divining that he was, via Madame Ambrat, up to date with the situation, she was gripped by a fit of bitter frankness.

"You find me changed, eh? Oh, no polite words! You're right. I bear no resemblance to the young woman with whom you once debated *Du Mariage*!"

He perceived, without hint of its depth, a secret wound, and protested, with spontaneous sympathy: "Monique Lerbier is extremely beautiful, and celebrated."

She did not reply, lost in her past.

He added, not without an imperceptible irony: "Haven't you now achieved equality with the most favored of those men whose privileges you thought so unjust?"

She had a desire to cry out: *What does it matter, since I've lost, in exchange, all the joy of living? I'm alone and aimless. Humanity disgusts me to the point that I no longer have any desire or strength to strive for anything whatsoever! But*

*vile as I find it, there's no one who disgusts me as much as I
disgust myself!*

All she said, pointing at the colossal stones, was: "Equality? Yes, in annihilation. It's this that offers you a lesson.
What rubble!"

The scattered blocks reconstituted, in their thoughts,
temples ruined for millennia. Dynasties and peoples agitated
their phantoms in the depths of the immemorial gulf. History
was strung out confusedly through space and time...crowds
had been born, suffered and died...and from that turbulence of
vanished dust, this was what remained: insensible stones, and
a memory as deceptive as forgetfulness.

She shook his hand hastily, and left him where he stood,
pensively. With an intrigued gaze he followed the elegant silhouette as it drew away, straightening up, at a swift pace. A
brazen mask over a dolorous face.

Philosophically, he continued his stroll.

Returned to the Rue de La Boëtie, Monique attempted to
work. The pencils and brushes would not stay between her
fingers.

She came back from her laborious whim further demor-
alized. What could she do? What would absorb her? Courageous, yes, she could have devoted herself body and soul to
any task. There was no lack of interesting ones, even impas-
sioning ones, including that of taking up that of Madame
Ambrat on her own account, and amplifying it...

So much misery to soothe, everywhere! So much to do!
she said to herself. *But one can only be altruistic on condition
of no longer thinking about oneself. Easy at forty, for Madame
Ambrat...*

Monique, being young, thought of nothing but herself.
The bad habits she had acquired, including the success in her
métier of luxury, wound around her like a thousand soft but
tenacious bonds...

She sent for the design of the incriminated backcloth,
and judged the brick shade, with its embroideries of fake en-
crusted gems, to be charming.

"What an idiot that Lair is!" she said to Claire. "I need to call in at the Vaudeville to see the set in place. What if I were to go now?"

"They're not rehearsing, Mademoiselle. It's Thursday, in the morning..."

"*Zut!* Show me the cerise velvet, then, for Monsieur Plombino's study."

"We don't have it yet."

Monique left it there. Sufficient effort for one day... At the same time, the end of the afternoon extended its familiar desert before her. How could she pass the time until the evening, when she could go to smoke the interminable hours away at Anika's? There was a rendezvous with Hélène Suze at the Ritz, who was piloting a young Swedish couple susceptible to making purchases...but the idea of interested politeness...! And the vision of the tea room, with its little tables covered with interminable cakes, and the tiresome repetition of jazz bands, the stupidity of small talk!

An increasingly frequent savagery succeeded her promiscuities with the society in which she, along with the Hélènes, Ginettes and Michelles, whether minister's wives or Marquises, were worth little more, if not even less, than a Carmen or an Irma.

She put on her hat and tailored jacket. She had adopted that uniform several days before, even in the evenings, having renounced the coquetry of her dresses since the last expedition. She thus had only one clasp to undo, and her skirt came off. And with Anika helping her to undo her bodice, she was immediately ready, at ease in the drapery of a kimono, for the quotidian ceremony.

I'll certainly find her in the process of smoking, she thought. *She must have received her drug. A good pipe! There's nothing like it!*

Suddenly decided, Monique calmed down. She was in one of those periods of intoxication in which opium was as necessary to her as air. She could no longer kick the habit. It

172

was necessary for her to inhale the pacifying smoke, or she would choke. A cold sweat of anguish chilled her flesh.

Often, ceasing after weeks of being absorbed in that slight intoxication, she had had those dolorous symptoms. She had then succeeded, with a renewed effort of will, in spacing out the sessions. She sensed that by a prolonged abstinence, she would recover for action a lucidity that was in the process of applying itself entirely, in a sterile fashion, to dreams. But this time, having taken the poison in massive doses, she experienced only one desire: to take more.

Brutalization? No, annihilation: the marvelous scorn for everything that was not the bliss of which, from the first pipe, she felt the benefit, and through which, by the twentieth, she was penetrated—she was penetrated to the extent of the supreme joy: dissolution; evaporation!

As expected she found Anika prostrate on her cushions in the dark. The minuscule lamp, half-dimmed by a silver butterfly valve, was gleaming faintly on the tray of utensils. One might have thought it a funerary nightlight.

"It's me," said Monique. "Don't move."

On emerging from the bright summer twilight, the studio with the hermetically sealed curtains, completely impregnated with the heavy odor, seemed as quiet as a great tomb. Already, however, Anika had turned the commutator. The lamp illuminated, with a ruddy glow, the recumbent smoker and the ritual apparatus. The violinist's face seemed corpse-like, the flesh plastered on the brown bone structure.

In a hoarse voice, she declared: "You've come at a bad time. No jam."

"I thought…"

"No. The fellow who was to bring it to me—good stuff, direct from London!—got himself pinched yesterday at the Saphir. Can you imagine? Not because of the opium—they didn't know he had it—but because of the coke! They confiscated the lot."

She sniggered. Loquaciously, with the mechanical volubility that the white powder produces, she uttered, in a single breath:

"They're annoying, all those morons in Parliament, with their laws! They make me laugh! Narcotics! They've got them. Père Hutier, merchant of virtue! You see that? So what if I want to intoxicate myself? To begin with, if they want to talk about poison, let them start with alcohol! But that, they don't dare. It's the bistro that nominates them..."

She lowered her voice, and continued, confidentially: "I've still got some snow, fortunately. Souillarde, who looks after the toilets at the Pelican, sold it to me. Look, that boxful! You see?"

Laughing, she pointed at a little enamel candy box.

"And then, I know where to find some. There's a pharmacist at Javel! You see? But for jam, nothing doing. Do you have any left?"

"Yes, the dregs of a pot..."

"Fish it out. You have a light? It makes no difference, go, stay. We'll smoke the drops. I've scraped out all the old pipes. Hold on, there's still the bowl of the big one—the ivory one...it's full of it. The drops are good, too. I don't know if I like them as much..."

She coughed, in spite of her armored throat, and repeated, hoarsely: "The drops are stronger. They intoxicate better..."

Like a drunkard, she needed stiffening.

She sighed: "All the same, if one didn't have that, in life...come on! Lie down...

"Wait until I put my robe on."

Monique, accustomed to it, got undressed in the gloom. Draped in a Chinese mantle, she took her place alongside the tray. As she rotated the butterfly valve of the lamp mechanically, the flame of which was inconveniencing her, Anika, who had taken advantage of the interval to stuff her nose, complained with an angry vivacity: "When you've quite finished shining the light in my eye!"

What has she taken? Monique thought. To the loquacious overexcitement of the cocaine, to which the violinist had been trying to convert her for several days, she preferred the silent vertigo of the opium.

Refusing the pinch that Anika, having calmed down, was holding out to her, she agglomerated into a ball a little of the black residue that would constitute her entire feast that evening. Once more, she would be dining by heart! But the drops, being too hard, did not roll up well, melting at the tip of the needle. That one fell back, sizzling, into the flame. She succeeded, however, in rounding out the heavy drop sufficiently, and, seizing her pipe, almost garnishing the bowl.

Then, putting the bamboo to her lips, she inhaled avidly, with a long aspiration. The smoke was so bitter that she spat it out, the ball consumed. Usually, when the opium was fresh, she swallowed the heady poison, savoring the delight of feeling it enter into her, liquefying her entire being almost instantaneously.

She set down the pipe and let herself relax on the cushions, dazed. The reek with which the studio was saturated, the insipid and powerful perfume of the black balm, had gripped her, and was carrying her away, under the violent breath of the first effluvium.

With a satisfied snigger, Anika exclaimed: "Well, my old lady!"

"Don't shout," Monika pleaded. "One would think it were a train going by!"

The noise reverberated within her, multiplied. But the sonorous wave soon faded away. The walls recoiled. Everything became distant—very distant—and simultaneously muffled, to the point that Anika's staccato verbosity was no longer anything but a whispered confidence. Time ceased to exist. Space was filled with a fluid softness. Ecstatic, Monique experienced a double impression of emptiness and plenitude.

"Say, then," jeered the voice, transposed as if it were coming from another world, "that it's having its effect! And if you'd taken a little coke...! Me, it's my third gram since yesterday. You see... There's nothing to say…they invented these drugs, you know, to cure you of seasickness. Existence, that makes me vomit! A good pipe, a good pinch! That puts the guts back in place. Suppress opium and coke, can you see that? They must be stupid! It's like a doctor who refuses you morphine when you're in pain! There are some who do that, on the pretext that people get a taste for it! One can't even kick the bucket in peace, then? What right do the filthy swine have to condemn me to life? It's my wreck, not theirs. In order that they can put on airs, in their boutique! You see that? Oh la la! Love, for a start, doesn't exist. It's just rumors that are put around. There are idiots who tear themselves apart when they don't get kissed. Pleasure? Yes, the ass! A cul-de-sac that you soon get to the bottom of. Art? Oh, my dear, where's my violin? Talent, yes, I had it, perhaps. Yes, yet, a great artist, that's understood. A long time ago. And afterwards? Chopin had talent, too. Only he was at least able to chew his notes…that sticks. Me, necessary to stuff myself…you see that? I played the music of others. Spoiled, see! Not even children. A good-for-nothing!"

Nervously, she opened her candy box and took out a copious pinch. An in an authoritarian tone, she said: "Take it, I tell you. It's the true remedy. With that, one can do without the rest!"

"No," said Monique. "I prefer your dirty drops."

The violence of the initial sensation had dissipated. Patiently, she set about fashioning her balls, and then cooking them, but she no longer succeeded in smoking them at a single draught. Then, nervous in her turn, and not finding the calm she was pursuing, she followed Anika's advice and took one pinch after another.

Far from relaxing her, though, the dangerous powder, ineptly dosed, exasperated her agitation. She suddenly thought that she had a wooden face, the nose, the forehead and the temples hardening, in an anesthesia so brutal that she felt that she was becoming a machine. In her turn, untiringly, she began to grind out words into the void. A complete insensibility stiffened her. With jerky gestures, she continued to perorate, incessantly.

All night long, separated by the tray on which the lamp went out at dawn, they conversed in that fashion, like deaf people.

When Monique woke up, chilled, it was after midday. The studio remained mysterious in its gloom. Anika was still asleep, so pale that she contemplated her anxiously. One might have thought that she was dead. She touched her hand, which was cold—but a faint breath was making the flat chest rise and fall, regularly.

Monique left without disturbing her.

That afternoon, although she felt ill, she called in at the Vaudeville. They were rehearsing with the sets for the second time, and the management had phoned that morning to say that Monsieur Lair wanted to see Mademoiselle Lerbier in person. When she went backstage, she stopped, bewildered, on hearing loud voices. It was Lair howling: "The Académie? I don't care! Your play isn't any better for that! It's shit, I tell you. There's only one thing here that matters—the stage set."

"But after all, Monsieur...!"

She recognized the irritated tone of Dussol's voice, immediately drowned out by the actor's roar: "Aah!"

Everything fell silent when she appeared.

Stupefied, Fernand Dussol contemplated his interpreter, who, seizing his hat, stuffed it on his head with a cold fury and went to the door, brandishing his cane. In distress, the stage manager and the director, Bartal, ran after him and pulled him back by his coat tails. All three of them were engulfed in a gap in the scenery.

Fernand Dussol looked at Monique and, his face red beneath his gray hair, told her what had happened. Banned until then from rehearsals by the autocracy of Lair, who would not tolerate, in his creation, any kind of interference, especially from the author, he had been obliged, wanting to avoid a scandal, to postpone his observations to the moment when the play, being ready, would be presented to him complete..."

"But why, Master, celebrated as you are, did you accept that?"

"It was either that or withdraw *Sardanapale*—and Bartal begged me not to do that. Thirty thousand francs of compensation to that animal, engaged especially!—or come to blows! And truly..."

"No," said Monique, smiling. "I can't see you..."

At that moment, dragged by Bartal, Edgard Lair reappeared, half by choice and half-forced.

She contemplated the famous poet, puny in spite of his large head, and the Herculean actor. He was Sardanapale himself, reentering his Estates as a king. The brick backcloth, fortunately, served as a diversion. He explained that, being dressed in a white robe, he wanted a black background.

"Wouldn't that be a trifle stark?" Monique objected.

Fernand Bussol having had the misfortune to be of the same opinion, the monarch looked him up and down.

"You're dribbling, Monsieur. Personally, I only drool when I want to." And, turning to Monique, he concluded, in a tone that brooked no reply: "I have spoken: black!"

She bowed, shook Fernand Dussol's hand—tremulous with disdainful rage—with respectful compassion, and left. Unhealthy, lunatics at liberty! She regretted having gone into that menagerie. Then, a fit of shrill petulance that she had just witnessed added sadness to her derision for the tragic farce in which she became wearier by the day of participating.

What had, for a moment, seemed comical had, in the frightful identity of its unexpectedness, became what, in reality, it had never ceased to be: black, as the other said!

The days that she passed, until the first night, were the most sinister she had yet known. They were nothing but a heavy sleep or an interminable yawn, between the morbid pause of the nights and the double asphyxia of opium and cocaine. She no longer ate, sated at the first mouthful. A taste of ashes rose to her lips.

She found herself once again definitively bruised by the tumble that had been her apparent ascension, and at the same

178

point of collapse as on the day when, in the vestibule of the house in the Avenue Henri-Martin, she had found Aunt Sylvestre crushed on the stretcher. She was lying at the foot of the big rock, on the reefs. The icy water was furiously turbulent, beneath an ink-black sky.

If Mademoiselle Tcherbalief had not constrained her, she would have left Lair Sardanapale to exhibit himself on the Assyrian terrace that evening without mingling her mechanical applause with the enthusiastic bravos of the audience. She held the cowardice of her action against herself, as one abdication more. But so what? She was only one step from inertia.

She was in the process of having an ice cream at the Napolitain with Baron Plombino, Ransom and Madame Bardinot, having encountered them at the exit, when a man on the opposite banquette, whose gaze had just attracted hers, nodded his head after a brief hesitation. Who was it?

That expression of a bilious carnivore, those cat-like-eyes and that russet beard? She could not remember. Conscientiously, the unknown man had resumed smoking his short-stemmed pipe, meditatively. But Fernand Dussol and his wife, who had just come in quietly, sat down next to him. She understood immediately that they were talking about her. Dussol waved to her in an amicable fashion. An instinct—curiosity regarding the one, sympathy for the other—drove her to get up in order to compliment the aged poet and his wife.

As soon as she spoke, Dussol introduced them: "Régis Boisselot...Monique Lerbier."

"I know Monsieur," she said, cordially shaking the large gnarled hand that he advanced toward hers, awkwardly.

"Everyone has read *Les Coeurs sincères*," observed Madame Dussol.

"Fifth edition," Boisselot grunted. "It's a small world, as is evident, Madame."

179

"But no," Monique joked, "Since it's four years since I last had the pleasure of meeting you."[22] For the benefit of the Dussols, she explained: "At the home of Professor Vignabos…a long time ago."

She glimpsed the astonishment of the novelist in the timid gaze that, not daring to look directly at her, peered at her covertly. Was she so ugly? She thought about Blanchet's expression from the other week. Boisselot couldn't get over it either.

"Yes…a long time," he murmured.

"To the extent that you almost failed to recognize me?"

He protested; "It's your short hair…besides, I recognized you first."

"With difficulty…"

He fell silent. It was true; she no longer had anything in common with the dazzling girl, the memory of whom had remained with him. A woman had been born, who must have been unfortunate, and driven back, bruised, into the depths of her own being. The butterfly had become a chrysalis again. How many tears there had been in suspense in those eyes that he remembered as blue, and now saw gray…a rainy sky…

He had finished his pipe. They chatted. The Dussols left; the conversation continued. They even—a sensation that astonished her—understood one another better. She rediscovered with pleasure the rudeness of intelligence and the brutal frankness that had once struck her without shocking her.

"You," said Boisselot, looking straight at her, "are in the process of doing something stupid. You're smoking?"

"So are you."

"Not the same tobacco! Mine stimulates; yours brutalizes…"

"And that's visible?" she said, turning to look at the mirror, which reflected her face, emaciated beneath the make-up."

---

[22] i.e., it must now be the end of 1924 or early 1925 in the story's internal chronology.

"A little," he growled. "You know that you have the face of a dog. The hollow cheeks...and the eyes! Opium and cocaine! I saw it right away. It doesn't help."

Gravely, she declared: "Yes, it helps."

"What?"

"The hours go by."

He became indignant. "You have need of that! And you think yourself intelligent? There are, however, things to do in life! Instead of contemplating your navel and weeping over your petty misfortunes! Do you know what misfortune is? I'll tell you. This morning, when I went into my kitchen to give my housekeeper an instruction, I found her with the bread porter: a tall old lady with a harsh expression. A minute later, Julia brought me my breakfast and said to me: 'Did Monsieur see the lady who brings the bread?' 'Yes, she has an ugly face.' 'Oh, Monsieur, the poor woman, she has a grief-stricken face! She looks sixty, but she's only forty-five.' 'What's the matter with her?' She's a refugee from the Nord. They are a calamitous people, you know! Listen to what the war has done to them. She lived in a village near Lille. By means of hard work, she and her husband were able to buy a little house. They had a shop that was doing well. It provided a living for them, with their two sons and their daughter. The war arrives. He husband and the two sons leave, One day, here come the Germans. She runs away with her daughter. A month afterwards, the little one, who was ill, learned of the death of one of her brothers. It turns her blood. A week later, they buried her. A beautiful young girl, Monsieur, who was their joy. Afterwards, they learned that their house, which was still standing, had been destroyed by an English shell—flattened. Then the second son is wounded, grievously. When the armistice comes, they're all three in Paris and starving, waiting for the indemnity, of which they haven't seen a sou yet. The father and the son are working in a factory. You think they're tranquil? The son can't go on; he's worn out, vomiting blood. And last year, it was the husband's turn. He's caught in a machine. A hand cut off and his skull caved in. Has to be trepanned. He

181

can't do any more. His eyes are feverish and fixed, to make you think he's going mad. Last night, he said to the poor woman: *At least I'm not doing you any harm when I'm suffering? What a shame it would be if I were doing you harm, you who've already endured so much!* That's what she told me, Monsieur. Today, she's the only one who can work..."

"That's frightful!" said Monique, upset.

"Do you think, after that, that one can feel sorry for your fate? You're at a loose end? Well, there are pains to soothe. Do you want the address? Yes, I can give it to you. When Julia had finished, I wanted it myself. How had I not sensed immediately how much that wreck contained of horror, resignation and sacrifice? I regretted not being able to shake her hand, to beg her pardon for all the harm that human stupidity and malevolence had done to her!"

They fell silent. The crushing burden of destiny weighed upon them.

"You're right," she murmured, with a confusion of pity and shame. "One only thinks of oneself! I won't forget your lesson." She looked at him with amity.

After a momentary pause, he went on: "If you're not capable of being a sister of charity, at least work, scratch! Look, me, my paper—it's not rich ground! It makes no money...but I'm not discouraged. I keep going..."

"All right!" she said. "Give me your pen, and I'll hand my brushes to you."

"No—no flattery! Perhaps I have no more talent than you, but I believe in the utility of effort for effort's sake. Everyone can't be Hugo or Delacroix, but it's already worthwhile to be..."

"Who?"

"Who? I don't know myself..." He searched, threw out a few names. He judged them, briefly and penetratingly. They discussed their preferences, often common. Monique, while yielding to the diversion of discussing arts and letters with the novelist, wondered why the sympathy between them had taken a turn in that fashion. He was ugly, and, even more than at

182

their first meeting at Vignabos', was exhibiting a ferocious spirit...

This time, however, Boisselot's surly abruptness did not displease her. Why? An obscure attraction toward someone encountered during a moment engraved in her memory? An invisible link to a past that had been sweet? But in that case, she would have prolonged the conversation with Blanchet in the same way, when they had met in the Louvre...

No, she thought, as she listened to the trenchant voice, *what interests me is the bluntness of his character. He's someone honest...*

The personality that Boisselot's speech revealed, and also the naivety that he must be hiding under this wild manner, seemed to her to be something so rare and so new that she suddenly appreciated the revelation.

Several times, perceiving the reproachful signals addressed to her by Madame Bardinot, she had dismissed them with a gesture: *I'm coming!* But the minutes went by, and she was still chatting.

"*Adieu*, deserter!" Ponette threw at her as she left, without stopping. She was thoroughly bored by the somnolent Ransom and the furious Plombino, who, when Monique had left them, had resumed talking about their interminable business affairs. She thought that young Lerbier was decidedly inane. Nothing to be done with such an idiot! To say no to millions when they were there for the taking, and nothing to give in exchange! To prefer that species of surly redhead to the Baron!

All three, reproving in a dignified fashion, went past the table where Boisselot, in order to watch them file past, stopped short. When Plombino, the last one to pass through the rotating door, his back bent beneath the sack that he always seemed to be carrying, had disappeared, Monique called gaily: "*Bon voyage!*"

"The fat one, though...the hippopotamus, as you call him...seemed sorely pinched."

"Poor man!"

Briefly, she told him about Plombino's unfortunate passion, and how, as the price of her clientele, she had made him one of the most important benefactors of the Nansen committee.[23]

"There's no philanthropist like the Baron," she concluded, ironically. "Don't mock him!"

"Baron?" exclaimed Boisselot, with feigned astonishment. "What's a Baron?" All that he knew about Barons was from having eaten, one day, a baron of lamb. A baron of Plombino seemed to him to be less edible...

She laughed. Like him, she found those titles of pseudo-nobility, which no longer corresponded to anything but the most stupid vanity, absurd: idiot traps with which the malign, speculating on endemic stupidity, had made into entitlements to income...

"And to think," Boisselot joked, "that there was the night of the fourth of August![24] Revolution, where are you?"

They suddenly perceived that the café was empty. The waiters were beginning to pile the chairs on the tables.

"One o'clock already!" said Monique, looking at the wall clock.

"That's true," said Boisselot. "How time flies!"

On the sidewalk, at the corner of the Opéra, they prepared to take their leave of one another, awkwardly. She was about to hail a cab when he asked her: "Where do you live? It's important, because of the quarter..."

"The Rue de La Boëtie, of course!"

He muttered: "You might not have had your apartment in the same place as your shop!"

---

[23] An organization for the relief of refugees founded by the explorer Fritjof Nansen in 1921; after his death in 1930 its mission was taken over by the League of Nations, but foundered in 1938.

[24] The occasion in 1789 on which the Constituent Assembly officially put an end to the Feudal system, abolishing all feudal rights and all class privileges.

She smiled, thinking—why?—about the bachelor pad in Montmartre, and replied: "Yes, I live in the entresol above it. And I hope that you'll do me the pleasure of coming to lunch there one day with our friend Vignabos."

He remained silent, flattered. Not banal, and simple, in spite of her renown! In sum, yes, he would willingly see her again. He shook the hand that she held out to him, amicably.

As she closed the door of the cab she said: "Agreed, isn't it? Oh—what's your address?"

"Twenty-seven Rue de Vaugirard."

"Au revoir. I'll send you a note..."

As the taxi drew away, she leaned out and watched the thickset silhouette drawing away at a slow pace.

Pleasant, that Boisselot...

PART THREE

I

They had only needed to see one another three or four times after their evening at the Napolitain. The troubled first light of desire rose between them, quickly blazing into an abrupt dawn.

First of all there was the lunch with Monsieur Vignabos in the delightful entresol in the Rue de La Boëtie. In Boisselot's eyes, Monique, through the sober elegance of the décor, in which all the trivia of her personal taste were displayed, had appeared anew: a kind of modern enchantress, in the palace of her fantasy!

It was not only there that she exercised the empire of elegance and carnal attraction, to which the surly writer remained sensible, all the more so as he did not want to let it show. Of humble origins, and retaining, from his difficult early days, dragged out for a long time in the Bohemia of Montmartre and the studios of Montparnasse, a reserve of appetites behind his disdainful pout, Monique had impressed him in everything that her luxury involved of novelty and appreciable pleasures. But she had, at the same time, completed his seduction by the finesse of her intelligence and the extent of the culture that she had revealed at the junctures of the conversation.

Although Régis Boisselot judged the intelligence of a woman sufficient if, being beautiful, she was capable of sensuality, and even had a secret prejudice against those who prided themselves on other concerns, he had found Monique's individuality to be one charm more. The fact that she practiced a métier different from his own and had succeeded in it had even given their camaraderie, to begin with, an equal footing

187

propitious to understanding. As an interior designer, she amused him, as much as she would undoubtedly have irritated him as a novelist...

Thus, respecting in her an equivalence on a plane in which their reciprocal development could not come into conflict, Boisselot, immediately accepted, had soon become Régis' quotidian friend. She had opened her heart to him and emptied it. Soon, he knew everything about her, and tenderness was born in him of pity.

They had only been going out together for a week when, one evening, after having dined in the Avenue Frockhet at the home of the painter Rignac, he was escorting her home on foot, as usual, and the inevitable came to pass.

He had not had any need to tell her that she pleased him—and how! His silence and his blushing spoke so clearly that Monique—touched herself by that unexpected sympathy, so rapidly developed—had been attracted toward what she increasingly divined beneath the rude envelope: a new soul and a tender heart. She called him, amiably, *My bear!* She told herself: *He's a child!* And she smiled in thinking, without displeasure, about his robust musculature...

That evening, as they went along the Rue Pigalle, past the shuttered windows of her bachelor pad, Monique instinctively slowed down. He knew that she possessed a small personal dwelling in that neighborhood, reserved for her vices: a smoking room. In Boisselot's eyes, that was the sole flaw in Monique, the one that degraded her because it brutalized her. The rest—the liberty of her morals—did not bother him; that was her business. In fact, beginning to count on some benefit for himself, he rather approved of it...

He had immediately guessed, having noticed the glance that she had darted at the ground floor, and sniggered. "Aha! This is it?"

The desire to stop had gripped him, and also that to flee. The opium, and everything that ensued—her artificial excitement, her cold debauchery—was repugnant to him, as something poor, a diversion of impotence, in confrontation with her beauty, of the health of lust. At the same time, the image of Monique, undressed and abandoned, surged forth. He had hesitated, immobile; his shoes turned to lead.

They did not exchange a word. They looked at one another, complicit. And abruptly, he followed her, like a lapdog. On going into the large room where the veiled chandelier produced a cellar-like light, and respiring the acrid reek of the drug, Boisselot had sensed, disagreeably, obscure grievances getting the upper hand over his desire.

"One might think it were a catafalque," he muttered, indicating the black curtains interlaced with gold, and the divan similar to an immense mortuary bed, with its tray of votive accessories.

She had wanted to demonstrate the virtue of the imaginary philter to him: "One little pipe! Only one..." But he refused the kimono that she invited him to put on, while she put herself at ease behind the tall lacquer screen. He did, however, sniff the light garment that lay like a shed skin on the back of the low armchair. How many partners, male or female, had already used it? He did not know whether the idea sickened him or excited him; eventually, he decided on disgust, and went angrily to lie down, waiting for Monique.

She came, draped in a plum-colored robe in which white ibises were pecking roses, but he only saw the supple play of her body beneath the soft fabric. Silently, he followed her methodical gestures, accomplished with a gravity that irritated him. He detested Monique, her absent manner, the distant impassivity that had overtaken her face, like that of an idol, as she took a long breath from the first pipe.

She had immediately fallen back with such a strange expression of ecstasy that he thought she was passing through her metallic eyes the lubricious cortege of all those past enjoyments. A dull hatred had then risen up, which burst forth when, obligingly, she wanted to cook a second ball in order for him to try it.

He had grabbed the needle brutally from her hand and thrown it onto the tray, which he shoved away with an angry fist, sending it flying into the middle of the room. The pipes rolled on the floor; the lamp went out.

She only had time to murmur "What are you doing?"

He was over her, insulting her with curt phrases: "Silly fool! Have you no shame? Do you take me for one of the dogs that lick your c…?"

Insensible to the outrage, however, and almost glad of the excess, in which she read more jealousy and lust than indignation, she had limited herself to placing a hand over his mouth.

Surprised, he had fallen silent, and kissed the odorous fingers mechanically. He felt her draw him toward her with the other hand, and saw the white breasts swelling under the parted robe…

Then, like a wild beast, he had collapsed.

There were seconds of vertigo, in which, lips joined, they were no longer anything but a single being, borne away by the same frenzy, uncoupling and coupling instinctively.

The shock and the voluptuous revelation, for one as for the other, had been too powerful. Passion was unleashed, unexpectedly, in both of them, and proportionately unreasoned, especially in Monique.

She had no need for Régis to speak to her again the next day about anything whatsoever to make her resolve to sweep all the bad memories away, resolutely…

"What if we were to rent Rignac's house at Rozeuil on the Oise? We could spend a fortnight there. Claire has no need of me to run things, and you'll have the tranquility to correct the proofs of your impending book?"

"All right!"

As soon as it was said it was done. Monique had taken away "her bear" after giving lengthy instructions in secret to Mademoiselle Tcherbalief. Above all, she had specified: "Don't let anyone suspect anything!"

Her bear! Since the day before, she had given that appellation a multiple meaning, both possessive and grateful. She felt that she was almost a new person. The suddenness of the attack had delivered such a blow to the old Monique, dispersed and bleak, that this one, vanquished, had come down to earth.

The indifferent was in love. She loved someone healthy, worthy and proud. She loved mentally as well as physically. She had suddenly recovered her footing on firm ground. Love: the sole fecund field of existence!

The fortnight they had spent at Rozeuil had been nothing but delight. The little house buried in the meadow under the tall poplars...the rustic garden hidden behind its thick hedges...the riverbank propitious to amorous afternoon siestas...the herbaceous Oise bordering the boat terrace...the excursions by dinghy to the little islets, their enlacements in the green freshness of the morning and the lukewarm blue of the night...the night, when, even more than by day, they savored the delight of their solitude...and over that divine sojourn, outside the world, like a magical envelopment from dusk to dawn, the friendly light of the moon...an enormous, gilded moon...a honeymoon.

The bear, by dint of being licked, bathed and caressed, had become a sheep. Monique, a shepherdess, recovered the soul of her childhood, an innocent ecstasy, in contact with the countryside, the crucible of nature. The lunches at the inn and the little dinners "at home"...the miraculous fishing in which the only catch he had hooked was an old shoe and she an aquatic root...the games left by Rignac, of croquet and badminton...all of it was marvelous to them, as so many discoveries. Every hour unveiled them to one another a little more.

Finally, when they returned, she was amused in childlike fashion by the great surprise prepared with Claire's aid, and by the ill humor of Régis, poisoned by the return to Paris and the forced separation. He lived in a small apartment with his mother. Where would they see one another in future?

The banality of hotel rooms was repugnant to him, and the ground-floor opium den even more so, witness to a past as it was that—infatuated to a far greater extent than he admitted—he could not think about without a hateful rancor. The bachelor-pad-catafalque—no thank you!

As for the entresol in the Rue de La Boëtie, where she boldly proposed that he should live henceforth with her, the publicity had seemed embarrassing to him. Poor, he had no intention of living with his mistress.

So it had not been without grumbling that she had succeeded, on the very evening of their return, in persuading him to come, once again, to the Rue Pigalle. Afterwards, they would search, they would see... He allowed himself to be convinced, cowardly before his pleasure, which had become a need. Monique enjoyed in advance the effect of her surprise.

When they had passed through the little vestibule, entirely transformed, into the large room, in which no trace remained of the former décor of nocturnal China, he had been unable to retain an exclamation.

"Why, it's splendid! You've found something else to rent? There's a second ground-floor apartment in the house, then?"

"No, it's the same one. Except that Claire, in accordance with my instructions, has modified everything. Do you like it?"

Flattered, he had contemplated that transformation, which the wave of a magic wand had accomplished, for him. A table shorn of ancient suggestions. Silence imposed on the evil hours in which, in spite of himself, his retrospective investigation was overly inclined to pay attention. He saw, in Monique's delicate gesture, a preventive submission, a determination of erasure, spontaneous and complete. She had exorcised the specter.

"Let there be no more question of it," the walls seemed to say, repapered in ocher, the color of marine sails, on which Rignacs and Marquets were hung, their Mediterranean skies trenchant against the orange-tinted background. "Here one can love, and forget," added the narrow double divan and the profound chairs upholstered in blue velvet, the low tables laden with favorite books and the florid shelves. Maryland tobacco in a Delft jar awaited the master's fingers, and a collection of short pipes was heaped in an onyx cup, ready for selection...

Bear as he was, and fundamentally remained, he had been touched to the bottom of his heart. After all, what right did he have to interfere, by manifesting reproach for actions that were no one's concern but hers? He had no right to judge Monique's past. To be able to enjoy the present: that was what intelligence commanded as the limit of his action...

He had drawn her to him, and had kissed her eyelids, bulging like petals over her closed eyes, for a long time. The entire visage smiled, joyously, in that offering of abandoned flesh. He had gazed at her, triumphantly. The rose petals re-opened, the pupils launched their glint of appeal toward the lover...a plea, a hope! An ardent plea, an infinite hope. With her entire being, Monique lifted herself up toward renewal...

The definitive gift of herself, she believed, at that moment, in which everything symbolized a resuscitated existence, singing the hymn of the metamorphosis: a gift solemnized by everything that each of them felt and did not say in their increasing fever, the irresistible magnetism that drove them and pressed them together, body to body.

Undressed in the same movement, they had taken hold of one another again, and fallen, enlaced, onto the nuptial divan.

Boisselot, leaning over Monique, gazed at her sleeping after the exhausting night. In that flesh, which he knew to be his even in the isolating reprise of sleep, he had wanted to be able to read, to pierce the enigma, of the mysterious depths of her being.

Her arms folded behind her neck, she was breathing evenly, pink in the coppery fleece of her hair. She woke up slowly under the fluid that enveloped her, perceived the meditative visage above her, and smiled.

They had lain down side by side, naked beneath the sheet that the morning had pulled up with a chilly gesture. Daylight filtered through the closed curtains, shading the dark blue of the velvet curtains with a softer hue. A ray of sunlight stitched its golden embroidery there.

"It's a beautiful day!" she murmured, putting her cool arms around the thickset neck, and drawing the cherished lips toward her mouth.

Then, gently pushing him away, she murmured: "You were spying on me, wretch."

"I was admiring you."

He had a spontaneity so sincere, such a tone of fervor, that she felt the words running over her skin like a caress. Then, with a seductive gesture, she hugged him, pressing her curly head against his breast.

Silently, they savored the sweet moment, she without thinking about anything except the restful abandonment, and the nenuphar lilies whose leaves their ears had still been brushing, the day before, on the Oise...

Monique allowed herself to be cradled, like them, but the sunlit current...

He respired the dark gold tresses, intoxicatingly. She raised her eyes, in quest of the response to her mute question: "Do you love me?"

But he limited himself to declaring: "What if you were to let your hair grow back without dyeing it? Their natural color, at the roots, is delightful."

"I'll do that if you prefer it."

He restricted himself to satisfaction with the promise. If he had spelled out his entire thought, he would have insisted that, as well as renouncing henna, she modify her bob. A woman ought to have long hair...

Bourgeois beneath his savage appearances, he was shocked by small details: symbols of apparent independence with regard to which he often took leave to tease Monique, without wishing to admit the sentiment of which his oblique reproaches were an indication.

Why be jealous? That would be too stupid. What had they associated, except the sympathy of their caprice and the pleasure of their senses? Honestly—before being his and when they had simply been friends—had she not confessed all her adventures to him, as to a fraternal confidant?

They had taken one another in awareness of the circumstances, freely and lightly. Jealous, today? By what right? He was not a brute, damn it! Never, before meeting Monique, had he known the intoxication of a durably shared amour. Frank to excess, to the point of violence, he had been unable to retain for long the women that his generous talent—and his male vigor, above all—might have fixed for him, if he had not driven them away, one by one, by a maladroit tyranny...

None, it was true, had conquered him more rapidly and more completely than "this damned girl" whose possession was as marvelous, three months later, as on the first day.

She raised her forehead and shook her thick curls. She had so much hair that, even though it did not surpass the nape of the neck, she would have been able, had she wished, to gather it into a chignon.

"Fundamentally," she said, "it's that you don't like my hair? Be frank."

"It suits you very well."

"But?"

He confessed: "Well, yes; it gives you a masculine look, which all the rest belies."

"That shocks you?"

"No...yes...it shocks me as a lack of harmony, that's all."

She smiled, without responding.

"Why are you smiling?"

"No reason."

Propping himself up on his elbow, he observed: "What are you imagining? I'm not so limited as to find it bad that Monique Lerbier has a gender, even masculine, if that gender pleases you."

She teased him: "Yes, you're a cave man. The proof!" She caressed the russet hair on his chest.

"I'm not a margarine gigolo, obviously," he conceded.

"Tyrant, what is it to you whether I do my hair one way or another, if this one suits me?"

"It went better with the Monique of old."

195

She went pale.

Suddenly anxious, he would have liked to take back the remark. A stone dropped vertically into a well, it had already stirred up, in the splash of the pure water, the muddy depths...

In her turn, Monique had raised herself up. She had a sensation of embarrassment at sensing that she was naked before that gaze, which the brutal evocation had darkened involuntarily. She stretched out her arm and seized a coverlet, with which she covered herself, mechanically.

He wanted to obtain a pardon for his awkwardness, and attested: "Do you think that I wouldn't care about the slightest things concerning you, including what people might think of you, if I didn't love you completely?"

"For me, there's only one thing that counts: what you think...and of the Monique of today. That's the only one that exists."

He shook his head. "A woman can't cut herself in two like a fruit, one side the past and the other the present. When one is in love, you see, and as soon as one is in love, the desired being forms an inseparable whole. That which is can't be detached, by a neat section, from that which has been. All the moments of an existence are connected. It's because I love you uniquely, and uniquely because I love you, that I can help thinking about the woman you have been, before being mine. That one, I hate."

"If you loved me as much as you say, you wouldn't hate her, you'd pity me..."

She was standing up. He imitated her, embarrassed in his turn by her nudity, and the sentiment that they had just become two beings tormented by the need to veil themselves, body and soul, from one another...

Was it necessary, then, as desire faded, for them to rediscover themselves as two adversaries after a truce? Frankness burned his lips. He had the skill to master it. Give her pain? No, that would be pure boorishness...giving rise to complaint.

He felt an irritation growing within him, the jealous suffering that even in the spick and span room, in which all their joy had just respired, the repainted walls caused him. The narrow divan disappeared; in its place there was the mortuary bed of the opium den, where Monique, gasping under other embraces, had rolled her enamored body, with the same sighs. And there, behind the partition wall, was the bathroom, immutable, with its bidet, over which so many before him had perched!

He dressed in silence, not wanting to stay any longer. He felt an instinctive haste to find himself alone, to control his tumultuous ideas.

She divined the drama that had been born within him after the fortnight of isolation, their lives transplanted into the paradise of Rozeuil...yes, the paradise! Had she, then, attained it only in order to lose it?

Instinct cried out within her, louder than pride. Fear folded up, dexterously. He turned his back, tying his shoelaces. She put her arms around him, and without appearing to perceive his sullenness, attempted a diversion:

"Don't forget to tell your editor that he'll have the ornaments for the end of the chapters tomorrow. They'll be engraved and printed today. I want there to be something of me in your book..."

He promised. He was touched, warmed by the tenderness that was burning under the ashes of his heart. In spite of himself, however, obsessive thought showed her to him as a charred hearth, blackened by all the fires of old. He did not know, blinded as he was by his possessive male egotism, the extent to which love, in a soul like Monique's, consumes all in a single devouring flame to create a clean space.

For her, from the moment when, having *known* Régis, she had chosen him, nothing remained, either pleasure or pain, of what she had been able to feel via others. From her halt at Rozeuil she had come back renewed: a happy Monique who, knowing the price of happiness, wanted to keep it.

Another woman...

197

II

The days and the weeks passed. They had bought a cheap automobile. They knew the intoxication of unplanned departures, escaping toward broad horizons. She had wanted a faster and more spacious vehicle, but he had opposed it, wanting to conserve the independence of his part-share. He was furious enough at being forced to allow himself to be driven.

Myopic and distracted, he had resigned himself to seeing her at the wheel. A few lessons had sufficed to make her a skillful driver, and him a conscientious mechanic: an inferior role about which he was the first to joke, pipe between his teeth, but which, fundamentally, without any doubt, humiliated him.

Monique became increasingly aware of the extent to which, satisfied in the flesh, they were unable to live in a communion of minds. He was so simple a companion. He had such a lofty view of events and people. He was pitiable, in spite of his impulsiveness. She appreciated, beneath the ever-displayed teeth, the weakness of a true generosity.

Were not their very quarrels—the peevishness that rendered him savage at the slightest recall of jealousy—proof of an exclusive, touching, almost flattering attachment?

When they had suffered the grief of his silences, the reproach of his allusions, all that sly and harassing guerilla warfare, she told herself: "How much he loves me?"

She even thought, for a while, that it would be pleasant to unite their lives more closely. What if he were to rent an apartment where she would be able to share more of his time? He could go to lunch every day with old Madame Boisselot. But he was fearful, given the infirmity of her age, of that semi-abandonment.

Monique was discontented with that partly divided existence, interrupted and punctuated by her business affairs, and especially by the obligation that Régis believed he had, not to sacrifice his mother by moving into his own apartment.

The precariousness and brevity of their meetings—except for the nights they spent together in the Rue Pigalle—left them with a thirst to meet up that their amorous reunions slaked periodically instead of appeasing: a bitter and tormented thirst.

Like a shrinking frame, re-gilded in vain, the ex-smoking room remained a bachelor pad constrained their love to a deadly cramping, incessantly turning their suspicious thoughts toward an involuntary hostility. Thus, she became disenchanted.

She began to be irritated by the dissonance, which she could not overcome. She resented him for it. She repeated to him: "The past is the past. Neither you nor I can do anything about it. Since I love you, isn't that enough for you?" He fell into agreement, admitted his absurdity—and almost immediately returned to the assault.

A somewhat unhealthy curiosity pushed him to an incessant need for inquisition. Not finding any purchase in the present, his obsession brought him back relentlessly to searching her memories. The most dolorous of all was that of Peer Rys. Régis had torn up the Samain and thrown it in the fire, unable to forgive *Au Jardin de l'Infante* its sprig of dried lavender, still odorous with erotic confession.

Not content with execrating those he knew to have enjoyed Monique, he wanted to know the names of all the others who had possessed her flesh before him. No matter how much he felt that he was its master, he could not tolerate that it had quivered beneath so many mouths before his.

Visions that his reason advised him in vain to drive away pursued him with precise visages and imaginary faces. They unfurled their living tableaux: an entire lubricity, which while exasperating his desire, infected it with gangrene.

With a profound sense of everything that might preserve their love, she opposed—too late!—those manic interrogations with a determined silence and the diversion of gentleness. She sought new abodes for their love. They knew the amusement of little unplanned trips and, fleeing the luxurious banalities of palatial hotels, the charms of country inns and provincial hostelries. But she always read the obsession in his anxious eyes when they relaxed their embrace.

After six months, Regis was struck by a great grief: his mother died. It was a melancholy truce, in which Monique was the consoler. Then they were able to realize the project they had cherished in the beginning, of belonging to one another more, in the warmth of a nest where nothing recalled the old days.

They diverted themselves in rejuvenating the modest apartment with tapestries and shelf-units in bright colors and rustic pottery. She made a large selection of books personally, and found him a monumental Norman table for writing in yellow oak, scarcely scratched by three centuries.

Every evening she came to dinner and slept there. She left at eleven o'clock in the morning. He ate lunch alone, while working on a sequel to *Les Coeurs sincères* entitled *Possession?*—for he was one of those novelists who has less imagination than observation, and depict themselves, involuntarily, in all his books.

For some time, Monique breathed more easily. Under Boisselot's influence, since the beginning of their liaison, she had reapplied herself to her métier, in which she saw a distraction from all the dangerous temptations that might have been offered to her in the hours she spent apart from him by the old customary circle of acquaintances and habits.

She had taken back—while retaining Mademoiselle Tcherbalief by associating her with it even more completely—the direction of the business. At the same time, she had made her a gift, in full entitlement, of her old bachelor apartment. Let there be no more mention of it! The installation that "Mademoiselle Claire" had carried out at the Plombino house had promoted her to a new status; having accepted the homages of the chagrined Baron, she even had unprecedented capital at her disposal. Being grateful to Monique, however, for having thus edified her fortune, the Russian preferred to remain second in title, without any risk, in an enterprise in which she was, in reality, the first.

Monique, leaving the general conduct of the business to her, had gone back with pleasure to her pencils and brushes: a partial reintegration of personality, but sufficient, in the interested calculation of Régis, to produce a result contrary to the one intended.

By steeping herself once again in the salubrious current of labor, Monique gradually drew from there an energy from which she emerged as if from a bath, her thoughts precise and her gaze clear. After the physical blossoming, she gradually recovered her mental health.

The occupation in which her lover had only seen a means of preserving, and reserving for himself, a monopoly of authority, rendered to the soul that he had wanted to dominate a consciousness of its own value: a sentiment that, on emerging from her fall, exalted Monique with self-confidence.

She began to find the despotism that Régis involuntarily abused less easy to tolerate. A revolt rumbled within her every time that he forced her to return to the shore from which she, in the meantime, had detached herself.

Everything served as a pretext for his maladroit observations. The most trivial incident unleashed the wild beast lurking beneath the civilized man. Followed by passionate remissions, the successive scenes were increasingly painful. Nothing, however, had yet attained the violence occasioned by an unexpected hazard: the reappearance of the naked dancer.

It was at a gala performance organized by Ginette Hutier, for the benefit of the Oeuvre des Mutilés Français, whose Hospice found its coffers empty after six years of existence. The unfortunates were taking too long to die. Peer Rys had been added to the program at the last minute. An announcement by Alex Marly—the stage manager for the occasion—had caused Monique to tremble at the same time as Régis. In the murmur of general satisfaction that rose up, concluding in bravos, he had leaned toward her, stabbing her with his gaze.

"Are you content?"

"You're mad."

She had never regretted so much the confidences that she had once allowed herself to make in the early days of their friendship, before the thunderbolt of slaked desire. Without waiting for the curtain to go up, he had left the place, instructing her to follow him. Wounded, she had refused—but when she saw him reach the door near to where their armchairs were positioned, she weakened. He was suffering because of her, and although it was an unjustified suffering, she was moved because she still loved him, almost as vividly as in the beautiful days at Rozeuil.

They did not say a word in the taxi that took them back. Each withdrawn to their own side, they climbed the slope of their thoughts, each gleaning an entire crop of bitterness against the other. When they were in the small bedroom, however, and he looked at her, hatefully, throwing off her coat and emerging, arms and shoulders bare, from her pearly dress, she could no longer bear his insulting silence. She came to him, conciliatory.

"Darling, I can't hold it against you, since you're unhappy…I'm suffering more than you, from the harm you're doing me without reason…you can see full well that I'm suffering with the torment that only you are causing..."

He pushed her away rudely. "It was me, was it, who slept with Peer Rys?"

She shrugged her shoulders. "Was it worth the trouble of writing *Les Coeurs sincères*, only to reproach me today for my frankness? Did I not have, before being yours, the honesty to confess all the sad truth of my life to you?"

"I didn't ask you to do it."

"Régis! It's not possible that it's you who are speaking! That confession, escaped from my confidence, my tenderness, and which you abuse in order to torture us today, you would have preferred that I hadn't made it! Are you forgetting that it was that impulse that brought us together? Would you have preferred that I had kept quiet, and that, having become lovers

202

even so—for that, too, was written—we had remained masked?"

"Perhaps."

"No, no! Neither you nor I could have done that! Or then we would neither of us be who we are, and we wouldn't love one another truly. Can there be anything hidden from one another when two people are in love? Can one love, truly, without knowing one another? Without knowing one another entirely and fundamentally?"

"No."

"Can you imagine me hiding from you, even when you interrogate me, at the risk of one day being found out? For now it's you who interrogate me!"

"It's stronger than I am."

"Yes, and it's for that reason that I did well to tell you everything beforehand. Think about it! Sooner or later, it would have been necessary for you to know. You wouldn't have suffered any less."

"That's true."

"You're reproaching me for my confessions. What would a dissimulation have been?"

"That's true. And yet..."

"And yet what? You would have wanted me to reply to your questions with false assurances? That I perjure myself? For you wouldn't have been content with my words—you'd have demanded my oaths! My darling, my darling, can't you sense that your love has consumed and annihilated all of that? That I'm only happy because I sense that we are living truthfully? Because there's only the truth that can efface, only the truth that can redeem, only the truth that is beautiful and good!"

He had kissed her forehead, and fallen silent with a somber expression.

She took him by the shoulders. "You're not ashamed of being in the wrong, of being unjust? Look at me, if you love me."

His gaze desperate, he murmured; "You know I do. Would I hate those who possessed you before me, if I didn't love you? Uniquely! Absolutely!"

"I, too, love you uniquely and absolutely!" she exclaimed. "What would you say, however, if I tortured you with the memory of your past mistresses? You had them, before me."

He stared at her so rudely that a chill penetrated all the way to her heart.

"It's not the same."

"What!"

He had turned his back, and began to get undressed, whistling.

Indignantly, she snapped: "Not the same? Explain!"

He took off his waistcoat, and dug his heels in: "It would take too long."

She cried: "You might have picked me up on the sidewalk and you wouldn't have treated me any differently! I'm not a whore."

"No. If you were a whore, a poor girl who lay on her back because it was the sole métier that society had taught her, I wouldn't use that language. One doesn't want to marry a whore." She started with surprise, but he went on: "One simply desires her, as one desires a slice of meat, or a book to read. One takes her for what she is. And if, by chance, one falls in love with her—why not?—one would have to be mad to be jealous of the lovers she has had, and which she couldn't not have had! For a start, one doesn't know them. Does she even remember them herself? There are too many. The crowd is anonymous. But you...you..."

She listened, dolorously.

"Who forced you to give yourself, like a madwoman, to anyone who came along? To fall for a cretin like your naked dancer because of his beautiful mouth? Not to mention the others, those whom you had the effrontery to name for me and those you were ashamed to display, because you're only too

204

well aware that it's dirty laundry, which it's better to lock away in a drawer!"

She put her hands over her face to cover the blush.

He shouted: "You didn't have the right! You should have thought that you might encounter a worthy fellow one day—as absolute as me—who would be able to love you, and that by disgracing yourself like a whore...worse than a whore...you, who were privileged by birth and by education, were forging his unhappiness and your own!"

She did not reply. She was trying to disentangle that which, within her, was striking truly, from that which was striking falsely. Certain words cut her to the quick, because they corresponded to the bruise of a regret. Others wounded her even more profoundly, so unmerited did they seem.

Finally, she said: "Let's not talk about it anymore, since you don't want to see what I've been before knowing you, and before everything! An unhappy woman... And since you've finally begun to be frank, let it be completely."

"Go on."

"You've just said to me: one doesn't marry a whore. Let's admit that, even though one sees it, after all, every day. But a widow, or a divorcee? Answer..."

He foresaw the argument, and muttered: "It depends!"

"No. Evasion doesn't suit you. Answer. If you loved, as you love me, a widow or a divorcee, would you marry her?"

"You're neither a widow nor a divorcee. With ifs, all reasoning becomes facile."

"I repeat that it's not a question of me. A widow or a divorcee, who had turned the four hundred tricks, about whom you knew nothing, except that you love her—would you marry her?"

"Of course."

"I no longer understand."

They were face to face, scrutinizing one another's eyes like mirrors.

He added: "A widow or a divorcee has generally submitted to her destiny. They're less responsible than you are for yours. They've obeyed the law."

"What law?"

Hearing laugher in advance, he snapped: "Well, yes, whether you like it or not, the law. That of men and that of nature."

"Of nature! *Hymen, O Hymenée!*[25] That's it, isn't it?"

"Well yes, that's it."

She burst into mocking laughter. "When I told you that you were a cave man! The little membrane, eh? The red stain on the marital sheet! And around the bed, the savages celebrating the sacrifice of the virginity! Go talk about that to the young women of today! It runs, it runs, the ferret, Mesdames! You're behind the times, Régis. The proprietary husband—ha ha! The lord and master!"

He grabbed her by the arms. "No—but the one who, husband or lover, imprints your flesh with a mark so profound that afterwards, when it's finished, you remain, even in the arms of another, his creature, his thing!"

"Oh yes, impregnation! The child of a second marriage resembling the first husband? Fiction. In any case, me, you know…no, Régis, no. First of all, don't worry—I'll never marry you, even if you beg me to. As for children, if I ever have any, I wouldn't want them to resemble you."

"Thanks."

She made a weary gesture. "What's the point of arguing? It's so individual, all that. There are mothers who die without

---

[25] This quotation, originally from Catullus, was best known in France at the time, with an additional prefatory O, as the title of a painting by Jean Luna that won a medal at the 1889 Exposition Universelle in Paris. Luna took it from a poem by Walt Whitman, in which the line is completed "why do you tantalize me thus?" The first term had changed its meaning in the interim because of the anatomical adoption of the name of the Roman god of marriage to denote the maidenhead.

ever having known love. A woman only awakes to life after being opened to pleasure."

He laughed: "Peer Rys!"

"Have I said that pleasure was all of life? Isn't mine there to proclaim the contrary? One is only happy when one is in love, body and soul."

He looked away.

She sighed. "It's you who taught me that, Régis. One is only happy on that condition...or, rather, one ought to be happy..."

They held themselves immobile alongside one another. She had a benevolent impulse, and drew closer to him. Then she saw that he was weeping. She was moved.

"Why are we torturing one another like this? There's nothing more degrading than a mediocre sadness. And it's futile!"

"One isn't rational when one's suffering." He was ashamed, and sank to his knees. "Forgive me—I'm a brute."

She had placed a hand on his head, and gazed at him, with more compassion than affection. He jumped to his feet and put his arms around her. How many times had their previous disputes finished like that, rolling in the reconciliatory bed? But this time, Monique declared, sadly: "No, Régis, no. I need you to leave me alone this evening. You've broken a bond between us. Tomorrow...when you've calmed down, when you've..."

But he violated her yet again. She fell, defending her body. And when, in the frenzy that overtook her, they had finished their spasmodic tussle in bestial cries, a great sadness invaded them. They did not fall asleep until morning, their limbs interlaced, and their thoughts distant.

From then on, an agitated life carried Monique away. She thought, with melancholy, about the peaceful hours of their love, when it had still resembled a sunlit sheet of water, with its flowers of forgetfulness. The paradise of Rozeuil, from which the demon had expelled them...yes, the demon, which had now taken entire possession of Régis. The evil had gripped him, hypnotized him. He no longer even tried to reason in order to overcome his jealousy. It overflowed from the past into the present, corrupting everything.

As unexpected as the disappointment was for her, and as bitterly as her pride suffered from having encountered, in the man from whom she expected liberation, a new form of slavery, Monique stuck to it, with all her carnal habitude, and all the regret of her error. Perhaps it could be mended? The worse maladies are cured, in the end. Who could tell whether all the intelligence and goodness that Régis had might not end up attenuating or even eliminating the venom?

Love and self-esteem were therefore in accord in inclining her to patience. For fear of exasperating the maniac, now inclined to be suspicious of everything, she consented to almost never leaving his side. She renounced the majority of her relationships and occupations. She let herself be taken over a little more every day.

He implanted himself as sovereign, relegated her to his shadow. She was the guardian of his work. She accompanied him whenever he wanted to go out. She only saw his friends, a few painters, avant-garde writers—rarely Monsieur Vignabos, with whom, since the day they had encountered Blanchet there, the conversation between them had ended up becoming embittered. It had sufficed for Monique to share the opinion of the professor; Régis had immediately taken the opposite line, furiously.

At length, that isolation inevitably had its effect: Monique was stifling, as if in a prison. She reacted, and their apparent peace abruptly ended.

"No," she protested, resolutely, when he tried to prevent her from accepting an invitation to Sunday lunch at Madame Ambrat's. "It's been two months that I've been refusing to go to Vaucresson—it's idiotic. You'll end up falling out with the entire world."

"I don't believe that Madame Ambrat is the entire world."

"You've already forced me to drop Vignabos—that's sufficient. I won't even mention the others. I'll gladly abandon them to you. They're a heap of idlers and bores whom one can balance like specimens. Yes, I know the formula—all the formulas: one rises by isolating oneself, etc. But Vignabos and Madame Ambrat! That's too much!"

He frowned. "Me, I say that it's enough. Do you think that I don't know why you want to go to Vaucresson on Sunday?"

"For a change of air."

"It's always the same song!"

"Perhaps it's funny. Elaborate!"

Two raps of the door of the room interrupted the response that Monique, riposte at the ready, had already divined. Mad! He was mad!

The housemaid, Julia, appeared, with a bandage over her eye. She was a replete and wheezy slattern, with a poor face corroded by vitriol—a souvenir of amour! Wringing her apron, she announced that lunch was served.

Sitting before the *hors-d'oeuvres*, they waited until they were alone. At a sluggish pace, Julia finally decided to leave the dining room. She had no other interest than watching her employers live. She lay in wait for their quarrels delightedly, avid for the slightest details. That was her recreation. Instinctively, she always sided with Régis; as a beast of burden, subservient to man, Monique's elegance and independence shocked her, fundamentally, in the darkness of her dungeon.

"May I know now what attracts me to Vaucresson?"

He hesitated, fearing to give substance, by making it precise, to the suspicion that was gnawing at him.

"As if you didn't know!" Mockingly, he sang: "*Parfum d'amour...rêve d'un jour!*"

She considered him pityingly. Madman, the first to underline thoughts that would never have occurred to her without him!

He could not bear her sympathetic irony, and mocked: "Vaucresson, where the friends meet! The true, the only ones!

Let's wager that we'll find there, as if by chance, not only the worthy Vignabos but also that excellent…"

"Blanchet, no?"

He parodied, with Max's voice: "*It's you who've named him.*"[26]

"Do you know what you are?"

"An idiot, that's understood. Not a blind man, at any rate. Do you think that I didn't notice your maneuvers, the last time we met? I say we because I don't know what you might do, apart from me!"

"Régis!"

"What? It's true. I'm stating a fact: I don't know. That's all."

"Can you suspect…?"

"It's always necessary to suspect! I know no other certainty than suspicion. Take care that you don't end up confirming mine by your indignation."

She fell silent, proudly. He took advantage of the fact.

"Do you think that I didn't notice your glances, when I was speaking, and your simpering, every time he opened his mouth! I wouldn't be surprised if you were already accomplices."

Julia came back in, carrying an unappetizing joint of beef with apples. She placed it on the table and changed the plates with sausage-like fingers with black nails. The relativity of things! Monique felt, more forcibly than usual, the kind of peevish poverty that everything around Régus exhaled: the narrowness of souls, the partitioning of walls.

Mechanically, she carved and served. They ate, like two strangers, at the same table. He could not contain himself any longer, pushed his chair back, and stood up.

---

[26] The line is quoted from Racine's *Phèdre*, spoken by the eponymous heroine when her interlocutor guesses the name of the person with whom she is in love (her husband's son). The actor who used the stage-name Max was one of the leading figures of the French stage during the 1920s

"You daren't deny it? I was sure of it!"

He paced nervously back and forth, as if in a cage.

"Sit down," she begged. "You're making me ill. Now, listen: I wouldn't stoop to trying to deceive you. It's so stupid, all that! So unworthy of us…"

"Sunday, then?"

"We're going to lunch at Madame Ambrat's."

"You go!"

She repeated, softly, but in a tone so firm that he did not renew his challenge: "We'll go. Either you give me that proof of intelligence—that's the only excuse I ask of you—or it will be finished between us forever."

He fixed her with the stare of a menacing cat, uncertainty shining in his pupils. Give in? Yes, perhaps…in order better to spy on them, to know…

She continued: "I don't want to become the victim of your manias. I intend to regulate my conduct as I please. Without respect for one another, there's no lasting love. Have you had enough of ours? One would think so, to see you so determined to destroy it."

He fell back in his chair, his head in his hands.

"No, Monique! I love you. Forgive me! I'll get better."

III

As they got closer to the Vert-Logis, Régis evoked the image of Madame Ambrat's house: the ground floor at the edge of the woods of Vaucresson, the pergola with its circle of visitors…Blanchet, naturally! And, increasingly silent, he became sullen.

He had tried hard to get a grip on himself, swearing to keep calm; Monique was right; it was stupid to spoil his own happiness like this! Why not enjoy tranquilly the miracle that such a love had realized in his life? He had never encountered, and would never encounter again, an individual who combined a more seductive beauty with as much real moral value.

Reproaching her, whether or not she was responsible, for a past with which, logically, he was and ought to remain uninvolved? Imbecility. Holding her independence of mind against her? Pettiness. Her fortune? A troubled sentiment divided him there. Sensible to the adornment of her luxury, and poor by comparison, he was humiliated by the fact that in that respect, too, she escaped the norm: the woman tributary, the man organizing…

"That way," he said, at a crossroads.

"No—there are the acacias. We're on the right road."

The auto sped on, to the regular throb of the engine.

Coiffed in a red leather beret, her neck bare in the unbuttoned coat, she was driving with attentive decision, so prettily tomboyish that Régis could not help admiring her, sulky as he was. Yes, all things considered, that was a new realization of feminine grace! A being still singular, although born in thousands of exemplars, with whom it was necessary to deal henceforth, as with an equal…an observation that, far from satisfying him, anchored in repugnance everything that was included in the word, discordant for him, "feminism."

"Well?" said Monique. "Was that it?"

The auto stopped outside the Vert-Logis. Buried beneath its porch of ivy, where the last climbing roses were shedding their red and yellow petals, the little white-painted lattice gate permitted the sight, beyond the lawn, of the small house, with its roof of old tiles.

"It's nice, it must be said!" Monique exclaimed. "Fundamentally, wisdom would be to live like this, close enough to come to Paris, when necessary, and far enough away to be in the open air."

The autumn afternoon deployed its bright serenity over the hedges. A light sky, the light so soft that one could not tell whether it was that of the end of summer or the rebirth of spring.

They parked the auto in a pathway and closed the gate. At the sound of the bell, Madame Ambrat appeared on the threshold of the house. She waved as a gesture of welcome, and hastened her brisk stride.

"*Bonjour, ma chérie! Bonjour*, Monsieur Boisselot. We were wondering whether you'd come. For, without reproach, you're making your visits rare! I don't hold it against you. The amorous are egotists."

She had taken Monique by the arm.

"Why didn't you come to lunch? There was pork with white beans! And the little Vouvray that Monsieur Boisselot doesn't detest..." She turned to him. "There are two bottles waiting for you, well chilled! Although you scarcely merit it, monopolist! Quickly, everyone's waiting for you."

"Who's everyone?"

"Your great friend Vignabos, Monsieur Blanchet and the Mutoys, whom you know."

Régis face grew longer. He hesitated as to whether to turn back. But they were already going through the drawing room, the center of the dwelling, one set of whose French windows opened on the garden, and the opposite ones on to the wood. He followed.

Monique paused momentarily. "How I love this room!"

"It's very simple," said Madame Ambrat.

"Exactly!"

It was restful, that intimate atmosphere, with the old provincial furniture, shining with the patina that familial maintenance confers, generation after generation. Monique particularly appreciated a vast cupboard with sober moldings that had come from Madame Ambrat's Touranian grandparents, a vestige of the ancestral home.

Régis felt the velvety wood in passing and thought: *You could fall into line; it's one up on the Lerbier style!*

As if she had divined his thought, she declared: "That's what the most beautiful modern furniture lacks; it's what time alone brings. A melting of the hardness of the corners—the enrichment of life."

He was about to reply: *Life! How malign it is...yes, of course; wait a hundred and fifty years and ours will sort itself out!* when a young girl came running from the pergola—where everyone had stood upon seeing her—to throw herself into Monique's arms.

"How beautiful you are, Riri! Are you well?"

The child raised her flaxen-blue eyes, beaming all over her little face, her chestnut hair knotted in a ribbon the color of her gaze. Her entire person replied, like a cry. Monique stroked the pert head, and congratulated Madame Ambrat: "How she's changed!"

The maternal face brightened proudly.

"Hasn't she? Go fetch two glasses, Riri."

They followed the joyful bounding of the soft calves with tender eyes as the whole frail body danced away. It was less than two years ago that Henriette Lamur—she was six now—had been taken in by the Ambrats. She was the daughter of a stitcher of boots who had died of cancer, or perhaps of poverty and physical exhaustion. The father, a zinc worker, a brutal drunkard, had abandoned the child, whom he beat, to the Oeuvre. Better than a renunciation of his rights—devoid of effective value in the eyes of the law, which respects paternal authority in the worst of brutes—a remarriage, fortunately followed by the emigration of the drunkard to the liberated regions, had permitted the Ambrats to undertake the definitive rescue in security. Of the humble victim, two years of wise education and tender affection had been sufficient to make another being. Transplanted, Riri was growing up right.

"What a success! You can be proud of it."

Madame Ambrat smiled modestly. "She's so sweet! And it's so pleasing to see a soul blossom that only needed love in order to live. I'm increasingly convinced that there are no true hearths but those of election. Riri loves me as if I were her mother, perhaps more. Family is just a word if it's founded solely on the prejudice of blood. Yes, every day I'm more persuaded: the true filiation is that of intelligence and heart."

"One can't suppress heredity," observed Régis.

"No, Monsieur Boisselot, but one can correct it to such a degree that it's transformed. Grafting is a beautiful invention! Why shouldn't one make a wild vine into a lovely fruit tree, when the stock of a bitter almond can produce exquisite peaches within two years?"

Monsieur Vignabos, who had taken possession of Monique, patted her hands amicably. Everyone bowed to her, with an urgency at which Régis had difficulty not taking umbrage. He found it difficult to accustom himself to being relegated to second place. Without warmth, he shook hands with Blanchet and received the banal politeness of the Muroys with bitterness. They were cousins of Monsieur Ambrat, the husband a notary in Langeais, the wife a discreetly self-effacing housewife: two aged individuals of no great culture, to whom the name of Boisselot evidently meant nothing. The Ambrats received them regularly once or twice a year, during each of their voyages. They held the Muroys in esteem for a rectitude and a mischievous tolerance, the smiling philosophy of one of those old-fashioned households matured in provincial peace, and whose only great dolor, stoically borne, had been the loss of an only son, Commandant Muroy, killed on the twentieth of August 1914 at Morhange.

The circle reformed under the pergola, enlarged. Riri reappeared, carefully carrying two glasses.

"Here, godmother!"

With the dexterity of a wine-grower, Madame Ambrat uncorked one of the bottles that was in the process of chilling. The pale golden wine sparkled in the misted glasses. The Muroys drew Riri toward them and caressed her; she resembled their granddaughter, a natural child of the commandant, adopted by them when they had opened their house to the grieving mother. With Madame Ambrat, they resumed their great topic of conversation, the Oeuvre, for which they were propagandists in Langeais. Two young boys had found unexpected parents, thanks to them, in Angers and Saumur.

"If only," Monsieur Muroy regretted, "our escapees didn't remain under the threat of being reclaimed, one day or another, by the authors of their evils! We continue to live, with regard to the legislation of childhood, under Roman Law. The father of the family has all the rights, and not one duty. As if childhood were not a social capital to be protected before any other!"

"Monsieur Blanchet has made that observation forcefully, in his study of the *Monde Nouveau*," remarked Madame Ambrat. "Yes, yes, my dear friend, you've rendered us a great service. Thanks to you, we've received a quantity of letters and requests at the seat of the Oeuvre. You don't realize how influential you are!"

"Blanchet will be the député for the Seine-et-Oise when he wants to be," said Monsieur Vignabos.

"I'll never want to. Lectures and articles, as many as necessary, but make speeches at the Palais Bourbon! Do you know what that reminds me of, Ambrat? Your windmills, on the hills of the Loire. Their sails move..."

"And turn in the void?"

"Exactly."

"But who will remake the laws," asked the notary, "if not the legislators?"

Blanchet sketched a vague gesture. "A time will come, perhaps sooner that we think, when we'll tire of Wordmills.

216

The world around us evolves. Under pain of suicide, we can't escape that law. The hour of action will chime."

"The revolution?" said Monsieur Muroy, unenthusiastically. "It requires, in order to succeed, more than a general staff and troops. It requires officers. Where are they? Without the Third, no 89!"[27]

The Bourgeoisie of 1922 ignores or misunderstands the C.G.T.[28] as the nobility and clergy did the Third. Have confidence in the People!"

"Well said, Blanchet," said Vignabos, supportively.

But the notary was uneasy. "A revolution, that's unknown—or rather, it's the eternal story: one overshoots the mark, and it's necessary to go backwards. What has Bolshevism brought to Russia? Can you tell me?"

"But Russia isn't France," Blanchet objected, "and furthermore, Russia's ruination and famine have other causes, more profound and more distant, than the communist utopia. Its failure even militates in favor of French reformists. Whatever happens, though, the nationalization of the land and major industry will survive the reign of Lenin in the ancient empire of the Tsars. Humanity entire will benefit, along with that infant and giant people, which we shall see grow when it emerges from its bloody convulsions. What do you expect? Nothing great is accomplished without struggle and pain."

Monique listened ardently to the generous voice. Conviction added to the resonance of its timbre a charm that even Monsieur Muroy had difficulty resisting. Only Régis enveloped, in the same ironic reproval, the speaker and his audience; *Baritone, old man—that always grabs them!*

---

[27] The reference to the *Tiers* [Third] is to the députés of the bourgeois "Third Estate" (as Abbé Sieyès dubbed it) who carried the Revolution through parliamentary process in June 1789.

[28] *Confédération Générale du Travail*: the central pivot of the trade union movement in France at the time.

He mocked: "Blanchet's wrong to reserve his talents for internal usage. With a voice like his, he'd be a minister in two years."

The professor sensed the aggressive thrust beneath the joke. "I'm only a humble professor of philosophy, my dear chap, and I only teach what I think."

The novelist excused himself perfidiously. "Why, I thought you had a chair in rhetoric. Forgive me."

"But I don't see that it would be disobliging," Blanchet riposted. "Rhetoric has its virtues. In any case, that's the first time I've heard a litterateur speak ill of it. You're spitting on your bread!"

Régis went pale. Touché! Beneath the tone of pleasantry, the points of the foils, with the buttons removed for them alone, were inflicting their wounds. It was a duel of words, of which only Madame Ambrat divined the gravity—and of which Monique, a judge as well as a witness, felt every thrust. It was for her that the two men were crossing swords with their gazes and their words—for she perceived with a sudden clarity, whose revelation gripped her, that it was not entirely blindly that Régis' jealousy had made Blanchet a rival. She took account of it, not so much from the ever-equable attitude of the professor as the secret exchange of sympathies.

During her recent encounters with Blanchet, a new sentiment had awakened in him. First a curiosity, and then an attraction, less banal than that of camaraderie, had succeeded his cordiality. She sensed, with the delicacy of instinct that all women have, flattered by pleasing, even when they have no intention of it, the progress whose crystallization had advanced in him every time they saw one another.

It was not only a kinship of intelligence, the impulse of intellectual amity that had brought closer to her, during each absence, the soul whose delicacy she had ended up appreciating fully. A more imperious magnetism was needling him…perhaps without him being aware of it? For nothing in appearances permitted anything to be distinguished in him but

218

affectionate respect. It required the feline eye of a jealous lover immediately to see it clearly.

At the same time, she interrogated herself. Gripped by Régis to the point that nothing except their pleasures existed, physically, for her, she did not discover anything for Georges Blanchet from the physical point of view: neither attraction nor repulsion. There was neither good nor bad: indifference...

However, on reflection, she admitted that he gained from acquaintance. Had not the first impression, when he had been introduced to her, been rather disagreeable? Nowadays, she took pleasure in seeing him again. She liked the broadness of his views, and above all, his faith, which did not exclude tolerance. Yes, a fine character!

She wanted to be absolutely sincere: would she have appreciated him to that degree if Régis, by his absurd suspicion and the clumsiness of his persistence, had not constrained her to pursue the comparison more than she would have done of her own accord?

No. If the image of Blanchet had taken on substance, to the point of often occupying her thoughts when she was alone, whose fault was it? Above all, that of the man whose coarse reproaches had galled her, less by virtue of their inanity than their injustice. A bruised heart, which needed tender and scrupulous care in order to be healed, Monique had only felt more cruelly the brutality of the hands that, in coming to bandage it, had torn away the bandage and scar alike at a stroke.

The old wound had reopened to the quick, further envenomed by an evil whose affliction Monique had not thus far suffered: the tearing of a heart that is detaching from the flesh to which a single but solid bond retains it. Every day, now, the virus became more active...

Thus, all three were approaching, without suspecting it, the critical moment.

Régis, unconscious of his imprudence, attacked his adversary. He was one of those whose violence carries them away, and he believed, at the same time, that he was surer of his victory than he was. Had he doubted his power, he would not have defended it so savagely.

"My bread" he growled. "You have the advantage of it!" He appealed to their old master. "Rhetorician, me! No! Which of the two of us? If there's one thing I hate, because I know of nothing more dangerous, and—in literary terms—more despicable, it's eloquence! Every time I can, I follow Verlaine's advice: I take hold of it and I wring its neck. Eloquence? It's an old luxury chicken that has lost her feathers, only good to excite that imbecile, the Gallic cock! Confidence in the People! But with two sous' worth of hollow claptrap, any ventriloquist can fool them!"

"It's true," conceded Monsieur Vignabos, accustomed to Boisselot's truculence, "that—judging from the reports of yesterday's parliamentary session—it suffices for an orator to have his little couplet, and to say the opposite of the preceding speaker, for the Chambre to applaud."

Blanchet smiled. "That's because, in general, nothing resembles the People less than its representatives! A clever monkey isn't a man. For every Jaurès there's a Pertout!"

The Muroys, uninterested in the argument, took advantage of the silence provoked by that remark to take their leave. Like the majority of people of their class, they found politics repellent. They saw nothing in it but a great alimentary cuisine, in which they were only concerned with the dessert. They left at a measured step, escorted by the Ambrats and Riri, who was holding her "godmother" by the hand.

"We were boring them," Monique observed, laughing.

Monsieur Vignabos nodded his head. "I fear so. And it's more serious because it's in the air, this growing disaffection of the people for the general ideas that, in the final analysis, orient and guide them. The party divisions and the personal fashion in which they're exercised when in power are gradually disgusting the best of public life. No one is any longer occupying himself with anything but his own business. The sense of national life has been lost."

Régis had stuffed and lit his pipe. He observed: "Then let's have no more talk of revolution! There's only the bourgeoisie, blinking their eyes, with their ostrich plumes. The populace does as they do. They don't care. You talk about the C.G.T.? It's half empty. They've stuffed our heads enough with principles…too many principles! What principles?" A grimace made him ugly. "A service stairway—and people sitting above every step."

"Be careful, my dear colleague," Blanchet mocked. "Paradox is also rhetoric."

"Paradox! Can you claim that we're not living today in the manor of the inverse? Everywhere—and everyone! Men, women, all in competition."

"Whose fault is that, Messieurs?" demanded Madame Ambrat, who had come to rejoin them, and had only heard the last remark."

"Not mine!" said Regis, drawing on his pipe, which glowed.

"Present company excepted, of course," she said, sitting down. "But ultimately, if anyone is responsible for the present anarchy, admit that, if it isn't you, Monsieur Boisselot, or these apostles"—Monsieur Vignabos and Georges Blanchet bowed, comically—"nor is it us poor women! If it only depended on our will, be certain that things wouldn't be going so badly. It's not us who would have let the war start! If we had a voice in the matter, there would be fewer taverns selling alcohol, fewer hovels causing tuberculosis and fewer prostitutes spreading syphilis. And there'd be more Maternity Wards and Hospices! Above all, there'd be more schools!"

Monique got up and went to embrace her friend. Régis blew out an abrupt jet of smoke. "A fine program! I recommend it to our friend Blanchet for his next electoral campaign. For you'll go that way, my dear chap! A hundred sous says that you'll be recruited! George Blanchet, socialist-feminist! It'll make you rich."

"At any rate, it would do good. I share Madame Ambrat's opinion entirely."

221

"Of course! One very small question, Madame: what about your electors? For a Madame Ambrat to be elected, it would first be necessary for women to be able to vote..."

"Yes, of course! As in America, England and Germany..."

"And in Switzerland, Belgium, Austria, Czechoslovakia, Finland and Denmark," Monsieur Ambrat listed. "It will be necessary for France to follow suit."

"The France of the Convention!" murmured Monsieur Vignabos. "The Emancipatrix...!"

"Let's return to the question," Boisselot continued. "Men responsible for the present anarchy—you make me laugh! Is it us who have taught your 'conscious and organized' citizenesses the steps they're following in the general saraband? Is it us who advise the female worker to squander her whole week's salary sticking her dirty feet into silk stockings and yellow bottines, or varnished shoes? Is it us who've shortened the skirts of society women in order to pray them to wiggle their very proper behinds in dance halls? Is it is who are responsible for the new mores of young women and the incurable vanity of feminine occupations? Mademoiselle Lerbier will excuse me—I'm not talking about her."

Monique did not blink, but the insult penetrated her, sharply.

Coldly, Madame Ambrat replied: "Permit the lamb to borrow the language of the wolf to reply to him: 'If it's not you, then it's your brother.'[29] Yes, it is men who have not only accommodated but further embedded feminine weakness in its habits of artifice, a second nature of deception and cunning. All the bad examples come from you, all the more inexcusable because you were, and still are, the masters. That said, Monsieur Boisselot, I will point out to you that there is as much error as verity in your paradox. You're over-generalizing. The wives, and even the young women, of France are not all like

---

[29] The quotation is from Jean de La Fontaine's fable "Le Loup et l'agneau" [The Wolf and the Lamb].

those you have depicted. Madame Muroy, if she were still here, could tell you, if I did not, that there are in the provinces, and even in Paris, a host of families in which virtue is more frequent than vice. That's obvious. And the spots that might appear, even on the sun, don't prevent the sun from shining."

Monsieur Vignabos rubbed his hands. Smiling, with an expression of approval, Monsieur Ambrat poured himself a finger of Vouvray. He blushed on perceiving that all the glasses were empty, and held out the bottle. "Oh, pardon me! But yes, yes! A little glass, Monsieur Boisselot. You like it. There are still, fortunately, a few of these good things on our native soil!"

"And then again," Blanchet added, "why judge a time or a society by one of its temporary aspects? First of all, indeed, as Madame Ambrat observes, what Boisselot sees is only what Boisselot sees. Secondly, what is ten years, or twenty, in the gaze of history? Who can tell whether, in the very anarchy, a new order might be in preparation? The new mores of young women, with the excesses that any apprenticeship in liberty brings, will perhaps embellish the face of the woman of tomorrow."

Boisselot sniggered. "*La Vierge folle*, introduction to *La Marche Nuptiale*, music by Henri Bataille!"[30]

"So what? Virginity, dear to the ancient buyers of spouses, seems to me to have no more importance than a milk tooth!

---

[30] The dramatist Henri Bataille (1872-1922) was very popular in the decade before the Great War, specializing in works about the effects of passion on human motivation and the oppressive effects of social convention, with a special interest in unconscious motivation. In between *La Marche nuptiale* [The Wedding March] (1905) and *La Vierge folle* [The Foolish Virgin] (1908) he produced *La Femme nue* [The Naked Woman] (1908) and *Le Scandale* [Scandal] (1909). His final work was *La Chair humaine* [Human Flesh]. He died before *La Garçonne* was published, but there is no doubt that he would have approved of the novel wholeheartedly.

And the superstition that certain people attach to it appears to me to be more a sort of sadism than a proof of intelligence. I'm of the party of Stendhal, for whom 'the maidenhead is the source of the vices and unhappiness that follow our present day marriages.'"

Boisselot mocked: "I'm not astonished by your indulgence for the Bolsheviks! Communism in love—it's an opinion."

Blanchet shrugged his shoulders. "It's not a question of communism, but simply of extending to young women our right to liberty and choice. It's absurd to condemn them in the thousands to abstinence, while we submit the dismal host of public prostitutes to the torture of forced pleasure. It's the celibacy of virgins that swells the number of prostitutes. Not to mention that, at present, our birth-rate is declining..."

"In truth," concluded Madame Ambrat, "one can never have too many children. Long live life!"

Régis was about to respond when he noticed that Blanchet's gaze was directed at Monique. At the same moment, she raised her eyes. She approved with a nod of the head, but she acquiesced with her entire being. Then he stood up, his expression so furious in its red beard, that Madame Ambrat jumped, as if a devil had surged forth from a jack-in-a-box.

"You scared me," she joked.

"Excuse me! With all your gossip, it's late and time to go home. I regret, my dear Blanchet, robbing you of an admirer. Are you coming, Monique?"

"Stay!" urged Madame Ambrat, upset by the impoliteness of the exit. "We'll finish off the pork with a nice salad...from the garden. Our friends aren't going back until after dinner, by the ten o'clock train."

Régis sensed that Monique, tempted, was hesitating. He played his final card.

"Impossible! Our headlights are broken down."

He was lying. Beneath a stare as heavy as a hammer-blow, however, she yielded, for fear of a scene.

224

Blanchet kissed her hand. She looked at Régis' face, white with rage, and loudly, like a promise, said "*À bientôt.*"

When the auto was garaged in the Place Saint-Sulpice, Monique and Régis went back toward the apartment in the Rue de Vaugirard without saying a word.

During the return journey, she had refused to enter into any conversation. Now that she sensed the unavoidable moment approaching, she was overtaken by an apprehension. If they went back in, the habitual argument would burst forth, following its fatal course: the deluge of reproaches, the hail of wounding words, and then, after the storm, the softening fall into the depths of lax pleasure, as if into a layer of mud from which she emerged more soiled every time.

She felt as if gripped by the throat, like an asphyxia, by the rarefied atmosphere of the small rooms, seeming all the poorer and emptier in advance, one that autumnal Sunday evening, whose splendor was suspended over the green Luxembourg: the dwelling where nothing was waiting for her; no intimacy, no tenderness...nothing but the visage of their grievances...

At the corner of the Rue Bonaparte she stopped. "It's a nice evening, and there's no dinner ready. There's no point going up three floors only to come out again."

"Time to rest before the restaurant?"

"No. Go back if you want to. I prefer to go sit down in the garden. I need to be alone. You can come to rejoin me."

He shook his head. "Let's go sit down."

They went through the large flowerbeds, where couples and families were amusing themselves in the magnificence of the fading day. She contemplated, sadly, the women hanging on the arms of their companions, the groups of children playing between the benches, around the groups of parents sowing and reading. She envied them their indifference. How many of those strollers bore, as she did, a soul in torment? She tried to read their secrets in their faces. How many seemed careless and resigned! It was as if, in the midst of that crowd, she were alone...

Régis was walking beside her. By extending her arm, she could have touched him. She looked at him, surprised to feel, so close to him, as if she were a hundred leagues way.

Finally, under the large tree that shades the statue of Madame de Ségur, they found two empty armchairs.

"Here isn't too bad," she said.

The silence weighed upon them for a little while longer. Finally, Régis, swallowing his rancor, found words that she did not expect, and which moved her.

"I don't deserve your love...if you do still love me. I behaved like a boor this afternoon."

He had raised his eyes, lowered until then, and implored her humbly. Surprised, she collected herself. She had been so sickened by his inexcusable attitude at Madame Ambrat's that she had kept silent since: a silence more scornful than any recrimination. Attack? He was not worth that honor! But she was on the alert, ready for any riposte...and now that unexpected humility disarmed her.

In her turn, she interrogated him, from the bottom of her soul: "Are you sincere?"

"Judge me henceforth on my conduct. For an hour I've been telling myself that I'm in the process of annihilating our happiness definitively. And I value it more than my life. Without you, what does all the rest matter? I can't do without you. You're more necessary to me than..."

He was speaking in a low voice, his expression obstinate. He sought a comparison in the absolute. She came to his aid.

"Than your pipe. How can I believe you, after all your promises, and today's fine result?"

"There's one means. That's to put me to the proof. Let's go away—we can do that—just the two of us. Let's go to Rozeuil. Rignac's house is available for rent, for the winter. He'd sell it, if necessary, if we wanted to buy it."

"Why would we do that?"

"To live there."

227

"You can't think so!"

"I think of nothing else. In anger, one says things devoid of rhyme or reason, stupid things that one regrets afterwards..."

"For example?"

"No, it's not a matter of the past. I was wrong! It's the present, and the future, that only depend on us. If you were good, you'd forget all the harm I've done involuntarily—yes, involuntarily. Because, deep down, I'm not malevolent. We can go far away from Paris, far from people. There's nothing keeping us here. Me, my inkwell, you, your paint pots, we can take our métiers with us."

"If we only had to carry that! One can change location, travel...but one doesn't transport one's métier in a suitcase. One carries it within oneself!"

"We'll leave the bad memories here. Everything in Paris pursues me, obsesses me. Those we'll rediscover in Rozeuil are those of our love; they'll remind us of our joys. Living alone, for one another, we'll be happy. I no longer have any idea but that one: to do anything in order to forget. To forget, to forget!"

His tone was so dolorous, with such a tension of determination and desperation, that she was troubled. What if what he said was true?

He sensed more stable ground, and advanced: "I'm only asking you this: let's try! If you can have enough indulgence not to give any more thought to my injustice! If you wanted to give me this proof that nothing, no one, retains you in Paris..."

The idea of Blanchet surged forth between them, immediately chased away by the ardent plea with which he tried to exorcise it, on seeing Monique's face darken again.

"To live far away from everyone, working, loving one another...cultivating our infinity like a narrow field. Perhaps then, the proof accomplished, you'd be the first to want to take back your words...and if I begged you, at this moment, to..."

He hesitated, blushing with humiliated timidity.

"What?" she said, unable to guess.

228

"I daren't say it. But it's burning my thoughts..."

"Speak."

He was afraid. His ears were still ringing with the trenchant phrase: *"I'll never marry you..."* Since she had pronounced the words, however, thus abruptly materializing a project about which he had only thought intermittently until then, those words had pursued him, with an increasing desire, as well as a regret. Marry her? The idea that had sometimes crossed their minds, each for their part, and which they had only mentioned in order to set it aside, had imposed itself subsequently, imperiously, on his reflections. Marry her! Yes...the sole means of having her henceforth to himself, wholly and entirely to himself...

She understood, and exclaimed: "Become your wife? Get married?"

"It's my only dream."

"To enslave me, isn't it? You believe you'd have more hold over me?"

"Who is retained by marriage, nowadays? Don't be afraid. Bluebeard's secret room is an old story...a fairy tale! No, to marry you in order that, even more, we'll make a single whole, we'll being to one another unreservedly..."

Everything in her protested, in an instinct of defense that resolutely urged her to reject, as the menace of a mortal danger, that unexpected proposition...and yet, she experienced in the incorrigible ingenuousness of her flesh and her heart, a swerve of indulgence, a semi-credulity... Rouzeuil? Who could tell? What would it cost, in fact, to try one last time...?

She did not say yes that evening. But a few days later, touched by the effort of affectionate repentance of which Régis gave evidence, she gave in. The auto took them, one misty morning, toward the house on the riverbank. Julia had gone on ahead of them the day before, with the trunks.

Was it the prism of the season? The warm light of the premonition of winter on the renewed décor, and in themselves? With its poplars with golden leaves, the nacre of the mists on the water, the reddening woods, they found Rouzeuil more moving, in the last suns of November, than they had in the spring of their love.

Régis had become once again the simple companion of the debut. The first week flew by, borne away in long excursions along the roads, the keen air on their faces, little villages passed through at speed. In the evening, huge fires warmed and lit the little dining room where, when the table was cleared, they laid out their white pages, staying up late, working with good humor.

She believed in the possibility of a miracle: a closeness sufficiently agreeable for her to overlook a quantity of faults that, in spite of his is good will, he could not avoid…and enough points of contact, in sum, for them to remain friends as well as lovers. As for the project about which he thought it politic to keep silent, but of which she sensed clearly that he retained the hope, she found the mere imagination of it repulsive.

Marriage! Never! With Régis less than anyone else. Free, she was, and free, she would remain! In any case, what could that legalization, in itself, do for her henceforth? What did it add to happy unions? Nothing. And to the others? A rope around the neck...

Reticences that he perceived in her, as she perceived them in him, and which darkened their interior skies in spite of them. The second week seemed longer to them than the first. The days were shortening, the morning gray, soon cold, and dusk fell rapidly on afternoons now woven with monotonous rain, reducing them to interminable hours of enclosure...

Separated from the external world, they fell back, like a fire to which no logs are added, on their own aliment. In vain they strove to galvanize the flame; there was nothing left but almost-extinct brands and ashes.

Only Monique had the courage to admit it, because she was not suffering from the observation. She believed that she had exhausted, in the matter of Régis, everything that she could expect, of good as well as bad. She was only connected to him now by the worn thread of the liaison itself. Had she given so much, attempted that last experiment, for nothing? Wounded pride more than affection; the torment of having believed that she had touched ground and finding herself drifting back out to sea, like a damaged boat...

This time, on discovering in a being that she had loved at first for his frankness and exceptional honesty, the same horror of the truth as in the most inveterate liar, the humiliation and the astonishment had been so great that she remained as in a stupor. Was it the others, then—Hypocrisy & Co., as Anika put it—that, being in the wrong, were in the right? Was she herself nothing but an abnormal creature, with her ever-more-unslaked thirst for sincerity and justice?

After a fortnight, exasperated by the rain that had not ceased to fall since dawn in squalls, she suddenly tore herself away from the window through which she had been watching darkness fall over the drowned landscape. A tempest!

"Ring for Julia to give us some light," she said. "Dirty place! Not even electricity!"

He continued smoking his pipe, without responding. When Julia had placed the two candlesticks that decorated the mantelpiece on the table, stoked up the fore and closed the shutters, he said: "It's nice here. You're difficult."

"You think so?"

"What is it that you lack? Come on, tell me!"

They looked at one another. The wind whistled through the windows. At a stroke as if it had knocked down the walls, they were abruptly invaded by the storm and the darkness. The frail scaffolding, the entire edifice of the fortnight, collapsed and dispersed.

"Go on!" he ordered, in haste to complete the ruination. "Well, I'll tell you myself! What you lack is Paris, and your..."

"Blanchet?" She shuddered.

"This time, there isn't even any need to name him! Monsieur comes in advance of the summons. Present! Just like that."

She disdained any disculpation, and opened a book. He snatched it away from her. "Answer me! It's not for nothing that a letter arrived yesterday from Madame Ambrat! A letter so interesting that you haven't even mentioned it to me, and of which I only found the envelope, torn into little pieces, in the waste paper basket. Oh, nothing but the envelope...look, here it is!"

He took the accusing jigsaw puzzle out of his blotting pad and showed it, stuck together again.

"Well done!" she said.

"What you lack, and what she's proposing to you—isn't she?—because she's not merely an old friend but a good friend, is a little visit to Vaucresson? That's it, eh?"

"That's it."

He stood up, with the same wrathful surge as the other Sunday, when he had dragged her away from the Vert-Logis. But this time he seized her by the wrist and shook her.

"Brute! Brute!" she moaned. "Well, yes, I miss Paris, and Vaucresson...and Blanchet, too, if that gives you pleasure."

Involuntarily, she compared the bilious and bearded face, with its murderous gaze and hard jaw, with the noble and delicate face that Régis himself had set before her, and which, by contrast, in the darkness in which she was struggling, appeared to her to be luminous, like nascent daylight.

"Let me go!"

"Never..."

He had shoved her away from the door, against the wall. Insensible to the blows with which she struck him, he maintained her there by the shoulders. At the same time, he shouted: "You confess, eh? I knew it. You've never been anything but a whore."

She pulled away with a desperate wrench.

He saw her already gone, lost. Then rage transported him. He vented the pus that was choking him; "You were made for one another! A whore and a pimp!"

She looked at him with a pity so insulting that he had a desire to hurl himself upon her and strangle her. "You can swagger! That doesn't alter the fact that you'll make a well-matched couple! It won't worry him, your bachelor life! Monsieur isn't disgusted, he'll eat the leftovers! Yes, yes, he has a great heart and a fine mind! A stuffy nose, but broad ideas! No, wait, I haven't finished! It's no good putting on your imperious expression. You've never been anything but a poor girl who's never understood anything, gone astray! Instead of starting out by putting yourself on your back for some passerby, you did it all because someone lied to Mademoiselle! You only had to do what everyone else does and get married, without so much fuss! But no! She wanted to reform the world! If all women did what you did, that would be a fine thing! And what's funny is that she believes she's honest! Honest—that's hilarious! Go, go back to your Blanchet—you're a fine pair!"

His spleen vented, he fell silent, grimly. She was still looking straight at him, pale, eye to eye. He yielded, and stepped back. Slowly, she went past him and opened the door. Half way up the stairs, Julia was squatting, listening. At the sight of Monique she came down precipitately, making excuses.

"I was coming to see if you needed wood. I heard Monsieur shouting. Poor little lady! It's not good sense to put him in such a state!"

"Pack my trunks."

"Madame wants to leave?"

The face of the stout old woman, streaked with scars, was impregnated with pitying criticism. The thick body wobbled on the threshold of the open kitchen door.

"I know that it's not my place to give Madame advice...but if it were me...to go away for silly things...it's not good sense."

Monique put on her waterproof, and pulled the hood over the leather bonnet that she had just unhooked from the coat rack.

Stupefied, Julia observed: "Well, if it were necessary to leave every time one spoke one's mind...but men are like that. They have to be the masters. That's understandable, as they're not the stronger. Mine, look, threw vitriol in my face. That didn't prevent me, when my other was dead, from going back to him. He was my husband, wasn't he? The vitriol was his right. And then, we didn't have children any more, they died. So we stayed together. He beat me hard, from time to time...but so what? He lost his temper for a minute. And then one says to oneself, he's bound to die one day! So, all that, that's what's driving you away? Stay, go...that man, he loves you, all the same. He's hot-blooded, it's true...but damn it, he's a man!"

Monique shivered, as much out of melancholy as disgust. That cowardly acceptance, that miserable adaptation! Julia suddenly appeared to be the incarnation of thousands of her lower-class sisters. Oh, that one hadn't had the leisure to linger over psychology! Analysis? Good for those who have nothing to do! She read, on the bloated and corroded face, centuries of humble pain and crushing servitude. What an abyss there was between them! Would it be filled in one day?

"I'm going to the village to order the carriage. I'll be leaving by the eight o'clock train."

"In this weather!"

The door closed. Vexed, Julia went back into her kitchen.

Monique went out on to the dark road. She had difficulty in assembling her thoughts. She walked as if she were being lifted up and carried along by the wind. Eventually, the first houses of Rouzeuil appeared; the lighted windows of the hotel were visible...

Before the surprised proprietress she recovered all her lucidity, and gave instructions in a clear voice. When she went back, under the rain that was lashing her cheeks, she breathed more easily. Finished! It was over!

From then on she did not depart from her calmness. She packed her trunks, tranquilly. Julia helped her, sighing. Behind the partition wall of the room, heavy footfalls were audible.

234

When Monique had finished packing her underwear, methodically, she went into the next room as if nothing had happened to fetch her satchel and her box of watercolors.

Régis planted himself in front of her. "So you think you're going to leave, just like that?"

"Yes. I'll leave you the auto. You can dine alone, with Julia."

She arranged her equipment and her brushes, indifferent to the fury with which she saw him trembling. Suddenly, he lunged forward, and slammed the lid of her box with his fist.

"Do you think you can leave me, to go to mock me tomorrow with the other? You're not leaving! You're mine! I've got you, and I'm keeping you! Leave all that—you're staying."

With a coldly determined expression she picked up the small bottles of colors, threw them in the fire, and calmly picked up her satchel.

Beside himself, he blocked her way, ordering: "Leave that! You'll listen or else..."

"Or else what?"

Abruptly rebelling against his stinging voice, she shouted: "You don't frighten me! That's enough! Nothing will prevent me from leaving! Nothing. You'd have to kill me to keep me here. For me, it's finished—over. Let me pass. You can console yourself with Julia. A housekeeper, that's all you need."

He saw red, but she marched toward him with such exaltation that he hesitated. At the same time, the sound of rolling carriage wheels surprised them. The driver appeared.

She hastened forward. "It's you, Père Brun! Come up!"

Swiftly, she went to her room, followed by Régis, disconcerted. At the sight of the man who was arriving, however, weakening, he turned round, went back into the drawing room, slammed the door violently and turned the key in the lock. Almost immediately, she heard the shutters open and close again, noisily.

235

Swiftly, she closed her trunks, which Père Brun took down one after the other, with Julia, the latter panting, her breasts collapsed beneath her caraco. Monique followed her, close behind her broad back, inclined over the weight of the burden. Haste impelled her to flee, to get away from that suddenly-hateful place and the wild beast locked in upstairs!

She did not take the time to button her coat, leaping into the omnibus on the roof of which the driver was securing the trunks. In the yellow light of the lanterns, the horse was fuming under the downpour. Julia was standing on the threshold, stunned.

Monique leaned out to say "*Au revoir*" and perceived Régis, at the open first-floor window, silhouetted in black against the luminous background. He was stuffing his pipe with grim rage. She threw herself backwards. The carriage moved off.

In an instant, the little house, Julia, Régis, everything, had disappeared. There was nothing around her but thick, damp shadow, a sensation of the end of the world: the deluge, in the dark…and within her, the lifting of an immense burden.

No one was expecting her in the Rue de La Boëtie. She was obliged to leave her trunks with the concierge, take a taxi and go to sleep at a hotel. She was so tired that she was no longer capable of reaction. She lay down, exhausted, as if she were, indeed, coming back from an exceedingly long voyage. Her nerves were so taut that she could not close her eyes.

It took her several days to recover her equilibrium. Her joy at having escaped the degrading torture was mingled with such a great fatigue that everything, no matter how trivial, exhausted her. She had to lie down. She seemed to be emerging from a deadly malady and waking up in the initial languor of convalescence.

Mademoiselle Tcherbalief, up to date with the adventure, which she divined from the half-voiced remarks that Monique, out of self-respect, wanted to silence, was a valuable friend to her during that time. She mounted guard around her chaise-

236

lounge, protecting her from visitors and importunate telephone calls, and monitoring the mail for surprises. Régis wrote one letter after another.

Far from being disturbed by the sight of that rude handwriting, however—which she had once applied herself fervently to the task of transcribing—Monique threw the envelopes into the fire without even opening them. They curled up and were consumed there, without any reflection brightening the bleak gaze with which she followed the dancing flame.

He did not content himself with writing, and presented himself several times, always pitilessly turned away. He returned from those fruitless attempts, head bowed, so somber, with the air of meditating some evil deed, that passers by sometimes moved away from him.

At the end of the week, at the insistence of the Russian, Monique decided to write to Madame Ambrat. The latter, ill in bed, had been unable to come to the Rue de La Boëtie to obtain news, but, surprised not to receive any reply to her last letter, sent to Rouzeuil, she had informed Monique in an affectionately reproachful note, both of her temporary indisposition and her desire to see her soon. When would she come? They would expect her at Vaucresson, without fail, on Sunday, for lunch—and preferably alone! There would only be Vignabos and Blanchet...

Blanchet? No! She did not want to see him again. Perhaps later...she had such a need to rest, to forget! Although he doubtless thought of her even less than she thought of him, and sympathetic as he was, she experienced a physical horror of everything that reminded her of Régis' poisoned love, a shadow of which remained over everything, and everyone.

Tempted nevertheless, Monique, having reflected, escaped by means of a categorical refusal and an insistent plea to her old friend to come and see her: "I have so many things to tell you!"

The next day, Madame Ambrat was there—and that evening, she took Monique back to Vaucresson with her.

V

Lunch was over. Elbows on the table, Monique, sitting opposite Madame Ambrat, was listening ardently to Blanchet, who was declaiming while peeling an orange.

"Come on, Ambrat. The question isn't a simple matter of knowing, in the case that Germany doesn't pay, whether we have a legal right to occupy the Rhineland in perpetuity. The law is one thing—the most uncertain and precarious of all—but the fact is another. The law, as it applies to peoples as well and individuals, has never been anything but an interpretation of interests. If you have the might, you have the right, by definition. Right changes its appearance when might changes camp! Are we sure of always having that? Will the life of the world, and ours, which depends on it, always be subordinate to that exhausting chimera? Are we going to be condemned to the eternal revenge of wars? So, it's not in law but in fact that, for me, the question is posed. What, in fact, is in the interest of France, inseparable from that of the world? The frontier of the Rhine, or Peace, guaranteed by the liquidation of an international debt? Peace—which is to say, universal labor, European solidarity."

"A fine dream!"

"It's sufficient to want it. There's no progress without belief in progress."

At that moment, the drawing room door opened. It was Riri, who, finding the speeches and the lunch overlong, had left the table, with Madame Ambrat's permission, taking her dessert with her, and who was now playing the mistress of ceremonies.

"Messieurs et Mesdames, coffee is served!"

And jumping up and down on the spot, she clapped her hands and burst out laughing.

"If I catch you…!" Monique said.

238

Amusing herself by pretending to be afraid, the child ran around the drawing room, and, almost overtaken, sought protection. With happy screams, she threw herself onto Blanchet's knees.

Madame Ambrat smiled. "Enough—you're annoying your Uncle Georges."

He held her back, stroking her hair. An aging bachelor, without any family that loved him, he found pleasure in his friends' hearth, in that chosen relationship.

"Oh, I beg your pardon," he said, taking the cup of coffee that Monique held out to him. "Thank you."

"It's sugared—your three lumps."

"Oh!" exclaimed Riri. "He's too greedy!"

Madame Ambrat scolded her, for form's sake, but all four of them laughed. It was pleasant in the bright room. The fire was crackling in the grate. The winter sun, outside, gilded the bare trees and the pergola, which a few leaves of virgin vines stained red in places.

"I'm going into the garden," declared Riri, when she had absorbed her sugar-lump from "Godmother's" cup.

"Go on, my girl."

Nestling her armchair next to the big cupboard, at the patina of which she was gazing amicably, Monique sensed the tranquility of a refuge. She appreciated the delicacy that her friends—Blanchet most of all, with an intuition for which she was grateful—had employed during lunch to deflect her thoughts away from the bitter slope.

They were changing her, those glimpses of a horizon so vast that she was hesitating on the threshold, her eyes still blinking from the darkness from which she had emerged. By dint of living in the egotism of her passion, she had ended up—she had realized—disinteresting herself in everything that was not her. Her...and him! And now she was rediscovering, with a pleasure whose vivacity astonished her, an entire field of limitless ideas. There she could breathe, after the asphyxia of the prison.

Régis? She no longer thought about him. He was dead to her, since the moment when he had engraved the final image in her memory, of that vindictive shadow in the window. She had torn him out completely, of her flesh as well as her mind—so completely that, although still in pain, she had turned, with the intuitive energy of the young, toward the remedy *par excellence*: the determination to be healed.

While the two men continued their discussion, Madame Ambrat watched Monique's meditation with an affectionate gaze. She was glad about the change that was already taking place in her. The poor child, who had gone so far in search of unhappiness, when happiness was perhaps there, close at hand! Were she and Blanchet not made to understand one another? Instead of being infatuated with Boisselot! She did not know anyone more antipathetic!

She drew her armchair closer to Monique and took her by the hand.

"You're looking well, my child. I'm glad to see you enjoying yourself here."

"The weather's so pleasant!" said Monique, looking past Blanchet and Monsieur Ambrat at the milky blue sky in which the sun was shining softly.

"That's true," said Blanchet. "What would you say to a turn around the garden? Riri's waving to us."

"At least put on your coats," advised Madame Ambrat.

A cold draught came in through the French windows, which Blanchet had just opened.

"We're all right as we are," he said.

They had already gone down the two steps, and were treading on the dry gravel.

"Wait there, Monique!" Madame Ambrat commanded. "I'll go find a shawl."

Alone, Monique advanced as far as the step, and followed the gesticulating Blanchet, elegant and brisk, beside Monsieur Ambrat, slightly stooped, with an amicable gaze.

Suddenly, she turned round abruptly, perceiving, by the fluid that ran through her, a presence...

The French windows facing the entrance gate had just opened. A man was silhouetted in black against the luminous background. She was so amazed that her exclamation died in her mouth.

With his hat on his head and his hand in his overcoat pocket, Régis was standing before her. Thin, his eyes hollow, he contemplated her with a haggard expression. She could only stammer: "What...you...here?"

"I've been watching you through the window since you got up from the table. I've come to fetch you. Come on."

"You're insane!"

He advanced, menacingly, reaching out with his free hand.

"Come on!"

She understood, by his murderous gaze. Astounded, she uttered an: "Ah!" so piercing that Régis paused, confused.

"You don't want to?" he murmured. "That's all right."

At the same time, he took the hand holding the revolver out of his pocket and took aim. Having run in response to Monique's cry, however, Blanchet threw himself in front of her, shielding her with his body.

The shot rang out.

Stupidly, Régis saw Blanchet totter and Monique, her neck splattered with blood, lean over to support him. Monsieur and Madame Ambrat, who had come running in their turn, irrupted into the room. The engineer ran at Boisselot, who, like a child, allowed himself to be disarmed. Madame Ambrat helped Monique to lie Blanchet down on the sofa.

Riri, attracted by the noise, was weeping noisily, hanging onto the cook's apron.

Monsieur Ambrat was the first to obtain a clear consciousness of the situation. "Marie," he ordered the servant, who was spinning like a top, "go fetch Dr. Luet quickly. Take Riri with you. There's been an accident."

Beside the unconscious Blanchet, Monique was sobbing, prey to a nervous crisis. Madame Ambrat came back from the dining room, where she had gone to fetch vinegar and a napkin, to bathe the face of the wounded man. His collar and waistcoat unfastened, the small wound could be seen through his open shot, close to the armpit. Anxiously, Monique was trying to find evidence of breath in the chest.

"But you've been hit, too!" exclaimed Monsieur Ambrat. "You've got blood on your neck. Show me…"

"It's nothing."

"Show me!"

After passing through Blanchet's shoulder, the bullet had grazed Monique's—a superficial wound, of which, in her emotion, she had not even felt the pain.

"What a brute!" Monsieur Ambrat raged. And only then did he think of turning round, as an administrator of justice, to confront the murderer...

There was no longer anyone there—nothing but the chair that Régis had knocked over a minute before. Boisselot, abruptly recovering consciousness, had fled.

Under the dabs that Madame Ambrat was administering to his face with the damp napkin, Blanchet uttered a long sigh and recovered consciousness.

"Ow!" he said, raising his head.

"Don't move!" said Monique.

On her knees beside the sofa, she had taken his hand and was squeezing it gently. He opened his eyes, smiled at seeing the three heads leaning over him, and reassured them.

"It can't be very serious! A bullet in the shoulder...I know that. They've already taken one out of me on the other side, in 1915…only that was a Boche bullet."

"Don't talk—you'll exhaust yourself," said Madame Ambrat.

"They won't have to go to the trouble of taking this one out of you," said Monique, leaning toward him. "Look what it amused itself doing to me on the way out."

He was so distressed by the sight of the red furrow that he went pale, on the brink of fainting again.

"A scratch! Don't be afraid..."

That was all she was able to say to him. She would have liked to cry out everything that was seething within her, her gratitude...the words pressed forward, impotently, and died on her lips. She was afraid of tiring him. She murmured:

"But for you..."

He replied, with a gaze whose involuntary fever gave the words their full meaning: "Don't thank me. It's so simple!"

So simple! The action, yes, he would have done that for anyone...because he was courageous and chivalrous... But—she was sure of it now—he was glad, above all, to have done it for her. The satisfaction that she read in his face filled her with a disturbance of which she was not the mistress...

"Ah! Here's Marie!" said Madame Ambrat. "Well?"

"The doctor was there. He's coming right away."

"Good. Put some water on to boil."

Blanchet waited until she had closed the door.

"Now," he said, "we need to agree...the revolver?"

Monsieur Ambrat pointed to it. "There, on the table."

"You were unloading it; we were chatting; it went off, accidentally. That's it!"

Monique and Madame Ambrat looked at one another. He had said it so naturally! She had tears in her eyes. How could she doubt that, in calculating in that fashion, he was, once again, thinking uniquely about her?

He added, for the sake of delicacy—for, as with the impulse that had driven him in front of the shot, he was afraid of seeming to burden his devotion with the slightest credence—"No one has any interest in a scandal."

"That wretch will get off scot free!" Monsieur Ambrat observed.

"That unfortunate," Blanchet corrected.

To hide her anguish, Monique had gone to the French windows, still open, to keep watch on the lawn. "Here's the doctor," she announced.

Monsieur Lumet, briefly acquainted with the facts, accepted the plausibility of the story of imprudence as if it were the most natural thing in the world. Having inspected the wound, and quickly reassured himself by virtue of the appearance to the two openings, he declared: "It's a matter of a week. Rest and washing. If the wound doesn't suppurate, it'll disappear. In the meantime, you need to put the fellow to bed for me. He's agitated enough like that."

In spite of Blanchet's forceful protests—rather than encumber his friends he wanted an automobile ambulance to take him back to Versailles—everything was immediately decided. Monique insisted on giving up her room; she would be perfectly all right on the divan in Madame Ambrat's. Swiftly, they put clean sheets on the bed and cleared the wardrobe and the drawers of clothing and toilette items.

Madame Ambrat and the doctor, supporting the injured man, had scarcely finished transporting him, undressing him and lying him down than Monique, having applied her own dressing, knocked on the door. She had assembled the necessities of primary care herself: cotton wool, oxygenated water, rolls of gauze. She had even put on a smock, borrowed like the rest from the house's small pharmacy, always carefully stocked.

In his fever, Blanchet smiled on seeing her come in. With the improvised nurse, the image of the Terrible Years reappeared in hallucination. He was in his hospital bed! Wounded, he had smiled the same ecstatic smile eight years ago, when he had saluted his resurrection, after the inferno of the trenches, on seeing the white form bend over him, and the benevolent eyes in which life was shining...

Georges Blanchet, once no more light-minded or egotistical than the majority, had found on his path through the war his road to Damascus. Having left as a dilettante, he had returned as an apostle. An excess of suffering, in which he had touched the bottom!

Like all those who had not emerged brutalized, he retained from his sojourn in the abyss a hatred and a love: a hatred of social lies, and a love for truth and justice. To tell the truth, though—it was necessary for him to admit it to himself—such a concept was that of an infinitesimal minority. Few men shared it, and even fewer women.

By abstracting himself thus into the solitary domain of ideas, he had, he thought, eventually desiccated himself. He felt that he was older, at forty, than his friends the Ambrats were at sixty. He often said to them: "I'm a finished man."

They invariably replied: "Because you're alone: get married!"

Then he went to take, from a bookshelf, his first book, and showed it to them, jokingly. *"Du Mariage et de la polygamie!* I'm like one of those cooks who don't eat their own cuisines! I might have written that marriage was an end, but I think it's a beginning! I've said that it had nothing in common with love, but I can't conceive of it without..."

"However," Madame Ambrat always replied, indicating her husband, "although it's true that marriage and love rarely coincide, they're not incompatible. Example! Let me make it! Someone will love you, and you'll marry..."

After his encounter with Monique at the Louvre, the sympathy established between them, tightened by a tacit understanding at every one of their subsequent brief meetings, far from loosening his refractory sensibility, had exasperated it. On seeing that woman, whom he judged to be of the elite, and with whom, unconsciously, he was already in love, in Boisselot's claws, he had been gripped by the same neurasthenia as in the muddy evenings in the ditch of earth...

And then, abruptly, the cry that had torn his entrails again! And the gunshot, after which he had woken up another man, in the soft bed in which they had laid him...and the apparition! The future surged forth again, with that white form, and the benevolent eyes in which life was shining...!

He closed his eyelids as Monique finished pinning the bandage. Exhausted, he sighed.

"His hands are burning," the doctor observed. "He needs to be left alone. Absolute calm! A little lemon water, if he's thirsty. Take his temperature every five hours. That's it. I'll come back after dinner."

"Don't worry," said Monique. "I won't leave him."

Silently, while the Ambrats went out on tiptoe with the doctor, she installed herself at his bedside. With an avid gaze, she interrogated the features to which suffering added a nobility. They entered into her, imprinting themselves so forcefully on the ardent wax of her offering that they effaced, in covering them over, all the faces of the past.

That man, so handsome, so intelligent and so good, who had spontaneously offered his life for her...would all of her be enough to recognize his sacrifice? She felt that she was a poor, sullied, diminished thing. And yet, she had never had such a surge of her entire being toward the need to believe, and the intoxication of love.

"No! Shut up! It's forbidden to speak to the nurse!"

"Since I'm doing well!"

"You're getting better. It's not the same thing. If you don't behave, instead of getting a book and sitting beside you, I'll go away."

He looked at her anxiously, but she caressed his forehead, and then, silently, sat down again. She had opened *La Chartreuse de Parma*, pensively...

It was the sixth day since "the accident."

"Isn't it odd?" she had said to Madame Ambrat. "That revolver shot, which exploded like a thunderbolt, instead of having tragic consequences, is in the process of putting things right! For Régis, it was like an electrical discharge, which emptied the pile...his furious jealousy left at the same time as the bullet. *Bon voyage!*" She followed him, with a complex thought, on the boat that was taking him away to Morocco at that very moment...

A note from Mademoiselle Tcherbalief had informed her, that morning, of the resolution and the accomplishment: Monsieur Boisselot had called in at the Rue de La Boëtie, and without any further commentary, had announced that he was going away for a long time...

On reflection, Monique was astonished not to feel any resentment toward him—an indulgent pity, rather. If he had loved her badly, at least—his odious violence had testified to it only too clearly—he had loved her as no one else thus far had... He had drawn her poisons out of her. The very memory of that possessive frenzy, now that she was free of it, revolted her less than it touched her.

She interrogated herself honestly. To some of the reproaches that she had thought at first to be unjust, did her conscience not find an echo? "An unfortunate," Georges had said, so generously. Yes, an unfortunate, but whose pain had, in its repercussions—she would have been very ingrate to forget it—caused two joys to flourish.

For no matter how she tried to put a muffler on her interior song, and, out of fear, to veil herself from the glint in the gaze that was, at that very moment, enveloping her and imploring her, they were both no more than one joy: a pure, child-like joy.

"I can see you," she said, raising a menacing finger. "It's naughty to take advantage of the nurse's distraction to continue addressing such language to her!"

"I haven't said a word!"

"But I can hear! Dear, dear Georges!"

Inconsequently, they resumed the everyday duet. They said the same things again, the alternating hymn that sprang unconsciously from their hearts. What need did they have to swear that they loved one another? What more evident sign, what more moving proof, could a man have given her? It was the certainty of their love that filled Monique with a supreme uncertainty.

The delicacy that he put into wanting to conquer her—as if he had not conquered her entirely at a stroke!—and the elegance of wanting no one but her, tormented her with an inverse scruple. Was she worthy of such a sentiment? Was she not bringing him a withered soul? A prostituted body? Did she merit that immense happiness? The desire by which he was illuminated seemed even more moving in its timidity than its intensity.

She lowered her head, blushing.

"I'm afraid that you only love in me a Monique who isn't the true one. Have I all the qualities that you suppose? There are minutes when I'd like to believe it…when you look at me as you're doing now. Then I imagine that I'm reborn, with my infantile soul, that nothing of my past exists, and that everything's beginning again."

Insistently, he repeated: "Nothing has existed! Everything is beginning!"

"If you only knew!"

Stirred in the depths of her memories, the lees rose up again…she felt a need to accuse herself, to excuse herself…but she had paid very dearly for a frankness for which Régis' jealousy still cried out the imprudence and the danger. Did she not, however, owe that confession, which she had made to the friend and from which the lover had suffered so much, whatever it might cost, to the person who, having saved her life, had become its arbiter? A mystic thirst to humiliate herself, as a punishment for her pride…the former rebel against the deception of brutality of men, the prideful bacheloress, found herself a woman again, and weak, before the grandeur of veritable love.

"If you only knew!" she repeated.

"But I do know! Yes, I know that you've suffered, like all hearts thirsty for the absolute. I know that, without you ever having done any evil to others, others have done it to you. What does the rest matter to me? It's the past, which belongs to you. There's nothing for me but life, and in consequence, in its highest form, love—that of free and equal individuals. One has no rights over the person one loves except those that are given to you. And it's only at the moment when one person has given themselves to another that they become accountable to the other."

She listened, as the woman taken in sin listened to the Savior.

"All that I know, Monique, is what you are: a proud and beautiful soul, launched toward everything that exalts the poor human will; an individual who loves truth and justice; an individual whom suffering, far from grinding down, has caused to grow."

"If only that were true!"

"Suffering, Monique, is the revelatory bath. A base soul remains corrupt therein. A noble soul is tempered by it. Have confidence! The bad days are over! The road has turned."

"How I regret!" she sighed. "How I would have liked to bring you a heart that had only ever beaten for you."

"You're weeping!"

"Yes, I'm weeping for little Monique, for her freshness, which I no longer have! I'm weeping in thinking about the joy she would have had, if your arms had been the first to embrace her! I'm weeping in thinking about little Monique, and Aunt Sylvestre!"

The touching voice penetrated him with its lacerating regret. He felt his own eyes moistening with tears.

"Don't weep! Don't weep, I beg you. You don't feel, then, that love—true love—bears within itself such a radiant light that it effaces all shadow! Don't think any longer about the nightmares of the night! We'll devote ourselves solely to living! We'll wake up with the dawning day..."

"My love," she murmured.

Her damp faced cleared like a dewy morning. He raised his arms. She let herself fall into them, inclining her upper body, protected by the smock, like a white shield, onto the bed. A kind of modesty that she had never experienced before held her against him. Neither of them thought, in the eternity of that minute, of plucking the rose of the kiss that parted their lips.

In his turn, she caressed her radiant forehead, and her fine coppery hair.

"Have no fear! You'll be loved..."

"You're so good!" she said, passionately. "It seems to me that I'm in a nest where no tempest can any longer reach

249

me. We're at the top of the tree, and around us, there's the solitude of the forest..."

And the end of the week prescribed by Doctor Lumet, Georges got out of bed, healed. The wound had not suppurated for an instant. The two scars had closed up under the budding of new flesh.

Around the drawing room sofa, on which they demanded that he lie down from time to time, the two women installed themselves, Madame Ambrat sewing, Monique chatting.

"No, you're not yet in a state to go back to Versailles. Your course can wait another fortnight. After the Christmas holidays, on New Year's Day. First of all, you're *my* patient. You have to do as I say."

She addressed him as *vous*, but the *vous* had, in its intonation, all the tenderness of the informal address that she had not yet dared to employ, even in the hours when their desires communicated freely: a respect for convention by which the perspicacious affection of Madame Ambrat was amused. Did they think that their amorous understanding didn't leap to the eyes?

"I'm your patient, it's true. But I've complicated the lives of our friends enough like this..."

Madame Ambrat placed her needlework on her knees. "Uncle Georges, you're annoying us!"

"And then, comfortable as I am here, my work, your business..."

"Say that you've had enough of us! Well, do you want me to tell you what you are, Uncle Georges? An ingrate." She smiled maliciously, uniting them in the same gaze.

In a grave voice, he replied: "No, my dear, my good friend! I'm not an ingrate. I'll always remember that it was here, on this sofa to which your authority enchains me, that Monique took my hands and squeezed them with a grip so strong that nothing will ever release them. It's to this house and to you, the Ambrats, that I owe my happiness."

Madam Ambrat stood up. Emotion was tugging at her stiff features. First she went to kiss "Uncle Georges" on both cheeks, and then came back to Monique, who had also stood up, mechanically, watched her do it, troubled.

"Now, it's my niece's turn!"

At that word, which caused their greatest memory of amity to surge forth, Monique thought she saw loom up, with her benevolent smiling face, the old woman who had been her educator: Aunt Sylvestre became confused with Madame Ambrat...

For a long time, Monique embraced the friend who had succeeded, in her heart, the one who had died. It was as if, through the mirage of the past, she were hugging a true Maman.

"Do you know what I think, my dear!" said Madame Ambrat, when she had mastered her emotion. "You just mentioned Christmas? It was four years ago, on the twenty-fourth of this month, that your poor aunt came to eat goose and black pudding.[31] That was the last time I saw her. Reunion Wednesday fortnight! We'll celebrate Christmas Eve thinking of her. She would have been so pleased about your happiness!"

---

[31] This calculation is inconsistent with the timetable of events previously set out in the story, Monique's affair with Boisselot and its aftermath must have extended over several months, so this Christmas, in the internal chronology of the novel, must be Christmas 1925, not Christmas 1924, as Madame Ambrat's "four years" would imply.

VI

Since they had each taken up the thread of their separate lives, Georges and Monique had seen one another every day. He had come to lunch several times in the Rue de La Boëtie. On the other days, she went to Versailles, generally in one of Mademoiselle Tcherbalief's autos, to take possession of the detached house in which he lived in the Avenue de Saint-Cloud. It was an old shanty, too big for him, but agreeable, with a kitchen garden, a chicken run and a garage, from which she had had the clutter removed in order to lodge the car.

The old maidservant who had been keeping house for "Monsieur Georges" for years had immediately adopted the intruder, divining that if she were not yet the master's mistress, she would soon be the mistress of the house...

One evening when, having arrived early by train, he had not wanted to let her leave again, and when she had accepted the unplanned invitation to dinner, Monique had been surprised by an elegant light meal, and when, admiring the table decorated with mimosas and roses, she expressed astonishment, he confessed: "Since the first time you came here, not a day has gone by without my having the dream that you wouldn't go back again, that I could keep you here...and it's thus, every evening, that the house has been waiting for you..."

Amicably, she contemplated the little drawing room where he worked, and where they were dining, and the familiar furniture... Yes, the universe was contained between these four walls!

He stood up, and came to kiss her hand. He was touching, with the ingenuousness of his joy and the feverish discretion of his desire...

Why, at the moment, having taken her in his arms and had finally dared to formulate his ardent prayer, had she gently shaken her head?

"No, not this evening, I beg you!"

In vain he had offered his lips, implored her with his gaze. She had modestly loosened the embrace. But on seeing him draw away sadly, she had swiftly taken his hand. "Forgive me, Georges! I don't know what sentiment I'm obeying. It seems to me that I'm not yet sufficiently worthy of you. Let me have a little time…you deserve…above all, don't put on that face, which pains me! I owe you everything; I belong to you…"

"So?"

"I don't know…no, no…not yet."

She would have liked to, on seeing him silent, so sad, as he accompanied her back to the station. She had regretted, throughout the return journey, the inexplicable contraction of the heart that had held her back, at the moment when everything within her urged her toward the common desire. What last hesitation had triumphed over her own consent, her tenderness ready to abandon itself?

It was a somersault of the unconscious, in which the transitory Monique, the one who had squandered her mind and her flesh, completed her disappearance, and from which the new Monique, entirely similar to the one that had opened with so much confidence to life, was beginning fearfully to bloom.

She had rediscovered her bridal soul, with a graver ardor under the same spontaneity, tender and youthful. Unconsciously, however, within her wiser allure and her charming reserve, a more feminine appearance was manifest. Mademoiselle Tcherbalief contemplated her with astonishment, reinstalled in her reception room in the Rue de La Boëtie.

Monique had had the Louis XV desk emptied of the papers that had been piling up in it for two years. Delightedly, with a facility of which she thought she had lost the habit, she drew in Indian ink, on the desktop…a project for an apartment: simple, a few large rooms, sober and bright…

"Why are you looking at me like that, Madame Tcherbalief…sorry, Plombino?"

"It's curious! It seems to me that you have something...a transformation! Ah! Your hair, perhaps? You're letting it grow?"

"Yes."

"I was about to cut mine! An idea of the Baron's... He wants me to look like you..."

"In that case, Baronne, stay as you are. Short hair is fine, for boys..."

"There!" said Mademoiselle Tcherbalief. "It's like your project for the apartment—that's new! Is Mademoiselle Lerbier thinking of becoming a Madame?"

Monique smiled. Madame Blanchet? A husband, children? Why not?

What had seemed to her, a month ago, to be an unrealizable dream appeared to her today to be a possible miracle. She was seeing with other eyes, because she was feeling with another heart. Already, involuntarily, she was making plans...

They would keep the house at Versailles for the spring and summer. In the vacations they would travel, and in winter...

Claire, still hanging on her question mark, looked at her, smiling.

"For the moment, Claire, I have an urge to move house, that's all. And since you're the proprietress of several buildings, and you have one for hire in the Rue d'Astorg...wait! That's not all. You have no more need, since the Baron's just given you his Mercedes, of your little Voisin, The ten horse-power saloon...?"

"No..."

"I'll buy it from you. Agreed?"

"Agreed," said Claire, habituated for a long time with "the Boss" no longer to be surprised by anything. "But not before the Mercedes is repaired. Friday, if you like?"

"As long as I have it by Christmas Eve. I have to take Monsieur Vignabos to Vaucresson, to the Ambrats..."

"That's fine! I only need it—I wanted to tell you, and that's the only reason I need the Voisin—because I'm going to Magny tomorrow…Anika's funeral."

"Anika!" cried Monique.

"Died yesterday, all alone, in an inn where she'd gone to earth some time ago…you didn't know?"

"No…it's so far away, all that…"

"Phlegmon of the throat."

"Poor girl!"

Monique saw her again, cadaverous, in the shadow of the smoking room. The entire past had just surged forth with its maleficent memories. Gripped by the fear of thinking of the fate that she had escaped, she mourned the dismal fate of the musician. At the same time, the band around her agitated its phantoms…Michelle d'Entraygues, Ginette Hutier, Hélène Suze, Max de Laume and Lady Springfield! And the others— all the others, even those to whom she had been indifferent: the Bardinots, the Ransoms, and those to whom she had given so much of herself: Vigneret, Niquette, Peer Rys, and finally Régis! She scarcely recognized their faces. They, too, were dead!

She chased away the painful vision, and said, sadly: "It's kind of you, Claire, to go to Magny—you who scarcely knew her. I'm sure there won't be a large crowd behind her coffin. She had so many friends! Add my flowers to yours. Poor Anika! Another one who fell victim to herself!"

In her clear voice, the Slav concluded: "You're right. One only has a single life—it's too stupid to spoil it."

Monique had stood up. Mademoiselle Tcherbalief, curious, would have liked to know more. Pointing at the ceiling, she asked: "So, when you're living in the Rue d'Astorg, what will you do with the entresol?"

"Expansion. That's your business. As soon as I've finished moving, you can apply your tricks of the trade up there. Make me something good…exhibition rooms for fabrics… Yes, I haven't talked to you about that. I feel the need to launch Tcherbaief & Lerbier, fashion designers. One can build the staircase here...look, it will come out there..."

She had taken a large white sheet of paper, penciled in the plans...

Expressions, gestures: such a decisiveness emanated, cheerfully, from her entire person, that Claire listened in amazement. Decidedly, her Monique had changed...!

"I'll drink a toast," said Monsieur Vignabos, raising his glass, in which the bubbles of the foamy Vouvray were bursting, "to the recovery of our friend!"

"And mine, my dear Master! No one's mentioned that!" Monique protested.

Monsieur Vignabos looked at her from the corner of his eye. Monsieur and Madame Ambrat consulted one another; they divined, beneath the joking request, a double meaning. All three of them perceived an accent of sincerity and profound humility therein, and also of pride, and were moved by it. In silence, however, they waited for her to explain...

Only Blanchet had divined the whole of her thought. He stood up briskly. He wished so tenderly that, except for the pious memory of Aunt Sylvestre, no recurrence should darken that happy evening for Monique! Deflecting the words from their true meaning, he raised his glass.

"Monique is right! I'll drink to repair the unforgivable forgetfulness of our venerated master, to the even more rapid recovery of our friend. That's what comes of being modest, Mademoiselle. People only talk about my wound, and pay no heed to yours! It's true that it's no longer perceptible!"

"Oh, if only one could say so!"

She inclined her head. On the snowy neck, at the junction of the shoulder, a pink line appeared, previously hidden beneath the black velvet of her dress, the neckline of which had scarcely plunged at all. The only jewelry she was wearing, at the end of a golden thread, was a little leaden ball, crushed at the summit, which Riri had picked up the next day at the foot of the stone doorpost where it had fallen.

Without saying anything, Monique had kept it, superstitiously. She would not have exchanged that little inert object, which, baptized in Georges' blood and her own, had marked them with the same sign for the most beautiful diamond. It was a trace of mysterious union.

While Madame Ambrat removed part of the remains of the Mont-Blanc dessert for Riri—the child had requested that it be set aside for her, along with a little of the goose and black pudding—Monique, eyelids lowered, evoked all the past that the anniversary symbolized for her: Christmas Nights when a little girl had died and a young woman born! Between those two poles of her life, a world of disappointments, a desert of sadness and ruins: a stage of her journey so long and so bleak that she had nearly succumbed. But for Georges…!

She opened her eyes to the gaze that was studying her anxiously. How good it was! How good it was to be around that table in that pleasant dining room, in the warm light: the simple joy of being there, all five of them, after the excellent supper in which, filially, she had taken the place of the absentee...

Aunt Sylvestre was there before her. The frightful image of the cadaver lying on the stretcher had vanished definitively. The benevolent old lady was there, alive, with the indulgent smile that she had had on the day they had gone together to the Rue de Médicis. Monsieur Ambrat was right: the dead one loves are not dead; they only disappear with the last memory.

Vignabos' study, Régis, Georges…the day of the tragic Christmas Eve, and, over all of that which was no more, the maternal visage that, during the long, bleak journey, she had ceased to see, and which reappeared today! Yes, there, living. *Aunt! Aunt!* she almost cried out with an irresistible need to be understood, and absolved. With a supreme prayer, which took the absentee as a witness, through those who had cherished her, and who, above all, adjured her, the sovereign judge, she confessed:

"No, Georges, don't deceive them. The recovery to which I was referring is the one that I owe you! In whom could I confide, if not to you and these old friends, who don't only represent Aunt Sylvestre to me, but my entire family— for let's not talk about my parents. For them I'm like a trinket that once belonged to them and has passed into other hands. When I see them again I have nothing to say to them, because if I didn't retrain myself I would shout at them: 'It's you, it's your rotten milieu that was the cause of the first of my errors!' With Aunt Sylvestre, I would have remained a simple, pure girl. Oh, I know full well that it's also my fault. Less absolute, less proud, I would not, on a night like this…I'm so, so ashamed of it! Too late! What do you expect? Once in the mud, one wallows in it…one wants to get out of it, but one can't. Then one rolls in it..."

She veiled her face with her hands.

"My poor child," said Madame Ambrat, "Why torture yourself like this? The past, at your age, is a small enough thing…when one has a future!"

"Fool," said Georges, supportively. "Dear fool, if anything could render you dearer in my eyes, it's the very excess of your scruples. Who, then, could think of reproaching you for the past when it extracts such a dolorous plaint from you? Look at me! There is only one thing in the world that matters: the minute in which we are living."

"It's because its light is inundating me," she said, raising her head, "that I tremble before my happiness. Are my hands clean enough to take gold out of it without soiling it?"

He seized her soft, delicate white hands and kissed them fervently.

"Verdure never grows back better than when the past has been burned. Monique, in the name of Aunt Sylvestre, I ask you to be my wife..."

"Can I…?" she stammered.

"Not only can you, my dear child," exclaimed Monsieur Vignabos, whose voice was quavering involuntarily, "but you should! My congratulations, Blanchet—your choice is good."

Monique, her face resplendent through her tears, let her hand fall into the one that was waiting, tremulously. He paled before the realized hope.

"And now, my children," said Madame Ambrat, I don't want to throw you out, but it's three o'clock, and by the time you get to Paris...what time is your train, Georges?"

"Four o'clock."

"That's true," said Monique. "I'd forgotten your lecture in Nantes..." She turned to Monsieur Vignabos. "And you, my dear Master, am I not taking you back?"

"No, since Madame Ambrat is doing me the kindness of putting me up."

"*En route*, then! We only just have time." As Monsieur Vignabos and Monsieur Ambrat made as if to accompany them, Monique added: "No, no—go back inside, quickly; it's too cold!"

Now, in the car that was bearing them away, they remained mute. A silence heavy with thoughts! Radiant in him, so tumultuous in her, they collided with one another and sprang forth—disorder, delight, gratitude, remorse—like a continuous shower of sparks.

They went forth in their enchantment, through the moonlit night and the misty wood, whose depths opened up before the dazzling flight of the headlights.

"Slow down, Monique. It's so beautiful."

They arrived at the turning at Bougival, going along the Seine. It extended like a silver streak with the blue shores of islets.

"Yes, it's beautiful," she murmured.

The vehicle had stopped. They took one another's hands. They did not speak, and yet confessed so many things. Suddenly, in the same impulse, their lips met. The time of a long oath!

Then, click, she put the car back in gear and they set off again, toward their happiness.

At the same moment, the Ambrats and Monsieur Vignabos were preparing to retire to their rooms.

"Do you know, my dear friend," said the old professor to Madame Ambrat as he went upstairs, "what else this proves? It's that, for a young individual who has not been entirely contaminated by social life, present-day mores are a terrible culture medium! There's our bacheloress. She's emerged from her double education—and the war!—with the thirst for emancipation that so many women, her sisters, have..."

"So many?" questioned Madame Ambrat. "Do you think so? The majority are resigned to their chains. Many, sad to say, are even attached to them."

"No matter! The elite draw the mass along. All of them bear a force within them beneficent in its power...a power of peace, justice and bounty. A force that will blossom! Count on that, my dear friend: on those who are doing, and will continue to do, increasingly, their share of the work as equivalents. Can one blame Monique for having gone on ahead, in her fashion? A false step, yes...but a step all the same."

"Admit, however," said Madame Ambrat, "that without Blanchet..."

"So be it, but to be just, add that without Vigneret... When a woman stumbles, *cherchez l'homme.*"

"The man, always the man!" grumbled Monsieur Ambrat. "Is it not more just to say that we're all playthings of energies that surpass us? Joy and dolor are blind. Only forces act. We're recording devices!"

Indulgently, Monsieur Vignabos concluded: "One more reason to excuse Monique. Does one think of the dung heap when one sniffs a flower?"

January-May 1922.

260

SF & FANTASY

Adolphe Alhaiza. *Cybele*

Alphonse Allais. *The Adventures of Captain Cap*

Henri Allorge. *The Great Cataclysm*

Guy d'Armen. *Doc Ardan: The City of Gold and Lepers*

G.-J. Arnaud. *The Ice Company*

Charles Asselineau. *The Double Life*

Henri Austruy. *The Eupantophone; The Olotelepan; The Petitpaon Era*

Barillet-Lagartousse. *The Final War*

Cyprien Bérard. *The Vampire Lord Ruthwen*

S. Henry Berthoud. *Martyrs of Science*

Aloysius Bertrand. *Gaspard de la Nuit*

Richard Bessière. *The Gardens of the Apocalypse; The Masters of Silence*

Albert Bleunard. *Ever Smaller*

Félix Bodin. *The Novel of the Future*

Louis Boussenard. *Monsieur Synthesis*

Alphonse Brown. *City of Glass; The Conquest of the Air*

Emile Calvet. *In a Thousand Years*

André Caroff. *The Terror of Madame Atomos; Miss Atomos; The Return of Madame Atomos; The Mistake of Madame Atomos; The Monsters of Madame Atomos; The Revenge of Madame Atomos; The Resurrection of Madame Atomos; The Mark of Madame Atomos; The Spheres of Madame Atomos; The Wrath of Madame Atomos* (w/M. & Sylvie Stéphan)

Félicien Champsaur. *The Human Arrow; Ouha, King of the Apes; Pharaoh's Wife*

Didier de Chousy. *Ignis*

Jules Clarétie. *Obsession*

Michel Corday. *The Eternal Flame*

André Couvreur. *The Necessary Evil; Caresco, Superman; The Exploits of Professor Tornada* (3 vols.)

Captain Danrit. *Undersea Odyssey*

C. I. Defontenay. *Star (Psi Cassiopeia)*

Charles Derennes. *The People of the Pole*

Georges Dodds (anthologist). *The Missing Link*

Charles Dodeman. *The Silent Bomb*

Harry Dickson. *The Heir of Dracula; Harry Dickson vs. The Spider*

Jules Dornay. *Lord Ruthven Begins*
Alfred Driou. *The Adventures of a Parisian Aeronaut*
Sâr Dubnotal *vs. Jack the Ripper*
Alexandre Dumas. *The Return of Lord Ruthven*
Renée Dunan. *Baal*
J.-C. Dunyach. *The Night Orchid; The Thieves of Silence*
Henri Duvernois. *The Man Who Found Himself*
Achille Eyraud. *Voyage to Venus*
Henri Falk. *The Age of Lead*
Paul Féval. *Anne of the Isles; Knightshade; Revenants; Vampire City; The Vampire Countess; The Wandering Jew's Daughter*
Paul Féval, *fils. Felifax, the Tiger-Man*
Charles de Fieux. *Lamékis*
Louis Forest. *Someone is Stealing Children in Paris*
Arnould Galopin. *Doctor Omega*; *Doctor Omega and the Shadowmen* (anthology)
Judith Gautier. *Isoline and the Serpent-Flower*
H. Gayar. *The Marvelous Adventures of Serge Myrandhal on Mars*
Léon Gozlan. *The Vampire of the Val-de-Grâce*
G.L. Gick. *Harry Dickson and the Werewolf of Rutherford Grange*
Edmond Haraucourt. *Illusions of Immortality*
Nathalie Henneberg. *The Green Gods*
Eugène Hennebert. *The Enchanted City*
V. Hugo, P. Foucher & P. Meurice. *The Hunchback of Notre-Dame*
Romain d'Huissier. *Hexagon: Dark Matter*
Jules Janin. *The Magnetized Corpse*
Michel Jeury. *Chronolysis*
Gustave Kahn. *The Tale of Gold and Silence*
Gérard Klein. *The Mote in Time's Eye*
Fernand Kolney. *Love in 5000 Years*
Paul Lacroix. *Danse Macabre*
Louis-Guillaume de La Follie. *The Unpretentious Philosopher*
Jean de La Hire. *Enter the Nyctalope; The Nyctalope on Mars; The Nyctalope vs. Lucifer; The Nyctalope Steps In; Night of the Nyctalope; Return of the Nyctalope; The Fiery Wheel*
Etienne-Léon de Lamothe-Langon. *The Virgin Vampire*
André Laurie. *Spiridon*
Gabriel de Lautrec. *The Vengeance of the Oval Portrait*
Alain le Drimeur. *The Future City*
Georges Le Faure & Henri de Graffigny. *The Extraordinary Adventures of a Russian Scientist Across the Solar System* (2 vols.)

Gustave Le Rouge. *The Mysterious Doctor Cornelius* (3 vols.); *The Vampires of Mars; The Dominion of the World* (w/Gustave Guitton) (4 vols.)

Jules Lermina. *Mysteryville; Panic in Paris; To-Ho and the Gold Destroyers; The Secret of Zippeliu; The Battle of Strasbourg*

André Lichtenberger. *The Centaurs; The Children of the Crab*

Jean-Marc & Randy Lofficier. *Edgar Allan Poe on Mars; The Katrina Protocol; Pacifica; Robonocchio; Return of the Nyctalope;* (anthologists) *Tales of the Shadowmen 1-10*

Xavier Mauméjean. *The League of Heroes*

Joseph Méry. *The Tower of Destiny*

Hippolyte Mettais. *The Year 5865; Paris Before the Deluge*

Louise Michel. *The Human Microbes; The New World*

Tony Moilin. *Paris in the Year 2000*

José Moselli. *Illa's End*

John-Antoine Nau. *Enemy Force*

Marie Nizet. *Captain Vampire*

C. Nodier, A. Beraud & Toussaint-Merle. *Frankenstein*

Henri de Parville. *An Inhabitant of the Planet Mars*

Gaston de Pawlowski. *Journey to the Land of the 4th Dimension*

Georges Pellerin. *The World in 2000 Years*

Ernest Pérochon. *The Frenetic People*

Pierre Pelot. *The Child Who Walked on the Sky*

J. Polidori, C. Nodier, E. Scribe. *Lord Ruthven the Vampire*

P.-A. Ponson du Terrail. *The Vampire and the Devil's Son; The Immortal Woman*

Edgar Quinet. *Ahasuerus; The Enchanter Merlin*

Henri de Régnier. *A Surfeit of Mirrors*

Maurice Renard. *The Blue Peril; Doctor Lerne; The Doctored Man; A Man Among the Microbes; The Master of Light*

Jean Richepin. *The Wing; The Crazy Corner*

Albert Robida. *The Adventures of Saturnin Farandoul; The Clock of the Centuries; Chalet in the Sky; The Electric Life*

J.-H. Rosny Aîné. *Helgvor of the Blue River; The Givreuse Enigma; The Mysterious Force; The Navigators of Space; Vamireh; The World of the Variants; The Young Vampire*

Marcel Rouff. *Journey to the Inverted World*

Léonie Rouzade. *The World Turned Upside Down*

Han Ryner. *The Superhumans; The Human Ant*

Pierre de Selenes: *An Unknown World*

Angelo de Sorr. *The Vampires of London*

Brian Stableford. *The New Faust at the Tragicomique;The Empire of the Necromancers (The Shadow of Frankenstein; Frankenstein and the Vampire Countess; Frankenstein in London); Sherlock Holmes & The Vampires of Eternity; The Stones of Camelot; The Wayward Muse.* (anthologist) *News from the Moon; The Germans on Venus; The Supreme Progress; The World Above the World; Nemoville; Investigations of the Future; The Conqueror of Death; The Revolt of the Machines*

Jacques Spitz. *The Eye of Purgatory*

Kurt Steiner. *Ortog*

Eugène Thébault. *Radio-Terror*

C.-F. Tiphaigne de La Roche. *Amilec*

Louis Ulbach. *Prince Bonifacio*

Théo Varlet. *The Golden Rock. The Xenobiotic Invasion; The Castaways of Eros; Timeslip Troopers* (w/André Blandin); *The Martian Epic* (w/Octave Joncquel)

Paul Vibert. *The Mysterious Fluid*

Villiers de l'Isle-Adam. *The Scaffold; The Vampire Soul*

Philippe Ward. *Artahe ; The Song of Montségur* (w/Sylvie Miller) *Manhattan Ghost* (w/Mickael Laguerre)

MYSTERIES & THRILLERS

M. Allain & P. Souvestre. *The Daughter of Fantômas*

A. Anicet-Bourgeois, Lucien Dabril. *Rocambole*

A. Bernède. *Belphegor*; *Judex* (w/Louis Feuillade); *The Return of Judex* (w/Louis Feuillade); *The Shadow of Judex*

A. Bisson & G. Livet. *Nick Carter vs. Fantômas*

V. Darlay & H. de Gorsse. *Arsène Lupin vs. Sherlock Holmes: The Stage Play*

Séamas Duffy. *Sherlock Holmes in Paris*

Paul Féval. *Gentlemen of the Night; John Devil; The Black Coats ('Salem Street; The Invisible Weapon; The Parisian Jungle; The Companions of the Treasure; Heart of Steel; The Cadet Gang; The Sword-Swallower)*

Emile Gaboriau. *Monsieur Lecoq*

Goron & Emile Gautier. *Spawn of the Penitentiary*

Rick Lai. *Shadows of the Opera: Retribution in Blood; Sisters of the Shadows: The Curse of Cagliostro*

Steve Leadley. *Sherlock Holmes: The Circle of Blood*

Maurice Leblanc. *Arsène Lupin vs. Countess Cagliostro; Arsène Lupin vs. Sherlock Holmes (The Blonde Phantom; The Hollow Needle); The Many Faces of Arsène Lupin; The Island of the Thirty Coffins*

Gaston Leroux. *Chéri-Bibi; The Phantom of the Opera; Rouletabille & the Mystery of the Yellow Room; Rouletabille at Krupp's*

Richard Marsh. *The Complete Adventures of Judith Lee*

William Patrick Maynard. *The Terror of Fu Manchu; The Destiny of Fu Manchu*

Frank J. Morlock. *Sherlock Holmes: The Grand Horizontals; Sherlock Holmes vs Jack the Ripper*

Jean Petithuguenin. *The Adventures of Ethel King*

Antonin Reschal. *The Adventures of Miss Boston*

P. de Wattyne & Y. Walter. *Sherlock Holmes vs. Fantômas*

David White. *Fantômas in America*

Pierre Yrondy. *The Adventures of Thérèse Arnaud*

SCREENPLAYS

Mike Baron. *The Iron Triangle*

Emma Bull & Will Shetterly. *Nightspeeder; War for the Oaks*

Gerry Conway & Roy Thomas. *Doc Dynamo*

Steve Englehart. *Majorca*

James Hudnall. *The Devastator*

Jean-Marc & Randy Lofficier. *Royal Flush*

J.-M. & R. Lofficier & Marc Agapit. *Despair*

J.-M. & R. Lofficier & Joël Houssin. *City*

Andrew Paquette. *Peripheral Vision*

Robert L. Robinson, Jr. *Judex*

R. Thomas, J. Hendler & L. Sprague de Camp. *Rivers of Time*

NON-FICTION

Stephen R. Bissette. *Blur 1-5. Green Mountain Cinema 1; Teen Angels*

Win Scott Eckert. *Crossovers* (2 vols.)

Jean-Marc & Randy Lofficier. *Shadowmen* (2 vols.)

Randy Lofficier. *Over Here*

ART BOOKS

Jean-Pierre Normand. *Science Fiction Illustrations*
Raven Okeefe. *Raven's L'il Critters; Rave's Faves*
Randy Lofficier & Raven Okeefe. *If Your Possum Go Daylight...*
Daniele Serra. *Illusions*
Randy Lofficier. *Over Here*

HEXAGON COMICS

Franco Frescura & Luciano Bernasconi. *Wampus*
Franco Frescura & Giorgio Trevisan. *CLASH*
L. Bernasconi, J.-M. Lofficier & Juan Roncagliolo. *Phenix*
Claude Legrand, J.-M. Lofficier & L. Bernasconi. *Kabur*
Franco Oneta. *Zembla*
L. Buffolente, Lofficier & J.-J. Dzialowski. *Strangers: Homicron*
Danilo Grossi. *Strangers: Jaydee*
Claude Legrand & Luciano Bernasconi. *Strangers: Starlock*
Thierry Mornet & Juan Roncagliolo. *Guardian of the Republic*
J.-M. Lofficier, M. Garcia, F. Blanco & J. Pima. *Strangers in a Strange Land*

Printed in the USA
CPSIA information can be obtained
at www.ICGtesting.com
LVHW041228051024
792934LV00002B/240

9 781612 273600